Safiyyah's War

PR/ 9100000817 0070 4R

'*Safiyyah's War* has the soul of a classic and the urgency of a story for our times. A tale of tolerance, unthinkable bravery, and heart-in-mouth true events. I loved this book'
KIRAN MILLWOOD HARGRAVE

'All at once, *Safiyyah's War* broke my heart and filled me with immense hope. With its unforgettable characters and exquisite storytelling, this really is an extraordinary book'
A F STEADMAN

'Safiyyah is a protagonist I was rooting for all throughout; a lovely, kind-hearted girl whose story filled me in turns with despair and joy. This book shines through with kindness and empathy at its very heart'
NIZRANA FAROOK

'I adored this book in all its intricacies. I cheered for and cried with Safiyyah — a testament to Khan's talent for storytelling — and enjoyed every word. *Safiyyah's War* has the makings of a classic'
AISHA BUSHBY

'A beautiful and sensitively written story which will stay with me for a very long time'
A M HOWELL

'Luminously written, this is an extraordinary story of bravery filled with truth and light and hope'
KATYA BALEN

'Beautifully written, full of compassion and hope, *Safiyyah's War* is an important and much needed WWII story that puts a spotlight on a rarely heard part of history. Safiyyah's story is a must-read in schools exploring WWII, to encourage empathy. The story is superbly told, with adorable characters. A special, heartfelt book that I'm glad exists' **A M DASSU**

'I was swept away by this richly evocative and beautifully told story. Heart-wrenching and hopeful, this is a book that shines a bright light in the darkness'
RASHMI SIRDESHPANDE

'Beautiful, vivid writing . . . A moving story of resistance and unity, the power of community and faith. I absolutely loved it' **RADIYA HAFIZA**

'A rich and inspiring story full of courage and resistance at the darkest of times'
ANNA FARGHER

PRAISE FOR SAFIYYAH'S WAR

Safiyyah's War

 HIBA NOOR KHAN

ANDERSEN PRESS

First published in 2023 by
Andersen Press Limited
20 Vauxhall Bridge Road, London SW1V 2SA, UK
Vijverlaan 48, 3062 HL Rotterdam, Nederland
www.andersenpress.co.uk

2 4 6 8 10 9 7 5 3

British Library Cataloguing in Publication Data available.

ISBN 978 1 83913 313 8

Printed and bound in Great Britain by Clays Ltd, Elcograf S.p.A.

For Sidi Abdel-Qadir Benghabrit and all the unsung
heroes who follow maps of light against all odds.
For every child affected by the darknesses
of war. May you be the last.

1

It is only in holy places of worship and libraries that you have to whisper, for they are both sacred in their own special ways. Safiyyah spent as many afternoons as she could here in the dusty stillness of the library, poring over atlases, maps and travelogues. Madame Odette, the kind librarian, never asked her unnecessary questions; she knew why Safiyyah came. Perhaps it was the same reason Madame Odette worked there. The promise of pages, the silence that seemed to shimmer.

Madame Odette would lead Safiyyah down the echoey hallway with its dark mahogany walls, her small heels clicking all the way to the World section. She wore pleated skirts and bright cardigans – Safiyyah's favourite was black wool with tiny colourful stitches all over, as if handfuls of sugar sprinkles had been thrown across it like confetti.

Safiyyah would choose where in the world she wanted to explore and Madame Odette would roll out the right maps and pile up helpful books on the leather-topped desk. The names of faraway places enchanted Safiyyah. Some in particular seemed to call out to her from the coffee-coloured pages of old maps: Jerusalem, Manila and Timbuktu summoned her in sacred hushed library tones. She whispered the names of cities, towns, islands and lagoons like secrets, feeling a thirst for the world.

Not everyone was allowed into these rooms whenever they liked, you needed permission and a special pass, but Madame Odette made an exception for Safiyyah. Two years ago when Safiyyah's father had first brought her to the library, Safiyyah had wandered off and found Madame Odette sitting behind her desk, chewing a strawberry bonbon.

'Sorry to disturb you, Madame. I'd like to see a map of Algeria, please. My grandma showed me one she has but it's ripped on the Tunisia side. Everything to the right of Annaba, El Bouni, Souk Ahras and Tebessa is gone and I'd really like to see the El Kala region properly.'

Madame Odette had stopped chewing and peered at the peculiar child with curiosity. The girl was wringing her hands nervously, and thick curls had wildly escaped from her plaits. She spoke softly but fast, and Madame Odette saw a spark in her eyes. Children rarely came to this part of the library and when they did, they never asked questions like this.

'D'accord . . . Is this for a school project?'

'No, I'm going to be an explorer. My grandma is from Tlemcen in the north-west and I know from there through Oran and Chlef to Algiers pretty well, but I can't continue to the east until I have the full map, of course.'

Looking surprised and quietly impressed, Madame Odette chuckled to herself and told Safiyyah to follow her. By the time her father finally found her half an hour later, Safiyyah had six different maps laid out in front of her and was contentedly sucking a strawberry bonbon. Madame Odette marvelled at Safiyyah's interest – it was like the lines and curves of the continents joined up with the patterns of her brain! Ever since then, she allowed Safiyyah access to whatever she liked in the library, and always supplied her with a stash of strawberry bonbons.

Today, Safiyyah popped one of the powdery pink sugar balls into her mouth absentmindedly. Goose bumps appeared on her arms as she traced her finger gently down the ocean. Safiyyah wore the special white gloves that the librarian had given her in order to handle this book. Its pages felt like delicate tissue, as if they might float away if ever the book's spine came unbound. Her pulse quickened as her finger reached Manaus, in the state of Amazonas, Brazil.

She could almost hear the intense pulsing and throbbing of the Amazon, an orchestra of a million cicadas, squawking parrots and howling monkeys. The best kind of music, it filled the room, interrupted only by the ticking of the grandfather clock in the corner.

THE TIME! Safiyyah remembered suddenly that she was supposed to have been home ten minutes ago and leaped up in a panic. She closed the atlas and the book with gilded pages and rolled up the maps carefully, grabbed a bonbon for the journey home and left.

Safiyyah ran as quickly as she could through the familiar streets, her schoolbag on her back. Her mother always told her to make sure she was home on time each day, and this would be the second time that week that Safiyyah wouldn't be. She wove through the streets and alleys, swerving to avoid two women wearing sunglasses and hats so huge it seemed the hats were wearing *them*. She dodged people chatting outside cafés, eating macarons and sipping coffee, shop carts laden with plump tomatoes and a hundred types of cheese.

All Safiyyah wanted was to get home and tell Setti everything she'd discovered about South America, but dread of her mother's inevitable scolding loomed like a cloud over her. Her mother hadn't always been this strict, it had only started in autumn last year when war was declared. Soldiers had dug bomb shelters around the city and handed out gas masks to families. Safiyyah knew it was only really because her mother worried, but there had been no bombs or danger or anything ever since and she longed for her to relax. She ducked beneath the low branches of a magnolia tree bursting with elegant pink flowers, panting and sweaty.

Almost in the 5th arrondissement where she lived, Safiyyah stopped to catch her breath for a minute, leaning against a lamppost. In between the noisy motorcars

4

spluttering and coughing out fumes, Safiyyah noticed a man standing in front of the shops on the other side of the road. He wore a black suit and had absolutely no hair on his head. He was crying silently, and the child holding his hand, not much older than Safiyyah's little sister, looked up at him anxiously. Safiyyah had never seen a grown man cry in the street like that before, and she felt bad for the young boy beside him. The whole scene disturbed her deeply, and despite the sun overhead she felt a chill in the air.

Safiyyah started running again, almost colliding with a bicycle as she looked back over her shoulder at the pair. She wished she could take them home with her, Setti would definitely know how to fix whatever the problem was. She always did. The man wiped his wet cheeks with a handkerchief, and then Safiyyah was round the corner.

2

The mosque's green roofs and white walls came into sight and Safiyyah began thinking up excuses as to why she was late again. She bounded through the doors and into the courtyard, relieved to see Setti there before she needed to face her mother. Her grandma was sitting beside the tiled fountain, a silk shawl the colour of biscuits wrapped around her shoulders. As soon as Safiyyah stepped into the serene courtyard she had known for as long as she could remember, she felt calmer. The bustle and smoke of the streets of Paris gave way to the sounds of gently trickling water and Safiyyah's footsteps on the shining white tiles.

Safiyyah breathed her grandma's scent in deeply as she sat down beside her: jasmine, musk and honey. She knew not to disturb the old lady, whose eyes were closed as she passed worn wooden prayer beads between her wrinkled fingers. She swayed slightly from side to side as she prayed, her shadow moving across the colourful, intricately patterned mosaic tiles framing the fountain.

Safiyyah looked from Setti's hands to the creamy wrinkled skin on her rounded face. The lines etched from age onto her forehead and at the corners of her eyes looked to Safiyyah like the lines on a map, as if the voyages and paths of Setti's life had appeared on her skin. Safiyyah's mother always said Setti was beautiful once, but to Safiyyah, her grandma was still the most beautiful human she had ever met. Safiyyah closed her eyes too, the whispers of Setti's invocations blending with the fountain's gurgling, and she felt suddenly exhausted, as if she could have lain down and slept right there.

'Safiyyah, darling, are you all right? You know you're late again, don't you? My goodness, look at you all pink-cheeked. Come, let me fix your plaits, there's nothing left of them! Where have you been?'

She moved to sit in front of her grandma, allowing her hair to be coaxed back into place.

'I went to the library after school, I had barely even got started and somehow it was four o'clock already! I hope Yemma won't be too angry with me . . .'

Setti laughed affectionately. 'I know what you mean, darling, time feels like a thief sometimes. Just remember each breath you are given is more precious than a pearl. If you use them wisely, don't worry about the tricks of time!'

'Is learning maps a wise use of my breaths?'

'I'd say so, yes. Although ultimately it depends on what you intend to *do* with all that knowledge.'

'Travel the world of course, Setti!'

Setti reached the end of her second plait, and turned Safiyyah to face her again. 'A very wise plan, but only if you take me with you!'

She winked at Safiyyah, her gappy smile almost reaching the white headscarf framing her face, deepening the grooves beside her eyes.

'There will come a day when you have the choice to use what you've been given in one way or another.' Setti became serious, stern almost. 'Choose courage and goodness, my dear. Maps have led many people only to terrible darkness; look at the horrors of what the French have done to our people in Algeria . . . There is no use in a million maps unless they lead you to light.'

'But what do you mean, Setti? What choice? What day?'

Setti's face softened, her coal black eyes twinkling. 'We *all* have choices, my love, all of the time. Forks in the road, twists and turns along the way. Sometimes there is no paper map, but really, the one that matters is the one in here.' She put her hand to her heart and then reached out and wrapped Safiyyah in a hug. 'All we have to worry about is choosing the path of light.'

Safiyyah didn't really understand what Setti meant, but she hugged her back anyway, breathing in her warmth. Yemma was for ever telling Setti to stop speaking in mysterious riddles, but Safiyyah didn't mind.

Setti tucked a curl behind Safiyyah's ear and handed her a half-moon orange segment, before placing another into her own mouth. The tart sweetness of the fruit exploded as Safiyyah bit into it. 'Sweeter than yesterday's, don't you think?'

Setti nodded in agreement, holding another piece up to the light to inspect it for seeds before handing it over. 'Oh yes, this one tastes of the Andalusian sunrise. I can tell it was picked with love.'

Safiyyah chuckled, closing her eyes for a moment to imagine golden light spilling over green hills in southern Spain. Setti had moved there with her family from Algeria when she was in her teens, and missed it dearly. Back in Algeria, Safiyyah's great-grandparents farmed vast rolling fruit orchards, and when they moved to Andalusia, Setti's father had taken young orange, lemon and cherry saplings with him. They had taken root in the fertile soil and so the garden of Setti's home was shaded by trees bearing sweet fruit like glowing gemstones. Sometimes Setti talked of the trees like they were her siblings. Like her, the trees had been uprooted and planted in a new land.

For as long as Safiyyah could remember, Setti was obsessed with oranges, lamenting the fact that in the colder climate of Paris there were no citrus trees. She could easily go without a meal but made sure no day passed without a zesty orange. She savoured the peeling process, inhaling the scent from the leathery peel and often infused oil with the rinds to rub into her skin.

Yemma joked that Setti had orange juice running

through her veins instead of blood! Baba teased that Setti could live without him but not without her fruit. She seemed to be able to produce them at will, there were always one or two in the deep pockets of her long dresses, and Safiyyah had recently seen three in Setti's gas mask case. Setti claimed to be able to tell where the orange had been grown by tasting it, always ready with a commentary on the balance of tang with sweet, the ratio of acid and sugar.

Safiyyah often thought that for Setti, her beloved oranges had come to hold everything she had loved and lost in her life. Her parents, her memories of home, her husband, even. A million moments, a thousand emotions wrapped up in this fleshy round fruit that burst when you bit into it. Perhaps that was why Setti could taste things in them that no one else could.

'Another!' Setti pushed a second orange piece into Safiyyah's hand. Setti had tried for years to save the orange seeds to plant them at the mosque, but it hadn't ever worked. A few times seeds had germinated and grown, but they stayed small and never got close to bearing fruit. She still hadn't given up though, and saving seeds was as much of a habit for Setti as grating the fragrant rind into yoghurt or stirring steaming pots of pulp into marmalade.

'SAFIYYAH! Where is that girl? My god, why does she torture me like this!'

Yemma's voice was shrill, panicked almost, arriving in the courtyard before she did. Safiyyah leaped up just as her mother appeared, and thankfully Setti came to the rescue.

'Sara, she's with me, don't worry, she is fine! I was fixing her hair.'

'Oh thank god, thank god.' Yemma breathed a sigh of relief, and so did Safiyyah. 'I thought you hadn't come home yet. Safiyyah, come on up, you need to get washed and changed before we eat. You can help me with the salad, Ammo Kader will be joining us for dinner.'

Safiyyah's eyes lit up at the mention of her father's dearest friend visiting them that evening. He wasn't really her uncle, but she called him Ammo as a mark of respect. She loved his company, he was always attentive to her and told the best stories. Safiyyah hoped she might get the opportunity to mention what she'd discovered about the Amazon jungle at dinner.

She followed her mother out of the courtyard and up the steps towards their apartment, trailing her hands along the hanging moon and star paper decorations she had helped to make the week before. She had glued gold glitter onto the shapes that her neighbours Ayah and Hafsa cut out to make them shine. They strung them from tulle ribbon and hung them outside their apartments for the festival of Eid. The three-day festival ended a few days ago, but Safiyyah still felt the sparkle of celebration in the air. A pile of gifts she'd received lay beside her bed, a heavy magnifying glass from her parents and tiny gold earrings from Setti among her favourites.

The children from the madrasah had a party in the grand prayer hall, playing games on the soft green carpets and eating pastries soaked in rose syrup. Now Safiyyah checked quickly through her pile of presents to make sure her burglar of a little sister hadn't stolen anything. Fatima was for ever toddling around taking Safiyyah's things and stashing them beneath her cot. Today it seemed she had chosen the bouncy balls Safiyyah had won during a party game. She made a mental note to re-steal them once Fatima had been put to bed.

The fragrances of cumin and mint filled the little kitchen as Yemma stirred the tomato and lamb stew she'd been preparing. Safiyyah chopped bunches of parsley, red peppers and wedges of lemon for the salad before laying out the big stripy mat across the living room floor, where they would eat dinner. She straightened the orange tassels at its edges and had almost finished assembling the intricately patterned plates and jugs on it when Ammo Kader arrived with her father.

As she went to hug them both, she immediately sensed tension in her father. Perhaps he'd had a stressful time at work, Safiyyah thought, but he'd be back to his cheery self once he relaxed and had dinner. But even half an hour later, with Setti, Fatima, Yemma and Ammo tucking into their food, Baba remained on edge, distant and anxious. His mood perturbed Safiyyah, as if his worries had crept across the room and gripped her too.

'What have you been up to, Safiyyah?'

Ammo's question startled Safiyyah, who had been pushing tiny beads of couscous around her plate for the last ten minutes.

'Ummm, in the library today I learned that there are beetles in the Amazon jungle that are even bigger than my hand.'

Ammo smiled and then pretended to shudder: 'Make sure you don't bring any of those back here when you go exploring!'

'Our Safiyyah is going to be the greatest explorer yet. And she said she'll take me with her! The next Marco Polo.' Setti winked at Safiyyah, grinning.

'Ibn Battuta travelled even further than Marco Polo,' Ammo replied, and then turned to Safiyyah. 'But you will go further than both of them.'

'Ah yes, Battuta! He was Algerian, wasn't he?'

Yemma chuckled affectionately at Setti's claim. 'No, he was from Tangiers, a Moroccan. Setti would claim Abraham Lincoln as Algerian if she could!'

Everyone laughed, including Baba for the first time that night, though within a minute all traces of joy had vanished once again.

Once everyone had eaten, he helped Yemma clear away the dishes and then set a tray of small cups of sweet mint tea down on the mat. Baba sat down again beside Yemma, placing his hand on hers. He took a deep breath with his eyes closed, bracing himself.

'The Germans entered France today. They finally crossed the border through Ardennes.'

Yemma gasped, fear flushing her face. Setti closed her eyes and mumbled a prayer. Safiyyah felt strangely numb and cold. She remembered the man in the suit and the chill that had swept through her.

'I saw a man weeping in the street today, Baba.'

'Perhaps he was Jewish.' Baba looked down at his hands sadly. 'We don't know what the invasion will mean for us as Muslims yet, but one thing that *is* certain is what it will mean for Jews.'

Safiyyah had a thousand questions circulating her mind, but she was told to go to bed early as the adults had important things to discuss. Fatima had already fallen asleep on Setti's lap. Her podgy little face was peaceful, entirely oblivious to the world changing around her.

In her room, Safiyyah pulled on her pyjamas in a hurry. What *did* this mean for Jews? Would there be bombs? Would people be hurt, or worse, killed? What was it that had brought the man to tears?

Safiyyah realised she'd buttoned her shirt up all wrong as she jumped into bed. She wasn't even remotely tired.

Her blankets, her pillow, everything felt cold. She tried to distract herself with thoughts of the humid rainforest, the heat of the Amazonian sun, but no warmth came. All she could think about was the little boy who had been holding the crying man's hand.

3

Safiyyah awoke early to the familiar crowing of the mosque's resident cockerel. For a few blissful moments she was oblivious to the news of the previous night, but as she blinked away the heavy hands of sleep, everything came flooding back. She'd slept fitfully, dreaming that she was trying to outline the borders of Luxembourg, France, Belgium and the Netherlands on a huge map. No matter how much ink she had pressed onto the paper, the lines just kept disappearing, as the ragged shape of Germany grew and grew, unstoppable like liquid spilling across the floor. Safiyyah shuddered and threw open the curtains. Clear skies, smudged with pale pink and orange settled her heart a little, and she dressed and ran down to Baba's office.

Baba could have earned much more money by working at a bank or somewhere else, but there was truly nowhere else he wanted to be. He took great pride in the mosque, which he called a shining gem of the community and the city. A person could come to wash the dust from their soul in the grand prayer hall, then wash the dust from their body in the steaming marble-tiled hammam. They could eat and drink to their heart's content in the courtyard, relax in the lush gardens, peruse the mosque shop or little library and even see a doctor there!

At weekends, after the Fajr prayers, her father spent a couple of hours with the Imam of the mosque. He was another, ammo Safiyyah was fond of, and since she'd learned to talk she called him Ammo Imam, literally 'Uncle Imam'. The Imam led the congregation for their five daily prayers and taught classes.

Ammo Kader was also there, he was the main authority at the mosque. As the rector, he oversaw things, made final decisions and liaised with politicians and other important people, while Baba assisted Ammo Kader and took care of everything technical and money-related. The men would drink coffee in Baba's office while catching up on the mosque's affairs from the week. Between the three of them, the mosque ran smoothly, serving people from all across the city and even beyond Paris. They jokingly referred to themselves as *les trois mousquetaires,* the three musketeers, and Safiyyah was an honorary member of the club.

The congregation and visitors to the mosque were for ever gifting the Imam presents such as runny honey like sunshine in jars, green and black olives, or sweet semolina halwa that melted in your mouth. A few years back, Safiyyah had heard her father mention that Ammo Imam had been given a box of Turkish delight. Knowing Ammo

Imam would share some with Baba at their morning meeting, she'd jumped out of bed before him, washed and dressed, and begged him to let her join them. Of course she didn't mention *why* she wanted to join them, and Baba was pleased at her interest (though as soon as he saw her ogling the painted wooden box on the table he figured out her true intentions). The squishy cubes of lemon, rose and pomegranate-flavoured joy didn't disappoint, and with a satisfied stomach and sugar-powdered fingers Safiyyah had curled up on the armchair and slept through the meeting.

Since then it had become a habit for Safiyyah to attend on Saturday mornings, and Baba had taken to involving her in his work where he could. Despite it being unusual for women to work unless they had to, he hoped that Safiyyah would later go to university and use her sharp mind to do something great. By enlisting her help with tasks around his office, Baba felt he was preparing her for something bigger one day. Yemma told him to leave her to do her homework and be a child, but Safiyyah enjoyed it and couldn't imagine not being her father's second pair of hands.

Now Safiyyah knocked on the intricately carved wooden door of the office. Her father's voice welcomed her from the other side and she entered and sat beside him. Bitter black coffee steamed in small cups on the table, and Ammo Imam offered her a white chocolate-covered date with a warm smile. It tasted fudgy and nutty and creamy and wonderful all at once.

'Ben Youssef brought them this morning to the prayer. His wife made them yesterday to celebrate their daughter passing her exams.'

'Excellent, masha'Allah. Try the pistachio one, Safiyyah, delicious,' Baba said.

'He was asking me my opinion on whether people should think about leaving the country now. Just until everything blows over . . .'

Baba raised his eyebrows. 'What did you tell him?'

'I had no idea what to say. God only knows what this war will bring. I just told him we'll know more in the coming days and weeks, and as we keep hearing in all the news, our army is strong and ready.'

Baba was about to respond but caught himself as he glanced at Safiyyah's anxious face. Instead he replied, 'Our soldiers are fighting the Germans right now and I'm sure they won't allow them to progress any further into the country.'

Safiyyah couldn't help but ask, 'Surely if our army was so strong, they would have stopped the Germans from crossing the border in the first place, Baba?'

Her father glanced at Ammo Imam for a second, and Safiyyah's anxiety became horror as she realised he had been thinking the very same. 'We'll go through our mosque safety measures again today. Come, Safiyyah, we have work to do. Insha'Allah, everything will be fine. I need you to type up two important letters, no time to waste.'

Safiyyah took a seat on the velvet-topped stool at Baba's desk. She rearranged his collection of paperweights, lining up the trail of camels in front of the Eiffel Tower. She wiped the dust off the surface of his old drum, feeling it vibrate at her touch. She had never once heard him play it, just as she had never heard him sing.

She had been told about his talent countless times by Setti, Yemma, Ammo Kader and others, but to Safiyyah it remained like a wonder from an ancient legend: marvelled at but never witnessed. Once upon a time her father had mesmerised crowds with his hauntingly soulful voice. He was often called upon to play the drum and sing at celebrations and religious gatherings. People would even travel from other cities to listen to him. Yemma said his voice was like rippling silk, that it filled the room and embraced everyone in it. When his fingers came alive and beat his drum, its rhythm transported her away from her burdens and from France, across land and sea to the heat and dust of far away. But that was before he became a soldier. Years before Safiyyah was born, Baba fought for France in the Great War and not only did it snatch away the hearing of his left ear, it also stole his voice.

When she was younger, Safiyyah had begged and bribed him to sing, to teach her to beat the drum, frustrated at his refusal. It wasn't fair that everyone else had heard him and she couldn't! She had since given up asking, but still wondered what he would have sounded like whenever she heard someone else's voice rise in song. Setti said his voice was still within him somewhere, the blasts and brutality had just pushed it deep into hiding.

Baba handed her two pieces of paper, one written in Ammo Kader's looping writing, the other in Baba's own neat, tiny script. Safiyyah loved the click-clack of the typewriter, and took pride in how quickly she could make perfectly formed letters appear on the page. She typed them up quickly, carefully, not paying much attention to what they said. Her mind was on what Ammo Imam had said. The man who had asked about leaving had a son in her class at school. Were they really considering packing up and fleeing France? Would her own family leave too? Ordinarily Safiyyah loved travelling, but now her mind was filled with thoughts of soldiers and invasions she didn't feel very adventurous at all.

Her father signed the letters, placed them in envelopes and dripped hot wax on the back. Safiyyah pressed his metal stamp into the runny maroon wax, waiting for a few seconds before revealing the perfectly imprinted pattern, her favourite part.

Next, she helped Baba carry buckets of sand to the top floors around the mosque, in case they were needed to put out fires during air raids. Then, in every courtyard, they stuck directions to the nearest bomb shelter written in red marker pen.

Her final job of the morning was to deliver medication to an elderly friend of Baba and Ammo Kader. As she stepped out of the mosque door onto the street, armed with a paper bag of medicine, Safiyyah nervously anticipated the city looking different. She half-worried she might see German soldiers, but of course they were miles and miles away, and the familiar roads and alleys were entirely unchanged. Shopkeepers were pulling up shutters, as if the buildings were opening their eyes from sleep. A baker arranged baguettes and croissants on a stall outside his shop, and two stray cats fought beside a row of bins.

Monsieur Cassin lived in the 4th arrondissement just across the river. He was always delighted to see Safiyyah; she had been delivering his medication once a month for almost a year now. His house was an old white building set back from the main street. With its intricate iron balconies and old trees separating it from the road, Safiyyah thought it looked very grand. But that was nothing compared to the inside, which took her breath away every single time.

When he was younger, Monsieur Cassin was a well-known botanist, travelling across India, Sri Lanka and Malaysia to research plants and trees. His spacious hallway was framed with tall palms, their long fronds fanning through the air, while feathery ferns spilled over the edges of their pots on the floor. On every step of the generous spiral stairway was a potted plant: some had leaves shaped like umbrellas, others like string threaded with tiny hearts. The copper hat stand had been taken over by heavy leafy ivy vines, as if Monsieur's single felt hat at the top had grown hair. It felt like stepping into a lush green forest, and it was the only way Monsieur Cassin knew how to live.

Safiyyah understood why he needed his plants, somehow it seemed easier to breathe in his home. A serenity descended on her when surrounded by the thousand leaves, beautifully alive, growing imperceptibly every second. Though she did wonder where he ate his dinner ... His dining table was covered with pressed flowers and leaves, a pair of tweezers and a scrapbook. He wore a green cardigan, as if to match his surroundings, and his willowy figure was bent at the shoulders, like a windswept tree.

'Welcome, welcome!' He cleared some straggly ivy and a messy sketchbook from a chair and beckoned to Safiyyah to sit down. He always insisted that she come in for a little while, and she was all too happy to oblige. He must have been in his eighties, and despite the fact that his knees weren't too good any more and he didn't make it out of the house much, he still made sure to always have a batch of mille-feuille ready for Safiyyah when she came. The creamy, custardy vanilla flavours melded delightfully with the light pastry layers as always, but Safiyyah resisted the urge to eat more than two. Her mother most definitely would not approve of dessert before breakfast! But then again, her mother hadn't tasted Monsieur Cassin's speciality.

'How is your book coming along, Monsieur?' Safiyyah's words were muffled, her mouth half-full of pastry.

'Quite well, thank you!' He heaved out a stack of papers he had typed up, so thick you could practically use it as a stool. 'I've just completed the chapters on medicinal uses of the jungle species, it felt like I'd never finish but finally the day has come!'

'*Mazel tov!*'

Monsieur Cassin's face lit up, he had taught her a few Hebrew words over the months and was impressed that she'd remembered how to offer congratulations.

'Thank you so much! I now really just need to get going on the appendix on insect species. There's a terrific book I once had that would be a useful resource, but I can't seem to find it anywhere . . . Knowing me I probably left it on a boat or something silly.'

'I can try and find a copy for you, I'm friends with a librarian, you see!' Safiyyah felt excited all of a sudden at the prospect of being able to help him.

'Lucky you, librarians truly are a wonderful species!

That's a terribly generous offer, but don't trouble yourself with an old man's little request, I'm sure you have far more important things to do.'

'Monsieur! This book is your life's work on paper, I can't think of anything more important.' Over the years he had written many articles and papers, but only since retiring had he the time to finally compile all the precious knowledge he had acquired. Monsieur Cassin looked so genuinely touched that Safiyyah worried he might shed a tear.

'How kind of you, dear child. I should be eternally grateful if you'd mention the book to your librarian friend, whether it is ever found or not.' He scribbled the book's name onto a little square of paper with a fountain pen.

'I'll do my best, I promise! My mother will be cross if I'm not back for breakfast so I must leave you now. Thank you for the delicious mille-feuille.'

Safiyyah brushed flakes of pastry from her dress, carefully stepping over plants towards the door. She put the scrap of paper with the name of the book into her pocket and headed back home.

4

As with every Saturday afternoon, Safiyyah was due to spend time with her best friend Isabelle. They had known each other since nursery, and been inseparable for almost as long. Despite being in the same class at school, Saturday afternoons were always the best, because it was just the two of them (and of course, there were no lessons or teachers to think about).

Today, Baba took Safiyyah on the Métro over to Isabelle's home in the 16th arrondissement. When they stepped back onto street level, the clothes on the passersby had become more expensive, the houses larger and grander, the cafés more upmarket. Even the dogs in Isabelle's district seemed chicer than elsewhere. A poodle with pink ribbons trotted past the steps up to Isabelle's apartment, its owner in a matching pink dress and hairband strutting not far behind. Baba said he'd be back in a few hours and said goodbye at the milky smooth columns flanking the entryway. The porter let Safiyyah in and she met Isabelle at the top of the wide spiralling staircase.

Saturday afternoons had been a tradition for the girls for years. Sometimes Isabelle would come to the mosque and the girls would spend time in the gardens. The comforting gurgling of the fountains had been a backdrop for games of tag around the mosaicked pillars, and for the girls sharing their innermost thoughts and secrets on the bench under the purple wisteria. Other times Safiyyah visited Isabelle's home, playing dress-up in her huge toyroom; Safiyyah made a surprisingly convincing pirate and Isabelle's favourite was vampire. Some days they'd play boardgames, or sit for hours making up stories about passersby on the boulevard as they looked out of the tall windows with steaming cups of chocolat chaud. Isabelle often spent Eid with Safiyyah and her family. Yemma and Baba always made sure there was a pile of presents especially for her. On a rare occasion when Isabelle's father was off work, he would take the girls out for treats. Once they went all the way up the Eiffel Tower and marvelled at their city sprawling beneath them, people like ants and trees like tiny florets of broccoli.

Isabelle's mother was usually fully dressed-up by the time Safiyyah arrived in the afternoon, ready to take tea at a friend's house, or prepare for some sort of fancy evening event. Isabelle's father worked in the French government and so her parents' social circle involved important ministers and ambassadors. When Isabelle's mother was out and her nanny Nounou was occupied in the kitchen, the girls would sometimes sneak into the dressing room. They'd admire the long brass rails of silk and velvet dresses, the colours of midnight, pearl, and everything in between. They'd try on dazzling diamond rings and emerald necklaces in front of the big antique mirror and pretend they were princesses, waiting to come of age. Today though, Isabelle's mother was in a dressing gown, her hair falling limply around her shoulders instead of immaculately swept up into her signature chignon style. Safiyyah had never seen her like this. Without lipstick or a glamorous outfit she looked childlike, vulnerable almost. She was sitting in the hallway speaking on the telephone, seeming panicked.

Instead of greeting Safiyyah as she usually did, with a big perfumed hug and a kiss on the cheek, she waved absentmindedly over her shoulder, and continued with her frantic conversation. Safiyyah looked at Isabelle quizzically, and all of a sudden noticed that Isabelle too looked worried. Safiyyah felt a lurch in her stomach: something wasn't right. She felt almost certain that it would be linked somehow to the invasion, and the creeping anxiety began to grip her again.

'Maman wants us out of the apartment for a bit. Nounou said she'll take us to the park for ice cream.' Isabelle's tone was urgent.

'Isabelle, what is it? What's wrong?'

'Come, let's go, I'll explain when we're there,' Isabelle whispered, barely making eye contact as they followed her nanny out of the door.

The five-minute walk to the park felt like five hours, with all sorts of horrible scenarios going through Safiyyah's head. As soon as they had their ice creams, they left Nounou on a bench and ran to the swings, out of earshot of anyone except a couple of little boys playing on the slide.

Isabelle took a deep breath, her face pale. 'Safiyyah, I think we're leaving.'

'Who's leaving? Where? What?'

'Papa wants us to go south, he said we'll go to our château in the countryside for now, and see what happens from there.'

'Why? When? For how long?' Safiyyah couldn't make any sense of it, but a bubbling panic was rising nonetheless.

'He said he doesn't want us to be in Paris any more, apparently things could get dangerous here. Worse than most people realise now. I don't know, Safiyyah, I really don't know, Maman only told me last night! I got home from school and they were both sitting at the dining table looking serious. I'm not supposed to be telling anyone really, but obviously you don't count.'

Isabelle visited their château in Provence usually once a year in the holidays. Going to the château for a while wasn't too awful, Safiyyah told herself, it'd be like the holidays, just not actually *in* the holidays.

'Right . . . when are you going and for how long?'

Isabelle sighed. 'I have no idea, I was simply just told that once I'd seen you and said goodbye I'd need to pack my things.'

'Said GOODBYE?! You mean *this* is goodbye? For what, a few weeks? Months?!' Safiyyah realised she was almost shouting. She felt physically sick. She remembered the ice cream in her hand when she felt something wet drip down her wrist. She'd squeezed the cone so hard she had crushed it. She bent down and wiped her hand on the grass. As she looked up she saw that Isabelle was crying.

'I asked them the same questions, I told them I don't want to leave. I have no choice, they've made up their minds and it doesn't matter how I feel. I think we might go tonight or maybe tomorrow, Maman is making the arrangements now. The war is coming, Safiyyah.'

'There's been a war on for months now apparently, but our gas masks lie unused and absolutely nothing has changed, why is now any different?' Safiyyah realised she sounded ridiculous, she knew exactly what had changed. She also knew that Isabelle was not at fault here at all, but still she felt angry.

Isabelle wiped her tears, 'It's different now, the Germans are in our country. Papa said they're advancing quickly.' She paused for a moment, looking almost guilty. 'If our army doesn't get control of the situation soon, he said we might go to England.'

Now Safiyyah began to cry. Hot, angry tears streamed down her face. She felt as if she was being abandoned, the thing most precious to her was slipping out of her grasp and there was nothing she could do about it. Like the ice cream that was now a sloppy mess on the ground, once it started melting, there was nothing you could do to stop it.

A shadow fell over Isabelle's face. Quietly she said, 'You could come with us. There's space in the motorcar and more than enough in the château.'

Safiyyah frowned. 'You know very well I can't come with you, there might be space for me but none for my mother, father, sister or grandmother. And anyway, it sounds like your father is overreacting; everyone knows how strong our army is.' She knew she was being unnecessarily cruel, but there was a knot in her stomach that she couldn't untwist. 'I'm not going anywhere.'

The pair were sitting on their swings in silence, avoiding all eye contact. Safiyyah pushed off from the ground, leaning back and then forward to pick up momentum. As she felt the breeze on her skin and through her hair, the hot anger within her began to subside. She swung so high she was almost in line with the top bar of the frame, the clouds seemed within reach. The feeling of exhilaration overtook the pain of Isabelle's news, the bleakness of the prospect of life without her best friend, and the anxiety about looming war.

She closed her eyes and breathed in deeply, comforted by swooping through the air.

Isabelle's swing was still. She was kicking pebbles on the ground. Safiyyah suddenly felt terribly sorry for the way she had reacted. She hadn't meant to hurt Isabelle, but she knew she had. Isabelle was an only child and Safiyyah as close as a sibling to her. She must have been dreading breaking the news to her ever since she'd heard it herself. Safiyyah scraped her shoes on the ground to slow her swinging, and remembered she had change from an errand she'd run for Baba one morning. She plucked two coins from her pocket and offered one to Isabelle, whose face lit up instantly.

Within seconds, the two were racing to the big stone fountain in the middle of the park. Nounou was too unfit to be able to run after them, if she'd wanted to, that is. She'd brought one of her romance novels to occupy herself anyway. Isabelle won by a couple of seconds, and both girls sat down on the edge of the fountain to get their breath back.

'I'm sorry you're leaving.'

'I'm sorry I'm leaving too.'

'And I'm sorry for what I said.'

'Come on, Fia, who has time for this?!' Isabelle joked. 'Make your wish and make sure it's a smart one!'

Isabelle stood up and faced the fountain with her eyes closed, her centime clutched to her chest. Safiyyah did the same. Just like they had done so many times before, in different spots around the city. Except this time, each knew exactly what the other was wishing for. They threw the coins in and watched as they floated slowly down at the feet of the carved statue, joining the hundreds of others. Both of the girls felt a little lighter.

'You'll come back to Paris, I know you will.'

'I'll write to you, promise to always write back?'

'Of course! As long as *you* promise not to replace me!'

'As if . . . I doubt I could find someone annoying enough to replace you with, even if I tried,' Isabelle joked.

'Haha . . . Seriously, though, make sure you stay safe.'

'It's not us we should be worried about . . . we're not Jewish, after all.'

'I don't get it, it's the stupidest thing I've ever heard, picking on people just because of how they worship God?!'

'Me neither . . . Hitler blames Jews for everything wrong with the world. The Nazis have been treating them horrifically in Germany already, and now they're spreading their evil further.'

'Ughh. My baba said Hitler is no better than the Devil himself.'

'And it's not just Jews, he says black people and those with disabilities are less human too! Definitely devilish.'

'I just don't understand why people support him?!

I saw a man crying in the street yesterday, I'm quite sure he was Jewish. I feel so sad thinking about him.'

'Did you know that Hana and Remy from school are Jewish?'

'Oh, yes. And Aharon is, remember he did his summer project on the synagogue he goes to?'

'I wish I could take them with me. And you of course.' Isabelle sighed sadly.

'I'll look out for them. I don't know how, but if it comes to it, I swear I will.'

'If there's anyone I'd want to look out for me, it would definitely be you, Fia. The stubbornest, fiercest and most loving person I know.'

Safiyyah grabbed Isabelle and squeezed her tight.

'Oh gosh, Nounou is shouting for us, look!'

Safiyyah glimpsed Nounou, red-faced in the distance, waving her arms around at them madly. They ran back, and tried not to giggle as she told them off for disappearing. It had taken her a full fifteen minutes to even notice they'd been gone, she must have been utterly engrossed in her book. They followed her back to the apartment, giggling at how flustered Nounou was and wondering if it was because of them or because of the love story in her novel.

Back at the apartment Nounou brought slices of onion quiche out for the girls, who were trying to occupy themselves with a game of chess. Neither could concentrate on the board, there were a thousand things they wanted to say to each other. Safiyyah felt something bittersweet rise inside of her; so much fondness for Isabelle and all their time together, but it was clouded with pain. She kept looking at the grandfather clock in the corner: it was almost time for Baba to collect her. Isabelle's mother was dressed now and had put out two suitcases for Isabelle to fill. When they glimpsed Baba through the window, just a few minutes' walk away, Isabelle ran into her room, returning with something in her palm. She brought it to Safiyyah, looking teary again.

It was a delicate silver locket, in the shape of a heart with looping patterns engraved across its centre. Safiyyah opened the heart carefully, holding her breath. Inside were two perfectly-formed pressed flowers, a tiny blue forget-me-not and a delicate daisy. Safiyyah knew instantly where they were from and her heart swelled. Last summer, the girls had gone with Isabelle's parents to L'Isle-Adam for the day. They'd sung songs in the back of the car with their sunhats on, watching the urban landscape of Paris turn to endless countryside. After wandering along the river in the sunshine, they'd sat down to a picnic in an empty field. In between sandwiches and sips of lemonade, the girls had picked wildflowers. Isabelle pressed them later that day, wanting to remember the trip for ever.

'For you,' Isabelle whispered.

Safiyyah wished she too had something to give to Isabelle, but all she could do was hug her as tight as she could. The apartment buzzer sounded.

Safiyyah stood back and took in Isabelle's straight sandy hair, the dusting of freckles across her nose and her wide, cucumber-coloured eyes. 'This isn't goodbye.'

Isabelle smiled. 'It's see you later.'

Safiyyah opened the door and traipsed down the stairs towards the lobby. She gave one last wave up at Isabelle, just visible through the iron balustrade before she moved out of sight. She held the heart-shaped locket tightly, as she felt her own heart sink.

5

The days passed in a blur. Safiyyah would find herself glancing back to catch Isabelle's eye in class, only to be met with an empty desk. None of the other girls' conversations or games seemed to interest her much. She wore Isabelle's locket and touched it for comfort. Was Isabelle happy at the château? Was Isabelle remembering her too? In the rush and emotion on Saturday, Isabelle had forgotten to give Safiyyah the château's address, and so all she could do was wait to hear from her. Baba promised Safiyyah that just as soon as Isabelle sent a letter, Safiyyah could write back and use his special wax seal on the envelope.

Yemma thought a visit to see Safiyyah's cousins might cheer her up, and so they went to Baba's sister's house for dinner after school. When they arrived, Tarek, who was sixteen, was busy repairing a toaster on the table. He greeted them with his usual cheerful smile. He'd just finished high school and wanted to become an engineer. He was always taking things apart and rebuilding them. He had made Safiyyah a ship once, with a wooden hull, thin wire coiled up to make the helm and squares of linen forming the sails. It sat proudly on a shelf in Safiyyah's room above the window.

Sumayyah was helping to prepare the food in the kitchen, but as always when her favourite cousin arrived, she rushed out to greet her. Sumayyah was a year older than Safiyyah and they shared a strong bond. Safiyyah knew she could count on her cousin to give her the lowdown on surviving high school, which she'd started a year before. Ibrahim greeted them next, wooden spoon in hand. He wanted to become a chef and was rarely seen without his apron on. The last of her four cousins was chubby baby Ahmed. Safiyyah gave his plump cheeks a big kiss and spun him around, making him giggle.

Fatima and Ibrahim ran off with Ahmed in tow, jumping on the bunk beds like crazed monkeys, while Sumayyah, seeing her sadness, led Safiyyah to her bedroom and asked what was wrong. It felt good to talk about how much she missed Isabelle and, by the time everyone sat down together to eat, Sumayyah had even made her laugh a little. As they moved on to dessert, it was Ibrahim who brought the dreaded topic of war back to the room like a stubborn grey cloud.

'My friend Gabriel from football club is moving out of Paris. His grandparents live in Scotland, so they are going before the war gets bad,' said Ibrahim.

Safiyyah was surprised to realise that she wasn't the

only one who was losing a friend to the approaching war. She felt the urge to reach out and hug her little cousin. He continued, turning to his father, 'Are we going to leave France too, Baba?'

Safiyyah looked at her own father, gauging his expression. Ibrahim had been brave enough to ask the question that had been on Safiyyah's mind all week. She wasn't sure if she felt more worried at the prospect of leaving or staying, but somehow, finding out either way made her feel sick. Baba looked resolute. Her uncle smiled gently, 'No, darling, this is our home. Everyone must do what they feel is right for them. Insha'Allah, we will be fine here.'

Safiyyah's father nodded at her mother. 'We feel the same. Our responsibility is to our community. The congregation, as well as our neighbours of all faiths, need us, and in difficult times it's more important than ever that we stick together.'

Tarek, who had been uncharacteristically quiet all evening, cleared his throat. 'Yemma, Baba, I'm going to fight.'

His mother choked on her tea, spluttering as she tried to catch her breath. His father asked sternly, 'What are you talking about, son?'

'I was asked to sign up to the army, and I accepted. I can't just sit here while France is taken over.' Tarek seemed calm, if a little defensive.

His mother began to cry, panic visible on her face. His father seemed angry. 'How could you do this without consulting us first?'

Tarek shot back, 'I *have* to do this. We don't know what's coming yet. Look at Belgium and the Netherlands. I won't sit back and watch everything be turned upside down. I'm a man and I'll fight like one.'

He got up from his seat and left the room, leaving a shocked silence, interrupted only by his mother's strangled sobs. Safiyyah counted the years between her and Tarek: five and a quarter. His words, *I'm a man* rang through Safiyyah's head and made her feel cold. They were children, how could Tarek be given a uniform and a gun and sent to fight Germans? He'd be in danger. Safiyyah had heard recently about how hospitals in Paris had been filling up with injured soldiers. There had been intense fighting in the countryside as the Germans pushed to take more land every minute. Safiyyah placed her hand over Sumayyah's. Her cousin looked absolutely terrified.

It felt like the cloud that had been menacingly hovering above had descended, engulfing the family in thick, dark gloom. Yemma tried to comfort her frantic sister-in-law, while Baba talked in hushed tones to Safiyyah's uncle. Fatima and Ibrahim, who were usually boisterous partners in crime were now sitting quietly in the corner. Setti rocked baby Ahmed to sleep, passing her prayer beads faster than normal through her hands. Safiyyah knew how pained Setti must be; she had sent away Baba, her own son, to fight before, and now it was her grandchild. She knew they must do what was needed to defend the country, but it still must be strange to see her children dressed in the French military uniform of the men who took away her childhood back in Algeria.

6

When Saturday afternoon next arrived and the absence of Isabelle felt sharper than ever, Yemma and Baba practically forced Safiyyah to the library. They were both convinced that a good map or two would lift their daughter's spirits. Safiyyah had half-heartedly agreed, but found some motivation in tracking down the book Monsieur Cassin needed. She bumped into Madame Odette beside the fiction section, the top of her coiffure just visible over the pile of hardback books she was carrying.

'Oops! Bonjour, Safiyyah! I haven't seen you for a while!'

'Bonjour, Madame. Shall I help you with those?'

Madame gratefully accepted. They carried their piles to a room behind her desk, depositing them beside the door. The light was off but Safiyyah could just about make out the outline of what looked like lots of boxes.

'Bonbon?'

The familiar chewiness, and the musky smell of the old leather armchairs, relaxed her.

'Not sure how much longer I'll be able to keep my

bonbon supply going, to be honest. All the good things are getting harder to come by with those greedy Germans trampling the north.'

Safiyyah shook her head in disapproval, unable to form words without drooling through her sugary stuck-together teeth. She pulled out the scrap of paper with the name of Monsieur's book and handed it to Madame Odette. 'A friend of mine needs this book to complete the volume he is writing, I wondered if you might have a copy? He can't get out of his house much, you see, his knees give him a lot of trouble.'

Madame smiled. 'It's very good of you to help him, Safiyyah. I'll have a look.'

Together they scoured the section that the book would have been in, without luck.

'One of the other libraries in Paris will have a copy I'm sure, I'll put a call out tomorrow. If there is a copy, I should have it in a week or so. Just check with me next time you're in, oui?'

'Thank you so much, Madame, it will mean the world to Monsieur Cassin!'

'What will you do now? Where do you plan to fly away to on a magic map?'

'Ummm, first I was going to trace the route that my best friend Isabelle might have taken to go to her château in the south, and then the route of my cousin Tarek, who will go to fight in the north.'

'Oh my dear, what joy will that bring to you? Come with me instead, I have some very important work and I could do with an extra pair of hands.'

Safiyyah was surprised to feel relief that she was no longer going to sit imagining soldiers spilling across latitudes, tanks and bullets flying over grid lines. Curious, she followed Madame to a store room on the second floor. She had never been here before and was intrigued by what she saw. Piles of books filled the floor, some short, some as tall as Safiyyah. The room looked like a city of books. Cardboard boxes lined the perimeter of the room, and a moustached man and a lady wearing a red neck-tie were filling them. Both of them stopped to smile and wave across the room at Safiyyah when she entered.

'What are they doing?' Safiyyah's curiosity had tripled.

'We are packing books to send to soldiers. If stories and words can bring even a tiny amount of joy and hope into the hearts of our men then we will pack all night. And judging by the requests for more that have been pouring in, these beauties are more powerful than most people think.' Madame Odette picked up a novel with the ocean on its cover. 'I know if I was stuck in a trench for weeks on end, books would keep me going. Even more than bonbons!' She winked at Safiyyah, beckoning her towards some of the boxes under a window.

Madame handed her a sheet of paper, and pointed

out the corresponding names of regiments written on boxes. 'Soldiers have requested their preferences, you see. Some want a good mystery, while others want a riveting adventure, or maybe even some romance. Some like to read non-fiction, a memoir perhaps, this gentleman here wants fishing magazines!' She pointed to a name on the list.

Safiyyah felt a new energy, a sense of purpose within her. She wove between the stacks of books, seeking out titles and wrapping them in brown paper before writing soldiers' names on and placing them in the boxes. As she folded the crisp paper around a book, she delighted in imagining the recipient eagerly ripping it open again. Safiyyah wondered if Tarek might request a book once he was sent away. When she came across *The A-Z of Building* and *The Greatest Engineers in History*, she asked if she could wrap them up and take them to him.

Safiyyah was reading the description on an orange clothbound poetry book when Madame Odette's voice made her jump. 'Oh, Safiyyah, is that a special edition? That shouldn't be here at all. Come, help me carry these downstairs please.'

'Sorry, Madame.' Safiyyah worried she had done something wrong.

'No, no, it's my fault, not yours!' Madame Odette showed Safiyyah into the room behind her desk. When she switched the light on, Safiyyah saw more books piled almost up to the ceiling, sealed boxes stacked atop one another. 'I'm sending the specials, the first editions and the rare collections away. Into the countryside down south for safe-keeping. My uncle has a large personal library in his farmhouse. They're far too precious to risk remaining here, only God knows what those Germans will do if they make it here.'

'But why would the Germans care about books?! I thought they just wanted our land, control over Europe?' Safiyyah was utterly confused, the image she had of German soldiers was definitely not bookworms.

'Ah, but you see, dear child, oppressors always fear the power of books. The truths and wonders that their spines bear threaten the injustice that the Nazis bring with them. It has happened throughout history, the light that a library brings is terrifying to the darkness of a tyrant. I've had word from libraries in Luxembourg and Belgium that the Nazis have raided their buildings, so thought it best to prepare for the worst. They've publicly burned books in German cities for years now. One thing the Nazis know is that you can't truly control a people without controlling what they read.'

Safiyyah shuddered at the thought of German soldiers in her beloved library. 'Will you be sending the maps away too?'

'I'm afraid rare and precious ones will have to go. Everything else will remain, and we will just pray and hope that the Nazis don't bother us too much.' She bent down to seal up a cardboard box, the brown tape shrieking as she pulled at it, as if it too felt pain at the situation.

Safiyyah wandered over to the back of the room and picked up a book called *David Golder* with a blue and beige cover. She checked to see if it was a first edition. Madame Odette noticed, her forehead creasing in concern.

'Safiyyah, leave those, please.'

Safiyyah placed it back on the pile quickly, wondering why Madame's face had changed. 'Is this a rare book?'

Madame looked uncomfortable, fear flashing across her face for a split second. 'The author, Némirovsky, is Jewish, Safiyyah.' Madame's voice was a whisper. She placed a black sheet over the three boxes at the back of the room, and ushered Safiyyah out, locking the door behind them.

'Will you send those boxes to your uncle too, Madame?'

Madame looked even more uncomfortable now, and she shook her head hurriedly. 'I haven't figured that out yet, but I know for sure I will not put anyone else at risk. My goodness, Safiyyah, what am I doing telling you all this? I shouldn't have answered your questions at all, I've burdened you with far too much.'

'I won't breathe a word to anyone, Madame, I swear. What boxes? What books?'

Madame half-smiled, looking relieved, though Safiyyah could see exhaustion, or was it worry, in the shadows around her eyes.

Four days later, Safiyyah and her family were back at her cousin's house. The Germans were now racing across northern France, with a trail of destruction in their wake. Tarek had been called up for training two weeks earlier than originally planned and the need for a sudden goodbye had come as a second shock to everyone.

As they stood beside the front door, crowding the little hallway to say goodbye to Tarek, Safiyyah could see that her father was holding back his tears. He almost went to hug Tarek like a frightened child, but instead he addressed him like a man, told him to be brave and that God would be with him. He seemed to strangle the tide of fear swelling within him, and told Tarek's weeping mother not to worry: 'The British alone are far stronger than the Germans. Tarek is joining the most powerful alliance.'

Once Tarek had hugged everyone twice, he lifted his backpack and calmly opened the front door. 'I promise I'll write to you soon. Assalamu alaikum.' *May peace be upon you.* And he was gone.

Once he was out of sight, his mother dropped to her knees and sobbed. Safiyyah could see that Baba could no longer contain his emotions as he slipped away to the bathroom and allowed his tears to silently fall. Just before he closed the door, she saw him cup his hand around his bad ear, perhaps trying to remember what it was like to hear in full. Safiyyah felt helpless. She didn't want letters from Isabelle or from Tarek, she just wanted *them*.

7

Safiyyah shuddered as her history teacher's chalk scraped the blackboard, squealing and groaning as he wrote the date: *3rd June 1940*.

Normally, this was Safiyyah's favourite time of the year: hot days with vast blue skies and long balmy evenings. Safiyyah's family would have enjoyed lively evening gatherings of song and worship beside the mosque fountains, the warm summer air thrumming with the beat of the drum. As *l'heure bleue* drew in and the stars began to twinkle overhead, Safiyyah loved to sit beside Setti, who would hum softly, swaying along to the tune. She'd watch moths flutter towards the flickering glow of candles, and often drifted off to sleep on floor cushions in the courtyard.

This year, things felt entirely different. Isabelle was gone, and Baba and Ammo Kader had no time for joyous gatherings. Everywhere she went, the atmosphere felt charged, tense. No conversation lasted more than a minute or two before turning once again to the topic of war, and almost everyone was worried about someone on the front line.

The newsreaders had been claiming that the Allied armies were holding the Germans back in the north, that the fighting would not engulf more of the country. But there were now rumours of an Allied retreat at Dunkirk, and Safiyyah could barely make sense of it all. She felt a pang of concern whenever she recalled Isabelle's words. *Things could get dangerous here. Worse than most people realise now.* As much as Safiyyah had tried to deny it that day, deep down she knew that Isabelle's father had access to insider information, and that he was a clever, careful man.

Now, despite the sunlight streaming in through the classroom windows and *la géographie*, her favourite subject on her timetable that afternoon, Safiyyah fidgeted. She couldn't keep her mind from wandering back to Saturday, when for the first time ever, Baba had asked her not to come to the morning meeting.

Safiyyah had headed to Baba's office. Instead of the warm welcome she was usually met with, she was turned away. Baba apologised at least, but she was barely given a sentence of explanation before he closed the door, leaving Safiyyah standing alone in the hallway. Apparently, the men had important matters to discuss that were confidential.

Safiyyah felt rejected and insulted. Since when could she not be trusted? She had always known not to speak of the mosque's affairs to anyone, and Baba had never cared about privacy in front of her before. He'd told Safiyyah to 'go and play with Fatima' instead. That had been the icing on the cake. It was bad enough that she'd been turned away, without then being patronised and told to go and *play*. It was as if Baba had forgotten the years of Safiyyah organising his files, typing his letters and running errands for him, and she was suddenly a little child, unworthy of his trust and attention.

It wasn't just Baba who was preoccupied and absent. Safiyyah's history teacher Monsieur Abrams now sat behind his desk, staring out of the window worriedly, as if Hitler's men were about to walk into the schoolyard. He tried to sip from his already empty coffee cup, appearing totally unaware of both the lack of liquid in it, and the chatter and noise rising in his classroom.

Monsieur Abrams spent his days bringing the wars of the past to life for his students, teaching the politics of persecution and the antics of armies. Now there was an army marching towards them, whose guns and grenades weren't confined to paper. In their first ever class of the school year, he had talked about the importance of studying history, that the lessons of old might be learned so that the evils of the past wouldn't repeat themselves. Safiyyah felt a deep pang of sympathy for Monsieur Abrams.

A black beetle moving slowly across the floor caught Safiyyah's eye. She'd been planning to go to the library to see if Madame Odette had managed to get hold of a copy of the insect book for Monsieur Cassin. She felt a rush of adrenaline at the prospect of being able to give Monsieur Cassin the last piece of the puzzle needed to finally complete his own book. She didn't want to wait for another two weeks to see him when his medication needed delivering. Besides, there was a chance Baba might end up demoting Safiyyah from that too, telling her to go and play instead . . . She felt a new swell of annoyance, and decided that she would go today.

As soon as the bell went for lunch, Safiyyah grabbed her bag and slipped out of the back entrance beside the lunch hall. Students didn't use this door, it was mainly for deliveries of food and school supplies, but Safiyyah being Safiyyah, she knew exactly where the long alley beyond the door led. After dodging dinner ladies, she half-jogged down the alley, littered with broken milk bottles and cigarettes. She had never skipped school before in her entire life, and was terrified that someone would run after her with a cane. Or worse still, tell her parents, who would definitely never forgive her for breaking their trust. Though when she thought of Baba, she reminded herself that he now didn't trust her anyway, and a little of her guilt morphed into fresh defiance.

The windy alley spat her out onto a bright square, lined with shops and cafés, just as she had calculated. At least the maps in her memory remained unchanged by the war, even if nothing else did. No one had followed her, she was free. Safiyyah took a deep breath in, but regretted it immediately when the stench of raw fish entered her nostrils. She'd figured the alley led from the school to this square, but hadn't realised she was standing right outside a fishmonger!

She set off towards the library at a brisk pace. The sky was a brilliant blue, crisp and clear, interrupted only by the silhouettes of rooftops and spires stretching up ahead. At the library, instead of Madame Odette, she was greeted at the front desk by a wiry gentleman with a whiskery moustache. His name badge spelled *Claude*.

'Bonjour. How may I help you today? The children's section is down the stairs and to the left.'

'Bonjour, may I speak to Madame Odette please?'

'Madame is currently in a meeting upstairs. She will be there for another hour at least.'

Safiyyah felt a twinge of disappointment, and resisted the urge to roll her eyes. Adults and their meetings!

'I wonder if she might have mentioned anything about finding a book for me?'

After a moment, Monsieur Claude's face lit up. He looked at Safiyyah properly now, as if he was noticing her for the first time.

'Ahhh, is it Safiyyah?'

'Oui.'

'Madame has told us all about you!'

He winked and reached into the desk drawer, pulling out what could only be a heavy book in a brown paper bag. Safiyyah felt a wave of relief and excitement as Monsieur Claude stamped the library card on the first page and passed it to her. Monsieur Cassin would be so delighted!

'Merci! Merci beaucoup! I will get this to my friend as soon as possible. Goodbye!'

By the time Monsieur Claude responded with his own goodbye, Safiyyah was already at the doors, clutching the book to her chest. As she stepped into the sunshine of the street again, she picked up an ever-faster pace, her happiness adding a spring to her step. She slid the book out of the paper bag. Its red leather cover was embossed with gold swirls at the corners. She opened it at a random page filled with intricate drawings of beetles from different angles, lines labelling different body parts with Latin-sounding names. Safiyyah put the book back in the bag, grinning, not caring about anyone thinking she was crazy.

As Safiyyah drew closer to Monsieur Cassin's area, she felt as if a pair of excited butterflies had escaped from the book in her hands and found their way into her stomach. She imagined Monsieur's reaction, she knew this book was worth more to him than gold or diamonds. Her anticipation grew as she wove through streets packed with office workers returning to their buildings after lunch, men in smart suits chatting and laughing as they walked. Two ladies who looked like twins walked arm in arm, intently discussing something in dramatic, hushed tones. A woman who must have been their maid walked two paces behind them, carrying a big blue hat box and too many shopping bags to count. A little boy clapped his hands in glee as his father carried him into a sweet shop. It occurred to Safiyyah that her classmates back at school would now be returning to lessons after their lunch break, and that she hadn't eaten anything since breakfast.

She was trying to work out what time she should arrive back at school in order to miss mathematics, but attend geography, when the wailing started.

8

It began as a deep, distant sound that grew in pitch and volume with every second, stopping Safiyyah still in her tracks. She'd only ever heard it before during an air raid practice with her family at home, and once at school. The haunting, falling and rising wail of the sirens had scared her on those occasions, but now Safiyyah felt terror like never before. This was no practice, and despite being on a busy street, Safiyyah was utterly alone. The howling seemed to fill the air around her, making it heavy and thick.

People were panicking and scattering in different directions. Safiyyah had absolutely no idea where the nearest bomb shelter was, and was too frozen in fear to make a decision about what she should do. She pictured her gas mask lying under her bed at home, and fresh terror engulfed her. If only the howling of the sirens would stop, she might be able to think straight. She knew she needed to move, but she couldn't feel her feet.

Safiyyah glimpsed the blue hat box disappear around a corner ahead as a stream of people jogged and marched past her. A young lady with an apron and baker's hat on walked slower than the others. She was guiding an elderly man whose back was hunched forward dramatically from age. His frail, trembling hands were clamped around his ears. His jaw trembled too, and he was shaking his head back and forth as he walked. Almost as if to say, 'Not again, not again'. Safiyyah thought of Baba, and all of a sudden tears began to stream down her cheeks.

She looked up, the sky was still a dazzling blue and there were no German planes in sight, but the wailing kept coming in throbbing waves. If she was killed right there by a dropped bomb, she would never be able to explain herself to her parents. Monsieur Cassin would never get his book, and whenever Isabelle finally did write, she would never receive a reply. Safiyyah wished she'd hugged Yemma, Baba, Setti and Fatima tightly this morning before she left for school.

Safiyyah stopped sobbing as she felt a warm hand on her shoulder. A red-haired lady nodded at Safiyyah before pulling her along in the direction that the hat box and baker woman had gone. As they turned the corner at the end of the street, they reached a wide square.

Approaching a tall sand-coloured building on the corner of the square, they saw a man in a suit shouting things frantically. He was standing on the steps of what must have been a shelter, with only his torso visible, waving his arms at the crowd of people approaching. They were too far away to hear what he was saying but within moments, the message had trickled through to people in front of them in the crowd. Safiyyah heard shouts of 'It's full already!' and 'To the Métro!'

Suddenly, a high-pitched, continuous whistle sounded from the sky, its scream becoming louder and shriller until it stopped altogether. The bomb exploded four streets away, and Safiyyah felt the shudder of the blast as everyone began to run. Some people separated from the crowd, presumably ducking for cover elsewhere, but Safiyyah and the lady continued running as fast as they could in the direction of the Métro.

The siren's wailing was interspersed with the sound of heavy gunfire in the distance. Another sharp scream came from the skies, Safiyyah covered her head with her hands, praying as she ran. Her ears throbbed as this deathly orchestra played relentlessly. Almost immediately, another whistle shrieked louder and louder above them, followed by the sound of shattering glass. Four or five white mushroom-shaped smoke clouds puffed out in the sky over the buildings up ahead. Safiyyah could just about make out huge flocks of panicked pigeons whirling and swirling in the distance. The Métro was only about a minute away and Safiyyah could see people running down the steps to it.

A force pushed Safiyyah off balance, everything spun into a blur and she felt a searing pain in her left arm as she landed on the ground. Once the world stopped spinning, Safiyyah realised with relief that it was a person running in another direction that had hit her. She'd fallen onto the ground beside a tree, and though the Métro was just feet away, Safiyyah had not pushed herself up before the next scream sounded. This time the explosion was closer and Safiyyah's head was thrown down hard to the ground again by the powerful blast.

She didn't know how long she lay there for. When she opened her eyes, she saw a discarded paper bag, striped pink and white with sweets shaped like fish spilling out of it, as if frozen while escaping. A lemon bonbon had rolled further away, smudged with dirt. Monsieur Cassin's book was underneath her, its corner digging into her stomach. Her ears rang as she slowly sat up, cringing as her shoulder hurt sharply. The sirens had stopped, the all clear sounded. Shocked-looking people were appearing from corners and basements and from the Métro steps. The red-haired lady was nowhere to be seen, and Safiyyah prayed she was safe.

Safiyyah scanned her body, touching each of her limbs. She was fine. She'd been saved. She wanted a hug from Setti. A lump rose in her parched throat and she began to cough. There was soil in her mouth, and Safiyyah had barely enough saliva to spit it out. Her legs felt strangely wobbly as she stood up, but she mustered all the strength she had left and began slowly walking towards Monsieur Cassin's home.

The streets were mostly quiet, people she passed were reduced to silence or whispers as they tried to process what had happened. The lunchtime laughter and frivolous conversation that had echoed through squares and floated from café tables earlier on had vanished. Safiyyah wondered if it could ever return again. The war was finally on their doorstep. She felt anger at the weather, how could the sun shine so brightly on such a dark day?

Safiyyah gasped at the sight of a building whose entire front wall had been reduced to rubble on the ground. She could see a kitchen, half of a staircase and what must have been two bedrooms on the upper floor. Its exposed front reminded Safiyyah of Isabelle's doll's house. Tears began to sting her eyes again as she thought of the people whose home it was. A horde of ambulances drove past and Safiyyah began to feel like her legs might give way soon. She held her breath as she turned the corner onto Monsieur Cassin's street, overwhelmed with relief when she saw it was unaffected by the bombing. Suddenly Safiyyah felt a new wave of fear as images of the mosque in ruins and rubble filled her mind.

It took all the energy she had left in her to knock hard on Monsieur Cassin's door. As soon as the door opened, Safiyyah held out the heavy book to him, its paper bag almost in shreds. Monsieur's wide eyes and aghast face was the last thing Safiyyah saw before she collapsed forwards into a blur of green fern fronds and ivy vines.

9

A few hours later, Safiyyah cradled her cup of velvety chocolat chaud, savouring the sweet, rich taste and the warmth that spread through her with every sip. She was propped up in her parents' bed, Yemma reading from the Quran quietly beside her. Snuggled under the soft blankets in the comfort of home, which she was overjoyed to find unharmed by the bombs, Safiyyah felt safe again.

Safiyyah was awakened by a noise in the early hours of the morning, and for a horrible moment thought she was back on the street again from the day before. The faint bang sounded a little like their apartment door, but on seeing her mother fast asleep beside her and hearing nothing more, Safiyyah relaxed again. Baba must have taken her room so as not to disturb her when she fell asleep earlier.

It was raining heavily now, a constant patter of water falling onto the tiles in the courtyard below. It felt appropriate, as if the sky had finally found its tears and was allowing them to fall for the sorrow of the previous day. The relentless raindrops pounding the tree leaves, window and ground outside lamented humans and their destructive behaviour. Grief swelled and burst from clouds in the sky that had seen everything unfold. Safiyyah felt soothed by the drumming melody of water falling from the heavens, and was lulled back to exhausted sleep.

She rose the next morning to find Fatima presenting her with breakfast in bed in the form of wooden tomatoes and toast laid out on her toy tea set. Apart from a faint ache and bruise on her shoulder where the person had run into her, Safiyyah felt fine. Monsieur Cassin had called the mosque after she collapsed in his hallway, and Baba had gone over immediately to collect her. After a once-over by a doctor and endless hugs and tearful kisses from everyone, Safiyyah had been tucked up cosily in bed. She had no idea what Monsieur Cassin had told Baba, but no one had asked her any questions about why she'd been there ... Whatever they thought had happened, somehow Monsieur Cassin had saved her having to explain herself, and Safiyyah was grateful.

Yemma said she could have a few days off school to let things settle and make sure she rested properly. Sumayyah, Ibrahim and their parents came to visit in the afternoon, and together they tuned into Baba's radio. The newsreader announced sombrely that forty-eight people had been killed by over a thousand German bombs. Ten of them were children. Setti hugged Safiyyah tightly and Safiyyah choked back her tears as she felt both of her parents' haunted gazes upon her.

One hundred and fifty-five planes had flown across their city, striking five schools and a temporary hospital. Ninety-seven buildings were destroyed and sixty-one fires started. Safiyyah tried to memorise the numbers and the areas affected in the hope that it would calm her rising anxiety. Saint-Germain, Montmartre, Versailles, Bois de Boulogne, Neuilly ... She couldn't get the names to settle on the map and the lines seemed to be swimming. Then it was the room that was swimming, Baba and Sumayyah and the table wobbling through Safiyyah's tears that refused to hide. Yemma switched off the radio as soon as she noticed her daughter's face.

Everything Safiyyah had been swallowing back down her throat and squeezing into her clenched palms came pouring out. She sobbed as she described the deafening sirens, whirring of planes, pounding of guns and the whistling of the bombs. Of her being frozen to the spot and of the red-haired lady. The full-to-the-brim shelter and the race to the Métro. How someone bumped into her and sent her flying. The smoke and broken glass and doll's house building. The toddler who must have dropped his sweets just after buying them and the old man covering his ears. How she'd felt scared she would never see her loved ones again and how much she loved them.

With each word that spilled out of her, Safiyyah felt a little lighter. When she finished, her own tears dried up, though now all the others' eyes were brimming. Setti raised her hands high in prayer and everyone followed suit. She gave thanks for Safiyyah's safety and health, and prayed for protection, peace and security of everyone in the world who was in hardship and fear. Yemma made chocolat chaud and they played boardgames late into the night, grateful for a little distraction and normality.

The next morning, a young boy arrived with a delivery for Safiyyah. Eucalyptus, ferns, pink peonies and some bright orange and yellow flowers she had never seen before were tied together beautifully with twine. A card lodged between them read:

> *Dearest Safiyyah,*
>
> *I do hope this finds you in a recovered and rested state, and that the shock of the other day is beginning to settle in your gentle soul. I cannot thank you enough for your incredibly kind and brave endeavour of uniting me with the precious book I was so in need of. I owe you a great deal, and have firmly included your name in the dedication section of my book. Entirely thanks to you, it should be finally ready to go to my publisher in a few weeks.*

Please take care of yourself and when you are
suitably recovered, you must visit me with your family. I
will bake a triple batch of mille-feuille for the occasion!
Your eternally grateful friend,
Adam Cassin

Safiyyah smiled to herself, perhaps the danger had been worth it after all. She read through Monsieur's letter another three times, before asking Yemma for a vase for the blooms, which she carefully placed on her windowsill.

'Safiyyah, put your shoes on, please. We'll be taking food and some bits and pieces downstairs for Khala Najma. Poor Najma's home was almost completely destroyed in the bombing, so she has moved to the mosque for now. Grab that bag with soap, towels and dresses, and see if you can manage this one with rice and potatoes too?'

Khala Najma was a favourite auntie of Safiyyah's. She was always busy, boiling pots of tea and baking biscuits for visitors to the mosque café, sweeping crumbs from beneath tables and lighting candles as the sun began to set. She was from India, apparently a grand-niece of a maharaja. Safiyyah's neighbour Hafsa said she'd run away from her family, following a sailor to Europe before laying her bags down in Paris. Yemma always said that Hafsa's mouth was bigger than her brain, and that she should think *before* she spoke rather than afterwards.

Hafsa did come out with ridiculous and often exaggerated stories rather a lot, but somehow Safiyyah felt that this one might be true.

Safiyyah was horrified for Khala. She remembered the building with its front blown off and shuddered. She ran back to her room and fetched the vase with Monsieur Cassin's flowers. Khala would surely need these to brighten up her new room more than Safiyyah did. Yemma and Safiyyah carried the things down to the small room behind the kitchens where Khala would now be staying. A mattress was rolled out in the corner, and a small pile of clothes sat beside it. Safiyyah recognised a carved wooden table from Baba's office in the room, and Safiyyah placed the vase in the middle of it. Khala Najma beamed at them, though the dark rings around her eyes gave her fatigue away.

'Welcome! Ah, you shouldn't have, Sara, this is too much, really! I can't express my gratitude honestly, and, oh Safiyyah, the flowers! How beautiful!'

She looked closer at the bouquet, fingering the purple petals on a tall flower, and gasped. 'I don't believe I've seen one of these for many, many years . . . Not since I left home, how did you . . . ? Where did you find this?'

Safiyyah felt a swell of pride, certain by the look of happy astonishment on Khala's face that she had done the right thing by gifting her them.

'My friend is a botanist, he's travelled the world

learning about plants and he grows hundreds, thousands probably, in his home! He even has a greenhouse in his parlour, perhaps he saved the seeds from his travels in India and grows them in there?'

Khala raised an amused eyebrow at Safiyyah, intrigued at where she might have heard of her Indian roots. Safiyyah panicked for a moment, hoping Hafsa had been right this time, but she needn't have worried.

'C'est magnifique. Perhaps it is so. Safiyyah, this has made me ever so happy! Come, I've prepared food, let us eat in the sunny courtyard.'

The three had barely sat down at the mosaicked table laid with stuffed pancakes when Ammo Imam burst through the courtyard doors. Safiyyah had never seen him looking even slightly flustered before, but today he seemed frantic.

'Quickly, bring water and food! We'll need the cups we use for Eid, at least one hundred, more if we have them. Many more refugees are arriving from the north and God only knows the last time they ate and drank.'

Safiyyah, Yemma and Khala Najma jumped to their feet. Yemma and Khala ran into the kitchen, standing on ladders to get down the huge trays and spare cups. As they set about filling them with water, Safiyyah emptied two big bags of biscuits stuffed with nuts and dates onto another tray, sugar powder and crumbs flying everywhere. Next she piled on all of the pastries and cakes that had been prepared for the café, and fetched the untouched pancakes stuffed with vegetables from the courtyard table too. Baba and Ammo Imam arrived to carry the big round trays out through the streets. Just as they were leaving the courtyard, Setti arrived from upstairs, Fatima in tow. She added a dozen sweet oranges that she'd pulled apart into individual segments onto one of the trays.

Safiyyah followed Yemma, Baba and the others onto the streets. They headed in the direction of the Panthéon, and within minutes, Safiyyah saw what had rattled Ammo Imam so. She had never seen that many people trudging along the cobbles before, far too many to count. The dense crowd trailed slowly, exhaustion visible on their faces. It was more than just exhaustion, it looked like despair. The people were silent, only the thunder of a thousand weary footsteps sounded. Safiyyah couldn't see where the beginning or end of the moving line was. Like a river whose water was heavy with loss.

A man around Baba's age limped barefoot, staring ahead as if seeing right through the people and buildings. Almost everyone's clothes were tattered and dirty, as if they'd been sleeping rough for weeks. A skinny donkey pulled a cart with mattresses tied to it, an elderly woman sleeping on top. Three young children who looked like siblings had dirty loops of yellow ribbon strung around their arms. Safiyyah wondered if it was to prevent them getting lost. Wheelbarrows, pushchairs and bicycles were weighed down with bags and sacks, precious possessions proving there was a life before this.

Safiyyah followed her parents. Baba approached the mass of refugees, and Yemma began handing out cups of water to people. Some people swigged the water back as if they hadn't drunk in days, offering nods of gratitude, while others walked on as if oblivious to anything around them.

Safiyyah handed out biscuits. A little boy clutching a photo frame and two books to his chest took half a pancake, his eyes lighting up ever so slightly at the sight of food. A woman with dirt on her face and in her hair popped an orange segment in her mouth. She closed her eyes when the sweetness hit, offering Safiyyah a tiny smile. A grey-haired man carrying a spade and a rake stuffed his mouth with pistachio biscuits. She cringed at the sight of an old woman's bloodied arm wrapped in a crusted scarf that barely covered the wounds. Safiyyah passed a pastry to a boy around her age who was carrying a small cat. Its body was twisted a little, in a way that didn't seem right, and Safiyyah hoped desperately that it was simply asleep.

Safiyyah didn't eat anything herself until dinner, and as they sat down in the apartment to plates of couscous and potato, she felt more grateful for food than she ever had before. Everyone was quieter than usual. Safiyyah mustered up the energy to ask her father the question that had been on her mind all day: 'Baba, where did all those people come from?'

He looked up from his plate at Safiyyah in alarm, as if she had discovered a terrible secret. 'Which people?'

Now it was Safiyyah's turn to be taken aback. How could he have forgotten the swathes of haggard people they had spent more than half of the day with?! Safiyyah looked at Yemma in bewilderment. Had Baba been sleepwalking as he carried trays to and from the mosque again and again? Yemma stepped in, shaking her head at her husband almost imperceptibly.

'Baba is very tired. He hasn't been sleeping well recently. The refugees came from the north of the country, Safiyyah.'

Safiyyah nodded, almost afraid to ask anything further. Baba looked apologetic now, Safiyyah sensed relief in him.

'Yes, of course, my dear, some are also from Belgium and Luxembourg. Their homes and villages have been ravaged and destroyed in the fighting against the Germans. They have walked hundreds of miles to get here, sleeping in ditches or fields or abandoned barns if they were lucky on the way. God only knows how many people began the journey and didn't make it here.'

'They've been dodging bombs and grenades on their journey here, one woman just kept repeating to me again and again: "My girl was on the bridge. Why did they blow it up . . . ?"' Yemma's voice cracked, she turned away to dry her eyes with a handkerchief.

'There were some Spanish people amongst them too. Imagine having to flee a civil war and then flee again . . .' Baba shook his head.

Setti spoke quietly, 'The cries from broken hearts speak only one language. Their screams echo up to the heavens like no other sound. My Lord, grant ease to the broken-hearted.'

She picked up the prayer beads that lay beside her, her plate of food barely touched. Even quieter now, Setti said, 'I fear we haven't seen the extent of the Nazi evil yet.'

Safiyyah felt a chill go through her. She wanted to ask Setti what she meant, but now her eyes were closed, only her fingers and her lips moved as she prayed on her beads.

10

The next day Safiyyah returned to school. Their art teacher was late to the lesson, and so Safiyyah crouched beside her friend Maria's desk, discussing the events of the day before.

'My maman locked us all in the house after school, she said it's not safe to be around the refugees.'

Safiyyah was confused. 'Not safe, why?'

Maria didn't seem much wiser than her. 'I suppose maybe because lots of them came from other countries . . .'

'And?'

Maria shrugged. 'Well, we don't know, they could be very dangerous!'

Hana and Amelie were listening now from across the room. Hana leaned over, looking unimpressed at Maria's comments. 'The dangerous ones are the Nazis, Maria. Not the hungry, injured civilians fleeing from them.'

Safiyyah smiled quickly at Hana. But Maria was getting visibly defensive. 'Well, it's better to be safe than sorry. And besides, Maman says soon we'll have barely enough food for ourselves. With all these refugees arriving, we'll probably starve to death before the Nazis even arrive!'

Safiyyah felt anger rising in her belly. 'Or maybe, Maria, if we all *shared* what we do have then everyone would be quite all right.'

Amelie chimed in, 'Yes, just because someone is from another country or town doesn't mean they have less right to food and a home.'

Hana looked at Maria defiantly. 'Or because someone is from another religion.'

Just then, their art teacher swept into the room, a flurry of a paint-stained apron and inky hands. She was breathless, wisps of hair escaping the mass that was bundled up into a bun and secured by a pencil.

'Oh no, I forgot the brush pots. One minute, I'll be back!'

She swept out just as quickly and chaotically as she came. A faint chuckle went through the class, she forgot something every single week without fail.

Henri and Phillipe sauntered into the class, relieved to see that the teacher wasn't in the room. Henri was making exaggerated gestures with his hands and ducking and dodging. Safiyyah figured from the *pkhow* and *crashhhhh* noises he was making alongside his movements that he was acting out some sort of military battle. Phillipe yelled in a booming voice, 'Blitzkrieg!' followed by a machine gun-type trill.

Safiyyah felt disgust at why anyone in their right mind would mimic guns and bombs. But then again, Phillipe and Henri were quite spectacularly dim-witted at the best of times. She fought the urge to throw her logbook at them. They wouldn't be so insensitive if they'd been caught up in the midst of it like she had. Before Safiyyah could open her mouth to say something, Amelie did.

'SHUT UP, you idiots!'

Phillipe glared at her. 'Bet you don't even know what blitzkrieg is, you idiot.'

Safiyyah shot back, 'No one wants to hear about German weapons while our country is being bombed by them!'

Hana turned to the boys. 'Exactly. And anyway, it means "lightning war", genius. And it's killing thousands of innocent people. It's senseless bloodshed and if you're moronic enough to glamorise the violence then do it somewhere else. If you had family affected by the destruction I bet you wouldn't behave so awfully.'

Safiyyah watched Hana in admiration. She was normally very calm and quite reserved, but Safiyyah had seen her passion pour out a few times before this, mostly during debate classes, in which her natural eloquence and articulation sparkled. It was like seeing a rose unfurl its petals, blooming spectacularly and suddenly. Her parents were activists, and Hana had grown up learning and caring about social justice. Even the teachers never failed to be impressed by Hana's powerful but compassionate arguments.

Henri slowly walked a few steps over to Hana's desk, before lunging suddenly and sweeping her books and pencil case onto the floor. He leaned down towards Hana menacingly. 'Well, *my* family won't need to worry, will they? No. They won't because they're not dirty Jews like you.'

Hana looked past Henri, as if oblivious to his words. She held her head up slightly in defiance, but Safiyyah could see a vein throb at her temple.

Phillipe was emboldened by his friend's bullish tactics: 'And besides, if it wasn't for *filthy* Jews like you, half of this wouldn't even be happening. You're the problem!'

Within seconds, Safiyyah had Phillipe pinned against the wall. She barely realised what she was doing through her rage, when their teacher ran back in, arms full of paintbrush pots. She stopped in surprise at the sight of Phillipe, red-faced, collar bunched up around his neck where Safiyyah had gripped it just seconds before. The teacher looked from Safiyyah to Phillipe, and scanned across the other shocked faces in the room.

Amelie was the first to speak: 'Safiyyah did nothing wrong, Madame, Henri and Phillipe were bullying Hana because ... well, because ... she's a Jew.' Her voice trailed off at the end, it felt crude and somehow too soon to use the word that the boys had spat out like poison moments ago.

Their teacher looked overwhelmed. 'None of that

here. Bottoms on seats. NOW! I will hand out your brushes and paints and you will work silently today.'

Safiyyah sat back down at her desk, ashamed at her outburst but feeling fresh frustration that their teacher was saying barely anything to defend Hana. She was an adult, she could have put the boys well into their places, but instead she told them to paint? She glanced across at Hana, who nodded at her gratefully, before lowering her eyes to her pencil and paper. Her previous defiant stance had melted into hunched shoulders. Safiyyah had never seen her look so vulnerable before.

11

Just as Safiyyah was giving up hope of hearing from Isabelle, but missing her more than ever, word came.

Safiyyah was fast asleep, dreaming that she, Amelie and Hana were being chased by Phillipe and Henri, who were sitting on army tanks with rage in their eyes. She was glad to be brought back to reality by Setti, who had sat down on the side of her bed, and even more glad when Setti handed her a cream envelope, with a twinkle in her eye.

'Isabelle!'

The last tendrils of her nightmare evaporated as she saw Isabelle's neat, curly handwriting on the paper. Two tiny pressed lilac flowers fell out onto her blanket, and Safiyyah couldn't help but smile and fill with warmth as she pictured Isabelle saving them for her. They were perfectly sized to fit inside the locket she still wore each day. Deep down with the way things were headed in France and beyond, she knew it near impossible that her friend would be returning any time soon. Somehow though, reading it as an inky fact dried onto paper would make it more real. Setti sensed her nerves, and nodded at her encouragingly. With a deep breath, Safiyyah read.

My best friend Fia,

I hope this finds you and everyone else safe and well, we are well too.

I'm so sorry for not having written sooner. Just days after arriving at our château, Papa began making arrangements for us to travel to England. I did write you a letter as soon as we arrived with details of our journey, which was quite eventful: we slept in the car on the roadside for the first night because of a flat tyre! We were miles away from the nearest village and so we had to share an apple and half a baguette between us for dinner, and apart from the chill that set in at night, it felt a bit like a mini-adventure. Like the ones in our make-believe games (thankfully minus evil pirates and man-size lizards though!).

Anyway, I wasn't able to send that letter because there were problems with the post in the local village, and by the time it was sorted, Papa had been called to London. Initially he wanted Maman and me to stay at the château, but she insisted we stay together, and I'm glad. It's horrid enough being separated from you as it is, without Papa being in a different country too. No trips to London though this time for us, we're staying

out in the country with a lady who is my grandpapa's
cousin. She's not bad I suppose, just a bit uptight and
moody. I think she finds Maman annoying, but it's
definitely mutual! On the whole she's all right with
me, she keeps chickens in her back garden and I get to
collect eggs, which is nice! Apparently food is rationed
in lots of places here, so we're lucky to have them. The
lilacs in the envelope are from her garden. Her home
is in Dover, really close to the sea which is amazing. If
you walk for about half an hour from her house, you
reach dramatic chalk cliffs, and the best bit is that on
a clear day, if I squint I can just about see France
across the water! It makes me feel a little closer to you.

I worry for you constantly, I still can't quite believe
that Paris was bombed. I was beside myself but Papa
phoned to reassure me that none fell near the mosque
or our school, and that you'd be safe. I've been
listening to the news of the Allies on the wireless, and
have been seeing lots and lots of Navy boats on the
Channel lately. The town is full of French and British
soldiers who've been brought back to safety here. I'm
praying and wishing that this will all be over really
soon and we can come back. I've no idea what Papa's
plans are, he works in London for most of the week
and comes to see us at weekends. He seems very on
edge and preoccupied all the time and I get the feeling
he might want us to move again . . .

I can't wait to hear from you, my address is at the
bottom of the page. Tell me everything, how have you
been, how is school, how is Paris? How is Fatima and
Setti and everyone else?

I know it's ridiculous but the other day when
Maman and I went for a walk and she fell asleep on
the picnic blanket, I ran to the cliff edge and shouted
a message for you across the sea. Just in case the wind
betrayed me and didn't deliver it: I miss you SO much
and cannot wait until we are reunited. Stay safe and
strong.

All my love,
Isabelle

Safiyyah was so engrossed in the letter that she hadn't
realised that Setti had snuck out to give her some privacy,
nor that she had chuckled out loud and tears had filled
her eyes at points. She felt relief, joy and sadness all at
once. It seemed a strange coincidence that both of their
fathers were tense and often absent. She thought of her
friend's gentle but unwavering optimism. How Isabelle
often considered things as adventures, even when they
were not going her way. She felt energised by it all.

Safiyyah immediately began thinking about what she
would say in her reply to Isabelle. As she brushed her
teeth, dressed and had breakfast, she felt lighter than
she had in weeks. All day at school she considered what

she would be able to squeeze into the letter, and wished she might have pressed some of the plentiful flowers from the mosque ready to send.

After school, she decided homework could wait and instead poured her heart out to her best friend. She barely noticed her hand aching and the indent the pen made on her finger until she had reached the end of the second page. Isabelle normally told her not to press so hard on the paper, but that wouldn't apply when the pen was recounting air raids, arguments, refugees and growing worries. On the back of the second leaf of paper, Safiyyah drew a map. She checked the grooves and ridges she'd carefully drawn for the outlines of England and France with a European atlas she had on her bookshelf – not bad, there were only two lines that needed adjusting. She drew herself at the top of the Eiffel Tower with binoculars, and Isabelle with an entourage of chickens at a white cliff edge, both searching for each other.

Once she'd folded the sheets into an envelope, Safiyyah felt about ten kilograms lighter, as if the tangle of heavy thoughts and emotions she'd been wrapped up in had been freed with every word she'd penned. She ran down to Baba's office to grab his wax seal. She knew he was out, but Yemma would be able to help her with it, using the stove in the kitchen. Her excitement cooled when she found the door to the office locked. It had never been locked before. Only people who had access into the apartments could get to the office, so Baba had never felt the need to lock the door ... Why all of a sudden now? Safiyyah couldn't help but think back to the last time she'd been standing in this hallway not even two weeks ago having been turned away. Somehow today, being shut out felt less personal than it had back then, but the frustration and confusion was still sharp within her.

When Baba arrived home, he seemed heavy and exhausted. As if his bones were made from lead and he'd been dragging them across the city all day. After dinner she asked, 'Baba, I need the wax seal, please, for my letter to Isabelle. I really want to post it tomorrow, insha'Allah. The office door was locked when I tried ...'

He looked at her oddly for a moment, as if he'd forgotten she was there. 'Yes. Yes, it is locked, sorry. I'll fetch it for you.'

Safiyyah made to follow him. 'Don't worry, Baba, I'll bring the letter down with me and we'll do it there, like normal!'

He waved her suggestion away as he left the room, barely looking back. 'You stay here, Safiyyah, I will bring the wax and stamp up with me.'

Safiyyah felt hurt bubble up in her belly once again. Setti tried to distract her with an offer of a cup of chocolat chaud. 'Come, dear child, help me grate the cinnamon, and I'll put cream in your cup too!'

Safiyyah barely tasted the creamy hot chocolate, watching numbly as Baba dripped the glossy red wax onto the envelope headed for England. One question pulsed through her mind relentlessly. What was Baba hiding?

12

A few days later, Safiyyah was on her way home from
school when she saw that the roads were much busier
than usual. Black and brown suitcases were piled high
on carriages, motorcars and motorbikes, and every
vehicle seemed full to the brim with people. These
people didn't look like the refugees that had filled the
streets before. Most of them were well-dressed and
looked wealthy. Safiyyah ran home to find Yemma
looking serious in the kitchen.

'What's happened, Yemma?!'

'The Germans are just days away from Paris.'

Safiyyah gasped in disbelief. How was this possible?

'They overwhelmed the Allies at the shores of Dunkirk,
then quickly turned south. It's been kept quiet in the
news for too long, making it seem like the Allies could
prevent the Germans from taking France, not wanting us
to lose morale ... But it sounds like we didn't stand a
chance, especially once the British started evacuating.
The Germans have blasted their way down the country
and I'm afraid it seems like Paris will be taken too. They
are more powerful than anyone realised and our cowardly

government has fled south. Our city has been abandoned. It is free for the taking.'

Safiyyah tried to fight her anxiety, but memories of sounds and scenes from the day of the bombing were overwhelming her senses.

'Come, sit down, darling.' Yemma hugged her tightly. 'We will be fine, insha'Allah. I can feel it. We will be brave, and we will be together. That's what matters. Now help me peel these carrots!'

Safiyyah began scraping the thin orange skin from the vegetables slowly, grateful that she had something to do with her hands. 'Where are all those people going, Yemma?'

'I think most of Paris will be going south into the countryside, perhaps they have châteaux there, or family they can stay with. Others might be hoping to leave the country altogether.'

'And what about Tarek, Yemma?'

Yemma's face flushed with fear, and Safiyyah saw her lip quiver slightly before she responded. 'Pray for him, Safiyyah, with all your heart. Insha'Allah, he will come back to us.'

Baba ate dinner with Ammo Kader and Ammo Imam in his office, as he had been doing a lot lately. Safiyyah was getting used to his absence a little, but it still hurt nonetheless. Worse than the hurt though was the creeping suspicion she felt.

Unusually, Yemma asked Safiyyah to read from a storybook for her, Fatima and Setti while they ate, and didn't say a word when Safiyyah spoke with her mouth full of rice. Even Fatima listened intently to the dramatic tale, eyes widening when Safiyyah made surprisingly authentic monkey and parrot noises. It felt good to escape into a treetop adventure for a little while, the villains in the story seemed tame and harmless compared to the ones who were marching towards Paris.

The next day Safiyyah watched sadly as the local baker frantically boarded up his shop. The grocer next door to him hadn't shown up at all, and the shutters of the jeweller and the tailor were down too. The roads were still teeming with vehicles, though now there were more people leaving on bicycles and on foot than the day before. Adults carried children, some had dogs on leashes with them. She wove through hordes of people, faces all painted with the same anguish and urgency as they turned away from their homes. An old cobbler turned the key to lock up his shop, suitcases at his feet. After he did so, he pressed his face and hands against the door for a moment or two, and when he turned around, Safiyyah glimpsed a single tear rolling down his cheek.

At school Safiyyah counted seven empty seats in her classroom, and she felt sad that she hadn't had the opportunity to bid farewell to Maria, Aharon and the others who'd left. Though part of her did feel a little relieved, because goodbyes were absolutely horrible. Her science teacher never turned up at school, and they were instructed to read quietly in his lesson.

On her way home, the flow of people fleeing seemed even more relentless than before. Safiyyah marvelled that there were even this many people in Paris in the first place! Some streets on her usual route home were blocked, and she began to feel frustrated as she realised how much longer the journey would take. She kicked a discarded juice carton. Would Paris be bombed again? If everyone around them felt it necessary to leave, then why was her own family putting her in danger by staying? Baba was probably too wrapped up in his own God-knows-what to even notice.

Safiyyah soon realised she was on a street she didn't recognise. She was so lost in her unhappy thoughts that she'd barely even noticed her surroundings. The street was spacious and leafy, and utterly deserted. The houses lining its pavements were grand and imposing, with iron railings and immaculate gardens. It seemed eerie, almost, to have gone from the overwhelming, chaotic exodus to this silent, abandoned street. Safiyyah figured that it was the wealthier Parisians who had left the city first; it was their glossy suitcases and expensive motorcars that filled the streets yesterday. She wondered how long these mansions would lie empty for. She remembered how long the Great War had gone on for – could it be years this time too? The houses were eerily quiet, as though they were haunted.

A noise behind Safiyyah sent her a foot into the air, yelping. She spun round, adrenaline coursing through her body, ready to run. The culprit was small, white and unbelievably fluffy. A blue-eyed cat looked up at her longingly, meowing again and again. It was ridiculously cute, and its little face made her forget all about ghosts and haunted houses.

Safiyyah crouched down and stroked its soft fur. It nuzzled its head against her hand and seemed to be comforted by Safiyyah. She sat down on the road and it put its paws onto her lap. The meows that had sounded frantic before became a soft purr. As she cuddled the cat, Safiyyah imagined this was what embracing a silky cloud must feel like. The warmth of the animal's body and constant gentle purring soothed her and all of a sudden, the chaos of Parisians fleeing their threatened city seemed much further away than the distance of a few streets. After a few tranquil minutes, the cat looked up at Safiyyah, its wide sapphire eyes imploring. It began meowing again.

'What is it you want, little fluffy-wuffy?'

The cat lowered its intense gaze, and Safiyyah couldn't help but feel like it was disappointed in her inability to know what it wanted. Was it hungry? Lost? She looked up and down the empty street, wondering where the cat had come from. Based on its spotless, glossy fur and perfectly fluffed tail, she figured there was no way it could be a stray. She felt around its neck for a collar, eventually feeling a thin satiny ribbon under the thick fur. A little gold coin strung through the ribbon had the name of a street engraved on it. Safiyyah walked to the end of the street she was on to check the navy sign, the cat following at her heels. It wasn't the same as the cat's home. She checked another adjoining street, unlucky again. Safiyyah sighed, but another drawn-out meow from her new friend pushed her to keep looking.

'YES!' Safiyyah yelled when just a few minutes later she found the street that the cat lived on. Her excitement began to subside as she took in the lifelessness of the place. She found number twelve, and the cat beat Safiyyah to the imposing blue door with its gold knocker. There was a large plank of wood nailed across the door diagonally. The cat leaped up onto a windowsill beside the front door. Safiyyah joined the cat at the window, but trying to see inside was no use as the heavy curtains were tightly drawn. It was obvious that no one was here any more.

She looked down at the abandoned cat, unsure of what to do next. Safiyyah wished she could adopt it, she'd dreamed of a pet of her own for years. Yemma wasn't a big fan of animals and had never agreed to Safiyyah's requests, even when Baba relented. Ordinarily, if she told Baba what had happened, he would come back with her with food for the animal, but nowadays she barely even saw him, and when she did, he seemed too preoccupied to notice her.

She decided to make a shelter for it in the front garden, and she'd come back tomorrow with food. With any luck there'd be chicken or fish for dinner and Safiyyah could sneak a few scraps from her plate and save them. She added the finishing touches to her makeshift cat hotel – some fallen leaves for padding and a frame of twigs wedged under a garden chair to form an entrance – before stepping back to look at her work. Not too bad, she hoped, although she reckoned it was dire compared to the plush sofas and abundant cushions the cat must have slept on in the grand house.

She encouraged the cat to enter the shelter, so it would know it was a safe place to sleep. She gave it one last cuddle before heading back towards home, hoping the crowds might have died down a little by now. She was barely halfway down the street when something white and fluffy trotted out in front of her. The cat was following her! Safiyyah laughed affectionately and bending down, scooped the cat up in her arms. She retraced her footsteps and placed it into its new little hut.

'I'm sorry, I can't take you with me, but I'll be back soon, I promise! I know you're hungry, just wait for me here.'

She stood to leave for a second time, but after only a couple of steps in the direction of home, the cat was at her feet again. They repeated this scene three more times before both girl and cat became exasperated. Safiyyah stood with her hands on her hips, the cat now sitting on her left shoe, purring quietly.

'Well, I suppose that's decided then. You're coming with me.'

13

The cat padded alongside Safiyyah as she figured out which route to take home. A few blocks from the street where the white cat had startled her she was startled again. At first, she wasn't quite sure if she had heard a voice. But then it came again, a loud whisper.

'Hey! Stop!'

Safiyyah resisted the urge to run. She knew too well that German soldiers were on their way to take Paris, and nobody could be sure of when they would arrive. Gulping anxiously, she spun around in a full circle. She was put out of her terror by the sight of a boy, half-hidden behind a wall. He was beckoning her over urgently, and as she approached him, she saw that he was around her age, perhaps a little younger. He was dressed scruffily in rough, simple clothes and his hair looked tangled and in need of a wash. She was almost a foot taller than the boy, and when she saw that he had kind eyes, her previous fear subsided completely.

'What is it?!' she asked.

He stepped out and looked down at his feet. Safiyyah's eyes followed his, and she gasped in surprise. In a cardboard box were three tiny kittens. There was a tattered piece of cloth in there with them, but all three of them were shivering. The black and white one let out a tiny squeak that must have been intended as a meow, while the other two snuggled quietly, trying to keep warm. Safiyyah resisted the urge to sweep all of them into her arms. Just as it occurred to her that these kittens might belong to the white cat who had been watching from behind her ankles, it wandered over to the box and hissed a little at the kittens. There was her answer. She scooped the white cat up in her arms, telling it to be nice.

'Where did you find them?' she asked.

'Behind a bin just down the street. There's no mother in sight and they won't last much longer without help. I saw you building a shelter for the white cat and all, and thought maybe you'd be able to help these ones too?'

Safiyyah was taken aback. 'You SAW me? Where were you hiding? I didn't see anyone around me on the entire street!'

He shrugged his shoulders. 'I see people, they just don't notice me.'

It felt creepy to Safiyyah, knowing she had been watched for probably an hour without realising it!

'Who even *are* you?' she demanded, rather impolitely.

'Name's Timothée.' He shrugged again, as if he was only half sure of the fact himself.

Safiyyah took in his worn-out appearance. 'You're not from here, are you?'

'Nope.'

She started to feel exasperated at his responses. 'Well, where *are* you from? What are you doing here?'

'I arrived in Paris last week. I come from Picardy, I'm a shepherd.' He paused, looking pained, before lowering his eyes to the kittens. 'Well, I was a shepherd. Dunno what I am now.'

Safiyyah's heart sank for the boy. She thought back to the swathes of refugees trailing through the city's streets, and imagined Timothée among them. Gently now, she said, 'I'm sorry for whatever happened to you. Are you here alone?'

He looked awkward, shrugging yet again as he spoke. 'I'm with my dad, but I guess he's only half here really. He hasn't been himself since . . . since we left. We woke up in the middle of the night and our fields, our barns, everything was blazing orange. My dad ran to fetch water, but once the shooting started, all we could do was run. His whole life, burned to a crisp for nothing.'

Safiyyah felt angry and heartbroken, and knew that it was impossible to find words to respond to such tragedy. She placed her hand on her heart, as she had seen Setti and Ammo Kader do at times, and whispered, 'I'm so, so sorry.'

Timothée gave a tiny nod, and bent down to stroke

one of the kittens. Its fur was a warm orangey gold, its eyes green. As he stood up again, he asked, 'Well? Will you take them? We've been sleeping on the floor of a kind of community building with lots of others from the north. Some nuns bring us food every couple of days but it's not much. Not the right kind of place for these guys.'

'Of course I'll take them,' Safiyyah replied. Now wasn't the time to think about Yemma or logistics, the kittens needed food and warmth.

Timothée seemed relieved. 'Thanks.' He picked up the box carefully, keeping it as straight as he could. The white cat in Safiyyah's arms turned its head away from the box of kittens sulkily.

'I live at the mosque. We should be able to go along this road and then take a left.'

'No, no, that way won't do, the streets are clogged up. There'll be roadblocks and police. Best to go back on ourselves and round the longer way.'

'How do you know all this?!'

Timothée chuckled. 'Being a shepherd gives you eagle eyes. Days on end of caring for a flock of sheep, watching out for predators and scanning the endless horizon for lost animals.'

'It must also make you patient.' Safiyyah imagined Timothée happy on his farm, sadness weighing her heart.

'Very patient. And stealthy too! You learn to get around

quietly, to blend in and camouflage with your surroundings to not disturb the animals. I've been herding since I could walk, about eight years now.'

Safiyyah nodded. 'That explains why I didn't know you were there for a full hour!'

14

Safiyyah and Timothée walked past deserted mansions. Many of the curtains were drawn, but some remained open, offering a glimpse into the lives of others. Expensive paintings adorning a wall, a dusty chandelier, cluttered bookshelves hung with pretty bunting. Through one window she saw cereal boxes on the table and a half-drunk glass of juice.

Two of the kittens were sleeping, while one looked wide-eyed at the world moving around it. Timothée whispered to soothe its nerves, and Safiyyah reached into the box every now and again to pet it softly. The sound of sweet birdsong filled the air as they neared the end of the street. It struck Safiyyah as strange. There weren't any trees on this road. In fact, there wasn't any green in sight at all ... She turned to mention this to Timothée, but he was no longer walking beside her. He was looking intently into the window of the house on the corner of the street. As Safiyyah caught sight of a birdcage in the corner of the room he was looking into, she realised he'd beaten her at solving the mystery of the whistles and chirps.

Timothée was shaking his head angrily. 'No one has been in or out of this house for two days now. Poor little thing.'

A small green and yellow bird was perched on a wooden bar inside the birdcage, its head cocked to the side. All of a sudden Safiyyah could hear pain in its song that she wasn't attuned to before. The bird was looking at them through the window, and its whistles became more urgent and shriller. It felt like it was trying to communicate with them.

'How do you know no one has been at the house, Timothée?'

'I've been searching the bins round here for scraps lately. Most people have either been in a mad rush to get out of the city, or already gone, so it's easier to not be noticed. I hadn't seen the bird before but I know this place has been empty for too long now.'

'What do we do?' Safiyyah felt adamant that they should rescue the bird, but had absolutely no idea how. She also knew that the kittens in the box on the ground needed care as soon as possible.

'Follow me.' Timothée was already trying to find handholds on the brick wall around the corner that led to the back of the bird's house. He'd scramble up a couple of feet but then slide back down to the ground; the wall was too high.

Safiyyah put the white cat down gently, and locked

the fingers of both hands together as she and Isabelle would to help each other get up to the first branch of a tree. She held her linked palms out towards Timothée, gesturing for him to step up onto them. He nodded in approval, and as he shifted his weight onto her hands, Safiyyah was surprised at how light he felt. She'd been bracing her arms for something closer to Isabelle's weight, but she needn't have. Despite being around nine years old, he barely weighed more than Fatima. He had a sprightly frame as it was, and his lightness made sense considering how he'd walked for miles and miles and had to scavenge for food ever since.

Thanks to her step-up, he just about made it over the wall and Safiyyah heard him land on the ground on the other side. All of a sudden she felt terribly conscious about what they were doing. She scanned all directions for signs of life, but it appeared to be just her and the cats.

'How are you going to get the bird?!' she hissed.

'The only way possible!' Half of Timothée's last word was lost to the sound of glass shattering, before a dull thud. Safiyyah was aghast. She'd never so much as stolen a penny sweet, even though all the other children had, and now she was breaking into a house!

Within a minute or so, she heard Timothée dragging something towards the wall, perhaps a garden table. Based on the squawking and screeching coming from the garden, he'd successfully rescued the bird. Then the top half of his body appeared over the top of the wall. He managed to balance himself on the bricks so that he could dangle the birdcage down just far enough for Safiyyah to catch it.

She breathed a sigh of relief when the cage was safely in her arms, and was mesmerised by the vibrant feathers on the bird inside it. She'd never seen a bird this close up before, and marvelled at the perfectly formed beak and claws, the iridescent sheen of its glossy feathers, and its curious eyes. There were thin black and white stripes on either side of its face that reminded her of a zebra, and there were splodges of at least four bright shades of green around its neck and face that she hadn't been able to see from the window. The bird was the brightest thing on the street. It was magnificent.

'*CHARMANT!*'

Safiyyah almost dropped the cage in surprise. She knew parrots could talk, but this bird was smaller and looked a bit different to the pictures of parrots she had seen ... Timothée leaped down beside her onto the street, and all of a sudden, Safiyyah felt very rude for not having introduced herself to the bird already, and for having underestimated its intelligence!

'Bonjour, I'm Safiyyah, and this is Timothée.'

'TIMOTHÉE!' Another shrill squawk, which delighted them both.

'I'm taking you home, little one. We'll get you some food and water and you'll be safe there, all right?'

The sound of a motorcycle driving down a nearby street reminded them that they probably shouldn't linger at the scene of the crime. Timothée grabbed the birdcage, Safiyyah the box of kittens, and they left, the white cat trotting alongside. They walked the rest of the way in companionable silence, their arms full, and their hearts fuller than they had been before.

When they got to the busier streets again, clogged up with vehicles and people, the white cat meowed and Safiyyah let it leap up onto her shoulder, where it seemed to settle. Initially it seemed alarmed at the chaos around them, startled by the growling of engines and the movement of so many people, but soon it grew drowsy, its head resting beside her ear. The warmth she had felt when she'd first met the cat just an hour ago was still there, and Safiyyah felt greatly comforted by this new companion. Though her arms ached as they wove around frantic people and dodged laden cycles and carts, she felt calm. Even when they drew close to Gare d'Austerlitz and she saw long snaking queues of people waiting to board a train to anywhere but Paris, her heart didn't quiver quite like it had before.

As they approached the mosque, Safiyyah said, 'You and your dad can come and eat with us?'

Timothée half-smiled, but shook his head. 'Thanks,

but my dad isn't in a state to meet people. I need to get back to him now.'

'I understand. Wait for a minute though, please. I need to get something.'

Safiyyah carried the box inside, leaving Timothée on the street with the birdcage. She bumped into Khala Najma on her way in, who looked shocked at the sight of the cats. Safiyyah handed her the box, and Khala peeled the sleepy white cat from Safiyyah's shoulders, still looking baffled. Safiyyah ran towards the apartments: 'I'll be back, Khala, give me two minutes and I'll explain! Oh, and they need milk!'

In the apartment, Safiyyah ran straight for Setti, almost entirely out of breath.

'I need blankets and food, someone needs our help! And we must be quick.'

Setti asked no questions and immediately set about wrapping some of the bread and bean stew that Yemma had prepared for dinner. She stuffed a fleece blanket, the food package and a couple of oranges into a bag. Safiyyah pulled one of her coats from her cupboard, a plain black one that a boy could wear, and added it in. Before heading downstairs, she dashed back into her room and put her pair of binoculars into the bottom of the bag, a little gift.

She sprinted back past a bewildered Khala Najma, onto the street, and was relieved to see Timothée and the bird still there.

'For you.' She shyly handed over the bag. She couldn't read the expression on Timothée's face, but he didn't seem happy, as she'd hoped.

He peeked inside. 'I don't need charity or handouts. That's not why I called you, I just didn't know what to do with the kittens. I can look after myself. Thanks, but no thanks.'

'It's not charity and it's not a handout!' She felt desperate to make him understand. 'You're a friend. And I hope you'd do the same for me if I'd lost everything.'

He pondered this for a moment, the bag still held at arm's length as if it was dangerous. He looked from Safiyyah, to the bag, and back again, and then nodded.

'All right. Thank you.'

'You're welcome.' Safiyyah felt relieved. 'Well, I guess you should get back to your dad now. I'll take the bird inside. If any more animals need rescuing, you know where to find me!'

Timothée smiled. 'You'll have to change the sign that says "mosque" to "zoo"!'

'Sounds like fun to me!' Safiyyah joked, before becoming serious. 'Take care, those evil soldiers will be here any day now.'

A shadow fell over Timothée's face, so dark that Safiyyah regretted having said anything. He spat his words out: 'I've heard people call the Nazis animals, but no animal behaves like them, destroying lives for no reason. Animals are more noble and courageous than Hitler's men could ever dream of being.' He was looking through Safiyyah now. 'I swear on my life I'll do whatever I can to resist and fight those cowards.'

'Me too.' Safiyyah placed her hand on her heart again. Timothée nodded at her and briskly walked away.

Safiyyah went back inside, placing the birdcage in front of Khala Najma, who had already put a proper blanket into the kittens' box and was pouring milk onto a teaspoon for them. Khala looked at the birdcage with wide eyes. She shook her head as if in disbelief, chuckled, and then pretended to look behind Safiyyah through the doorway: 'What's next? A giraffe? A chipmunk?' Her wide, deep-set eyes glittered as she laughed, and Safiyyah couldn't help but picture her in princess attire. 'Well, young lady, I can't imagine your mother will want this rabble in her apartment, so if you're about to employ me as zookeeper, you'd better explain!'

Safiyyah was all too happy to tell Khala Najma everything (minus Timothée's window-breaking), while the kittens hungrily licked drops of warm milk from the spoon. The bird drank its fill and Khala found a bag of sunflower seeds which Safiyyah poured out for it.

'You've had quite a day, Safiyyah, haven't you! I expect your family will be wondering where you are. I'll take care of our new friends until we figure out what to do with them, don't you worry.' Safiyyah felt a pang as she saw the white cat looking up at her longingly again. How she wished she could take it home with her, but she knew Yemma would never agree.

'Are you sure, Khala? I don't want to just dump them on you!'

'I'm sure, sweetheart. Who in their right mind – other than your mother! – would say no to three gorgeous kittens and this fluffy beauty! My father used to have birds just like this one. He's more beautiful than a precious emerald.' She gazed at the bird dreamily. 'I used to spend hours in our huge aviary . . . it was filled with plants and birds of all colours. Where did you come from, Mr Parakeet?'

The bird was quiet for a moment, before squawking, '*CHARMANT!*', making both Safiyyah and Khala Najma crack up. Safiyyah hugged Khala Najma tightly before she left, grateful for her help.

'Ahh, Safiyyah?' Khala Najma called out as Safiyyah walked away, 'it looks like we have a problem. A white, fluffy one!'

The white cat had followed Safiyyah, once again. Safiyyah knew it would be no use setting it down with Khala Najma again. She kneeled down to pet the cat, before telling it: 'Come on then, it's worth a try with Yemma surely. You're just as stubborn as she is!'

Safiyyah began to feel nervous as she walked up the stairs with the cat. Surely Yemma wouldn't turn away the helpless little thing?

She needn't have worried, the cat won everyone over instantly. Even Yemma, who normally kept anything on four legs at arm's length, stroked and admired the animal. The cat enjoyed the attention from Yemma, Baba and Setti – Fatima's tail-pulling not so much.

But then Yemma said, 'We can't keep it here, Safiyyah, you know that, don't you?'

'Come on, Yemma, please, it needs us!' Safiyyah pleaded. 'And, Setti, you always say that we have a duty to God to care for all creatures that need us . . .'

Setti laughed, nodding and winking at Yemma. 'This girl of yours, Sara, very wise and pious!'

Yemma chimed in, 'You can care for it very well *outside* of our home! I have enough on my plate without an animal to worry about inside the apartment.'

'It's already been abandoned once, Yemma! I can't, I *won't* abandon it again.'

'Don't be so dramatic, Safiyyah, it can stay in the courtyard downstairs.'

'I promise I'll look after it! I'll feed it and take care of its litter and everything, you won't have to worry about it at all! I need it here with me.'

Yemma's face was stern. Safiyyah lowered her eyes, sighing. She started to think she would have to accept defeat and send the cat down to the courtyard, when Yemma said seriously, 'I have one condition. It is NOT allowed in my kitchen!'

Safiyyah looked from Yemma to Baba in confusion. Was that a little smirk on Baba's face? He said: 'Well, if the cat is moving in with us, it most definitely needs a name!'

It took Safiyyah a few moments to process the news, and as soon as it sank in, she was squeezing both of her parents tightly and squealing. They all agreed that it seemed like a female cat, and began excitedly suggesting names.

'Bouffée! Because she is like a little puff of white smoke,' Baba suggested.

'How about Nuage, a perfect white cloud?' Yemma chimed in.

Setti asked Fatima for her opinion, and she responded by pointing at the cat with a loud 'Baaaaaaaaa!'. Clearly her sheep and cats were muddled up.

Safiyyah considered how the cat's generous long fur floated around her body, making her look almost round. She was small and perfect, and the sweetest thing around.

'Bonbon. Her name is Bonbon.'

15

Safiyyah awoke in the dark to Bonbon standing on her and licking her face. She had slept on and off through the night curled up at the end of Safiyyah's bed. Then, in between naps, Bonbon had climbed halfway up the curtain, giving Safiyyah a fright when she fell back down. She'd also meowed at the moon for about ten minutes, making it rather hard to sleep, but Safiyyah didn't mind. She figured it might take a little while for Bonbon to settle in – after all, she'd lost everything she'd ever known, overnight, perhaps.

The licks tickled Safiyyah's cheeks. Bonbon's tongue felt like sandpaper! She pulled the cat down next to her, giving her a squeeze. 'Hey, you'll get to sleep all day today, but *I* have to go to school! Not fair! At least give me another few hours of rest!'

Bonbon wasn't having it though. Her official decree was that it was playtime. Safiyyah tied some orange wool to the end of a wooden spoon and let Bonbon go wild chasing her new toy. Somehow Bonbon's presence in her life made everything seem brighter.

Safiyyah and Bonbon had just drifted off to sleep

again when they were shocked awake by the sound of a man's voice booming through a loudspeaker. It was morning now, but Safiyyah couldn't make sense of anything. Disorientated, she wondered if she was in a strange dream. On recognising the German accent of the echoing voice, she realised that she had awoken into something worse than any nightmare. This was what she had been dreading for weeks now. This was what *everyone* had been dreading. It was what had caused two million Parisians to throw their belongings into suitcases and abandon their homes, to board trains and bicycles with no known destination. The enemy was here.

Panic filled Safiyyah's body, and she leaped out of bed and ran into her parents' room. Baba was already dressed, looking out of the window. Yemma sat in bed, still, worry lines creasing her forehead. Safiyyah could barely make out what the man was shouting, and his voice was growing fainter now, as if he had moved into the distance.

Baba turned and gave her a hug.

'What are they saying?' she whispered, half not wanting to know the answer.

'They're driving vans around the city, telling people that we now have a curfew of eight o'clock in the evening.'

Safiyyah's breathing steadied a little. She had been anticipating the announcement being about imminent bombing or violence. This didn't sound too horrendous.

'Why?'

'Control, I suppose. Control is power. I was out earlier and spoke to people who'd seen hordes of German soldiers marching into the city from the north and west in the last hour. There are military tanks rolling down the Champs-Élysées with marching bands, and they're putting up that blasted swastika flag at the Arc de Triomphe.'

Yemma said something in Kabyle, her mother tongue. Safiyyah hadn't heard the word before, and based on her mother's tone, figured it was probably an expletive. Then Yemma spoke sternly to Safiyyah: 'You are NOT to leave the mosque without permission, do you hear me? It's not safe out there. If you don't believe me, just ask your grandmother about how brutal military occupations are.'

Safiyyah didn't know if she felt more horrified at the prospect of not being able to go out, or of seeing the streets filled with Nazi soldiers. Both seemed suffocating and awful, and she felt another twinge of anger at her parents for remaining in Paris, when so many others had left. A lump rose in her throat, and she left the room. Bonbon meowed at her in greeting from the foot of her bed, and Safiyyah picked her up for a cuddle. Setti wasn't in the apartment, so Safiyyah headed down to the courtyard, Bonbon still contentedly in her arms. She felt relieved to see her grandmother sitting beside the fountain in the garden.

Safiyyah set Bonbon down to explore. Setti smiled at Safiyyah, offering her a warm, fragrant hug. The square turquoise tiles on the ground of the courtyard were dazzlingly bright in the morning sun.

'What will happen now, Setti?'

'I don't know, my dear.' Setti handed Safiyyah a piece of orange that she seemed to have produced from nowhere and sighed loudly. 'These blue-green tiles always remind me of the sea.' She dipped her hand into the lower bowl of the fountain, splashing drops of water onto the tiles and on her dress. 'When I missed my family in Spain or in Algeria, I always thought of the sea. The seas connect us all to each other, across the entire world. Water is ancient, and always flowing. These drops of water could have once been in a cloud over Africa, or in a lake in America. They could have been someone's tears of laughter or sorrow once upon a time.'

Safiyyah pictured Isabelle, squinting out over the English Channel. The spray from the waves crashing against the rocks falling around her like rain. Setti and Safiyyah stayed in silence at the fountain, each lost in their own ocean of thoughts, until Yemma called for breakfast.

For the rest of the day, Safiyyah distracted herself by helping Khala Najma take care of the kittens, who were settling in well. She named the ginger one Croissant and the tortoiseshell one Crème Brûlée (Crème for short). The black and white one was called Chien, because he behaved more like a puppy than a kitten, and even wagged his tail a little!

The parakeet seemed to be content at the mosque too. They opened the door to his cage, hoping he might fly around the courtyard to stretch his wings and feel the wind on his feathers, but he stayed firmly put. They tried coaxing him out by putting food on one of the tree branches and by playing games, but he wasn't interested. Khala Najma suggested that perhaps he just wasn't quite ready to be free yet. They named him Émeraude, after the bright green of his feathers.

Safiyyah's weekly Quran lessons had been put on hold ever since her teacher, a university student named Yusuf, had joined the army. The men in the mosque congregation had more than halved, and now it was mostly the elderly or very young who remained. It still alarmed Safiyyah when she'd see the men gather to stand for prayer, barely filling a few rows now, when before they would spill from the prayer hall out into the courtyards. Safiyyah was beyond grateful that Baba's deafness meant he was exempt from being called up a second time.

Usually, she and the other children who lived in the mosque would sit with Yusuf and read aloud from the holy book in the prayer hall. He would correct their mistakes and help them to memorise short chapters in Arabic. Whenever a child reached the end of a chapter, Yusuf would pull a toffee out of his pocket and reward them. Safiyyah missed his gentle encouragement and melodious voice.

Today, Yemma told her that one of Setti's friends would teach the lesson instead, and seeing as none of the children had gone to school, there was no point in waiting until the evening. Safiyyah sat beside Hafsa and Ayah, who each lived with their families in other apartments like Safiyyah's. They'd known each other since they were tiny, and had grown up playing together. Safiyyah was nearly two years older, and they'd drifted apart a bit over the years. Now she was glad for their company, it made her feel a little less panicked and alone. As soon as they started talking though, she realised she'd have preferred silence. Hafsa said she had heard that the Nazis would soon be raiding their homes and searching for Jews, and Ayah described the parade of soldiers she had glimpsed earlier that morning on her way back from her grandfather's house. The conversation was so grim that Safiyyah was grateful when the old lady teaching them told them all to shush and to turn to the right pages of their Qurans.

The lady was rather bossy and didn't have any toffees to hand out, but still Safiyyah found herself melting into the words as she recited them. She ran her finger across the page as she read, the rhythm of the curvaceous, elegant script soothing her as she spoke it aloud. Rocking her body gently from side to side, she focused all her attention on her own rising and falling voice. The voices of the other children also reciting their verses melded and drifted around her like honey, and she felt the stiffness in her body soften. Everything around her blurred a little into the background and Safiyyah allowed herself, for the first time in a long while to let go of some of the worry she had been holding. The hour-long session passed quickly, and Safiyyah found herself desperately wanting to hold on to the meditative state for longer. As the children packed away their Qurans and the carved wooden stands that they read them on, Safiyyah felt calm and somehow still.

16

Yemma refused to send Safiyyah to school for nearly a fortnight after the Germans entered the city. At first, Safiyyah quite enjoyed herself, but by the end of the second week she felt she might go crazy. She was so desperate to be back in the world, to have the freedom to wander the streets and trace the maps of her mind once again that the fear she'd felt of the Germans was dulled. She pleaded and begged with Yemma to let her out; Hafsa was still attending school and *she* was fine!

When Yemma finally relented, Safiyyah was beside herself with relief, and also nerves. The night before her first day back, it took hours for her to fall asleep. Soon after she had drifted off, she was awoken again. She thought she'd heard the faint rattle of a key, and the clicking of the door of the apartment. There were no more noises, but she remembered that this wasn't the first time she'd heard their front door open in the middle of the night. The night after the bombing, when she was sleeping with Yemma in her parents' room, something similar had happened, but she'd been too exhausted to investigate. She was wide awake now, adrenaline coursing through her body.

She got out of bed, careful not to disturb Bonbon in the process. Fear of finding a burglar in the hallway gripped her, but as she peered around her door, it was empty. She breathed a sigh of relief. It would be near impossible for someone to break into the flat anyway, considering how it was tucked away within the mosque complex. Besides, nothing had been stolen the last time she heard the noise. This also reassured her that it wasn't to do with German soldiers, because the other time there had been none in the city. So what was the noise?

She lingered in her doorway for a few moments, listening for anything amiss, but there was nothing. Her parents' door was closed, she could hear Setti's soft snores from her room. Moonlight streamed into the hallway from the living room window; on any other night Safiyyah would think it looked ethereal and beautiful, but tonight it just felt eerie. Should she just accept that she had dreamed the noise? She didn't want to worry her parents unnecessarily . . .

Safiyyah sighed and turned to go back to bed, when she noticed something. Baba's shoes weren't on the rack beside the front door like they normally were. The instances of him behaving strangely, locking the office door and not allowing her in, all came flooding back at once. Safiyyah tiptoed across the hallway, checking in case the shoes had fallen behind the rack, or had been placed under someone else's, but they were nowhere to be found. She inhaled sharply. Where was Baba going in the middle of the night? Did Yemma know? The only way she could prove her suspicion would be to look inside their room, but that would definitely wake them. The last thing she wanted was Yemma getting angry and changing her mind about letting Safiyyah out of the mosque. She went back to bed, replaying the changes she'd seen in Baba over the last month or so again and again, until sleep overcame her.

In the morning before school, Baba's shoes were there on the rack. Baba had finished his coffee and was dashing out of the door before she'd even sat down at the table, so even if she'd mustered the courage to bring up the mystery with him, there was no opportunity. Yemma asked Safiyyah to collect Setti's medication from a pharmacy on her way home, reminding her for what felt like the seven hundredth time to keep her head down and stay out of trouble.

'The pharmacy is on your way, straight in and then straight back home, all right?'

Safiyyah nodded, rolling her eyes a little. She was still distracted by Baba's mystery. She carried the uneasy feeling in her gut with her across the streets to school. It only deepened at the sight of the eerily empty roads and lifeless shops, and it changed to queasiness when she glimpsed a German soldier. He was kicking an empty packet of cigarettes with his big boot, his helmet glinting in the sun. Safiyyah kept her eyes to the ground and quickened her pace, relieved when she turned into the school gates.

The third lesson of the day was cancelled, and the children were instructed once again to copy paragraphs out of a grammar textbook. The more bored she got, the less legible her handwriting became. After the agony of copying out another entire page, Safiyyah's head was slumped on her desk, and she began to regret having persuaded Yemma to release her from the mosque. She came to school to learn, and she wasn't doing anything close to that. Clearly the teachers couldn't care less about their classes any more. And as the empty chairs now made a majority, the classes were ghosts of what they once were. Safiyyah dearly missed some of the children who had left, and wished that she could swap them for Henri and Phillippe, who were still there, and more annoying than ever.

Safiyyah decided enough was enough. At least she was a little freer here than she had been at the mosque, there were no adults keeping watchful eyes on them. Besides, the last time she had skived from a lesson, no one had even noticed. Not that she wanted a repeat of that awful day, but there wouldn't be German bombs falling from the sky now that Paris was full of German soldiers . . . If she kept out of the soldiers' way, she should be fine. If the purpose of school was education, she'd surely learn far more useful information being in the library or at Monsieur Cassin's home than from the tattered textbook on her desk.

Safiyyah was becoming more and more convinced by her own logic. The voice within her that was still screaming in fear of the German soldiers quietened when she turned the page and saw another dense spread about semicolons and colons. When the sleepy-looking cover teacher left the room, waiting to be replaced by another, Safiyyah slipped out. She could get to Monsieur Cassin's home via quiet streets and alleys, while the library would require her to walk down busier squares and main roads. Somehow she felt she'd be less exposed and less likely to bump into Germans on the backstreets, so Monsieur Cassin's it was.

Safiyyah planned to stop by and give him some company for a while. She hadn't seen him since the bombing all those weeks ago. Baba had taken over the delivery of his medication, but Safiyyah missed Monsieur Cassin dearly. Now, she checked her watch: she needed to ensure she left with plenty of time to make it back home when she normally would, collecting Setti's medicine on the way. She mostly kept her head down, walking as quickly as she could without jogging. She took a route that she hadn't been on before, and this meant that her mind was happily occupied with mapping out the directions. Concentrating on which alleys opened where meant far less room for anxiety and nerves, and before she knew it she was turning onto Monsieur Cassin's street, shaded by the canopy of tall trees that lined it.

She froze in her tracks as she heard a rumbling sound in the distance. At the end of the long street, a small truck roared as it struggled along the bumpy road. Safiyyah knew immediately from the khaki green colour, huge tyres and the tarpaulin sheet stretched over its cargo bed that it belonged to the German army. She was relieved to see it turn around the corner, disappearing from view. That was lucky timing: she'd managed to avoid being seen by a single soldier so far today and for that she felt glad.

As she approached Monsieur's home, excitement rose in Safiyyah. He might have completed his book by now, perhaps even have sent it off for publication! She would persuade Baba to buy a copy, and make sure Madame Odette stocked it in the library too. As she crossed the road, from the corner of her eye she saw something white flapping. A crisp sheet of paper lay on the pavement, one of its corners lifting in the breeze slightly. Strange, the rest of the street was tidy and free of litter . . .

Out of curiosity, Safiyyah picked up the paper. It had typewriter text on half of it, and was labelled *page 1272.*

Her eyes skimmed across the words, realising quickly that it was about the growth patterns of alpine plants. *Grassland flowers. Altitude adaptations. Slow-growth. Tree lines.* It was all very scientific and she could barely make sense of it, but what she did know was that it must have something to do with Monsieur Cassin. She took it with her towards the house, and her feelings of puzzlement deepened when she retrieved a second piece of paper from the steps up to the front door. It clearly belonged to the same piece of work as the first, but this one was no longer bright white and pristine: pale brown prints of a shoe marked it.

Safiyyah knocked on the door, feeling apprehension all of a sudden. There was no way that the footprint on the paper could be Monsieur Cassin's – why on earth would he ignore a bit of paper on his own doorstep, let alone step on one that likely held his own work . . . ? He usually took a little while to come to the front door, but far more time had passed than normal now. Safiyyah knocked again, harder this time. Perhaps he had gone out . . . But if he had then surely he would have noticed the paper and done something about it. No, he had to be at home. So why wasn't he answering? Safiyyah resisted knocking a third time, remembering how Baba always said it was bad manners to pester someone like that. Privacy must be respected. Maybe Monsieur Cassin just wasn't up to seeing her today. She sighed, not quite content with this thought.

Safiyyah turned and sat down on the second step. She needed to think. She kicked a broken strand of ivy beside her, wondering what she should do. The ivy landed in the shrubbery that reached up past the steps. A jagged piece of terracotta poked out from the dense green, and Safiyyah leaned across, spotting a broken plant pot lying upside down. She lifted out what remained of it carefully, soil falling onto the plants below. Some sort of flower bulb fell out too, and Safiyyah wondered how and why the plant had been chucked here like this. Judging from the way it was cracked, it had already been broken before it was discarded here. It occurred to her suddenly that there was no ivy anywhere nearby either. The broken strand must have come from the plant in his hallway . . . Why on earth were Monsieur Cassin's plants and papers outside like this?

An image of the army vehicle trundling down his street just ten minutes ago filled Safiyyah's mind. She swallowed hard. Something was amiss. Panic got the better of her, and leaping up again, Safiyyah banged hard on the door, all thoughts of respecting privacy long gone. Her fist hurt from pounding the wood, and there was still nothing from inside. Just as she was considering running to fetch Baba in desperation, something made her try the big gold doorknob. She felt slightly sick as it gave way without resistance when she turned it. It had been unlocked all along.

'Monsieur?' Safiyyah whispered, met with silence broken only by the creaking of the front door as she pushed it open. There was soil scattered all over the wooden hallway floor, two of the big palms lay on their sides, white pots with gaping cracks snaking down them. Safiyyah held her breath, surveying the chaotic scene. Soil spilled down the stairs, pots were upturned and smashed everywhere she looked. Another lonely sheet of paper lay discarded in the adjoining doorway of the front room. Safiyyah braced herself as she stepped into the room.

Monsieur Cassin was huddled in the corner, sitting on the floor, simply staring into space. The once-brimming bookshelves that lined the walls were now bare, making the room feel like an empty shell. Here too, the large potted plants whose leaves fanned out in all directions and whose vines had adorned the walls, lay sprawled and broken across the ground. The room that had always astounded her with its verdant beauty now looked naked. Safiyyah could see that Monsieur Cassin was sitting on soil, his trousers marked by it, but he was entirely in a daze. He looked like a lost little boy, waiting for his parent to come and take him by the hand. The sight of him, forlorn and alone on the floor, made Safiyyah want to cry.

She tiptoed over the smashed terracotta and tangles of roots towards the old man, who all of a sudden seemed to be as fragile as delicate porcelain. His duck egg blue typewriter was on the floor beside him, the O and P keys broken off. He didn't look in her direction as she came closer, nor when she sat down beside him quietly. He didn't look physically hurt, and yet he looked utterly broken. Safiyyah reached out and touched him gently on the arm closest to her, almost worried that he might shatter into pieces when she did so.

'Monsieur?'

He seemed startled, at first barely recognising Safiyyah. Before now she had never seen him without a warm smile on his face, and a part of her felt she didn't recognise him either. After a few moments, he opened his mouth to speak, but barely any sound came out. She rushed to fetch a cup of water from the kitchen, which had also been ransacked. Sugar and flour sat in messy heaps on the floor with potatoes and onions, cupboard doors remained flung open and a chair from the dining table was on its side. Safiyyah picked up a tin of beans from the ground and set it aright, feeling fury bubble inside her. Who would do this to a kind old man like Monsieur Cassin? She knew it was the Nazis, perhaps even the ones in the truck she'd seen, but *why* had he been targeted like this?

Monsieur Cassin took the water gratefully, and after a few sips his hoarseness had gone. Safiyyah took his hand in hers, his palm hardened from decades of caressing earth and vine. It felt cold and clammy, and trembled a little.

'Dear Safiyyah. What brought you to me in my hour of need, I do not know. But you are a light in this darkness I find myself in.'

There was still a distance in him. He wasn't making eye contact as he normally would, in his expression was a haunted blankness.

'Monsieur, what happened?'

He sighed deeply.

'I should have known they would come for me. I even had a letter from a historian friend in Poland a month ago warning me. They've been targeting well-known Jewish academics for some time now in other occupied countries, but I just didn't think *botany* would bother them . . . I suppose I was in denial. How naïve I have been.'

He shook his head vigorously, and though she still didn't fully understand what had happened, Safiyyah desperately wanted to push away the despair she could sense behind his gaze.

'Monsieur, you weren't naïve, you were just being hopeful. It's not your fault!'

'I should really just be grateful that they didn't take *me* away to be packed off to some sort of concentration camp . . . But they've taken my work, and to tell you the truth, I don't know who I am without it. I completed my book a mere three days ago, and every last word of it has been taken. Viciously stuffed into a soldier's bag as if it contained deadly state secrets.'

She jumped up to retrieve the pieces of paper she had found outside the house and brought them to Monsieur Cassin. 'I found these on the street on my way here.'

He glanced over them wearily, then cast them aside as if the sight of them was causing him pain. He let them fall down onto a messy pile of plain white paper. 'Two soldiers barged in unannounced, taking me totally by surprise. I was actually just coming downstairs after having had a nap. I'm always terribly sleepy these days. They started on the bookcases, yanking heavy volumes down and sweeping whole shelves clean. All my encyclopaedias, novels and journals, thrown into their vehicle outside. Then they began combing the house, God knows for what, but in their careless, senseless mission, the younger of the two brushed his arm against poison ivy foliage in that corner.'

He pointed to the bay window at the front of the room, and Safiyyah noticed a small upturned pot of the plant that Monsieur had warned her to stay away from when she had first visited him.

'I was about to warn him not to touch it further but the other one shouted at me to shut up and leave them to their work . . . He ended up handling the plant quite a bit. They pointed their guns at me and made sure I stayed silently in the same room as them at all times.'

Monsieur's voice cracked a little, and Safiyyah took his hand in hers again, squeezing it tightly. 'It serves the stupid man right to have touched the ivy! Will it feel like nettles?'

'Oh it's much worse than nettles, Safiyyah, and yes, I suppose you're right.'

'Even your plants were resisting the Nazis for you, Monsieur.'

'They were here for over an hour, and I spent that time hoping that somehow they miraculously wouldn't seize my manuscript. It was sitting on my desk beside the typewriter. I couldn't hide it because they were keeping an eye on me constantly. After raiding upstairs, the younger soldier's reaction to the ivy began to develop on his skin, and he descended into a rage. I began to tell him it was the ivy, and even tried to explain what he could do to help, but he wasn't listening. He flew into a fury and began smashing the pots and ripping the vines and tearing the plants to the floor. It hurt so much to watch that disrespect. Much more than seeing my rare books being manhandled. The plants are living things! Then they came for the manuscript, and all my notes. The itching on his skin seemed to have propelled him into an animal state, he was sneering at me and growling in German as he stashed the pages into his bag. I'm not surprised that pieces of paper escaped onto the street in his madness.'

'But what will they do with it now, Monsieur?'

'Who knows? Perhaps they'll throw it onto a big bonfire along with other books and work by Jews and people with darker skin. That's what they've done elsewhere with thousands and thousands of books. What *is* certain though, is that I shall never see it again.'

As his voice trailed off, Safiyyah pictured Nazi soldiers cheering barbarically as they threw books into a roaring fire, its orange flames reaching up taller than buildings into the night. A shudder passed through her shoulders.

'But why?!'

'They pillage anything they see as contrary to Nazism. Me simply existing as a Jew is enough for anything I say to trouble them. By confiscating my writing and reading, they're silencing me, excluding me. And all of us. When they shatter glass and clay, they're shattering hearts too. But to them, our hearts might as well not exist.'

Safiyyah remembered what Madame Odette had told her when she was taping up boxes of books to hide. She wanted to scream. She understood why Monsieur Cassin seemed quiet and distant from the words he spoke. If he allowed himself to move closer to their reality, it would simply be too much to bear. He needed to remain as numb as possible. If he let himself realise the full weight of what had happened, it would crush him. His face crumpled all of a sudden, the little bit of colour that had been in his cheeks disappearing completely.

'It was all for nothing. Just like that, it's over. All those years . . . I feel sure I'll never write again.'

Safiyyah watched helplessly as devastation sank deeper into Monsieur's being. He looked around the room frantically, as if searching for explanations in the air.

'It's not like my work is politics, or history . . . I-I write about trees and flowers for goodness' sake. Leaves, rain . . . Butterflies . . .'

He whispered the last word, his palms thrown up in disbelief, and it seemed to drain all of his strength from his body. He covered his face with his hands, bending forward like a child. Safiyyah wanted to take him by the shoulders, to look him in the eyes and tell him that he was wrong. It was *not* all for nothing. It couldn't have been. She wanted to tell him that he hadn't been silenced forever, that this wasn't the end. Even though it made no sense, she felt it ferociously in her heart. But how could he even begin to think about writing the book that had taken him decades to write for a second time? And even if he did, the Nazis would never allow it to be published . . .

She tried to think of the examples that Monsieur had passionately told her about before, in which miracles happened in nature, in which hope prevailed. But no words formed in her mouth, there was absolutely nothing she could think of to say that seemed appropriate. She felt utterly helpless, and wondered if she should go and fetch Baba now, but somehow it also didn't feel right to leave him alone in this way.

Her eyes turned to the disordered stack of unused paper beside her. She thought about loading a sheet into the typewriter, but decided against it. Her brain felt chaotic, and she couldn't help but replay Monsieur Cassin's last sentences over and over again. *Butterflies. Butterflies.* Safiyyah took a sheet of paper in her hands, feeling its cool, stark smoothness between her fingers. Isabelle had taught her how to make origami butterflies two years before, and Safiyyah tried to remember how it went. It only took two attempts for her to perfect the paper creature, her hands remembering the folds and creases better than she thought they would. She held the three-dimensional white butterfly in the palm of her hand, its wings folded into elegant points. It was beautiful. She placed it between her and Monsieur, who was still cradling his face in his hands, his breathing uneven.

Safiyyah took a second piece of paper and began again. This time the complex folding and unfolding, measuring and pressing, tucking and turning took her less than two minutes. She curled the ends of the bottom wings around with her nails until they curved prettily, reaching up like question marks. Monsieur Cassin had lowered his hands from his face and was quietly observing her now. Safiyyah could see the remnants of a tear streaking his wrinkled cheek. She tentatively placed a piece of paper in front of him, and took another for herself. As she'd hoped, he picked it up, and waited for Safiyyah to demonstrate.

About twenty minutes later the pair were entirely surrounded by their creations, the butterflies glowing white on the floor around them. They'd settled into a comfortable rhythm, with the only sound in the room the rustling and creasing of paper as it was worked by their hands. Monsieur Cassin's breathing had now steadied, he'd become totally engrossed in the butterflies. Both he and Safiyyah stopped to look around them, almost surprised at how something as flat and unremarkable as a sheet of plain paper had taken beautiful form.

'A kaleidoscope of butterflies,' Monsieur breathed.

Safiyyah imagined them coming to life, one by one, floating and fluttering into the space around them. They would disperse with their delicate wings the thick sadness that had made the air heavy, whipping up a comforting breeze to gently embrace Monsieur Cassin. She gazed at the old man sadly, knowing that she needed to get back home before Yemma started to worry. She wouldn't put it past her mother to send out a search party if Safiyyah was even ten minutes later than expected.

'I'll be back. I promise I'll be back soon.'

Safiyyah hoped her words gave even a tiny bit of comfort to her friend, despite the helplessness she felt within her. Monsieur Cassin nodded, before reaching for another sheet of crisp paper, and beginning to fold.

As she hurried through the streets, thoughts of being scolded and grounded were far from Safiyyah's mind. Rage at the injustice of what had happened rose inside her with every step she took. Under the fury, questions circulated in her mind like tea leaves swirling in steaming tea as it's stirred. What did Monsieur Cassin mean when he said he should be grateful they hadn't taken him to a concentration camp? Was he in serious danger?

17

Safiyyah was a few blocks from Monsieur Cassin's home when she remembered Setti's prescription that Yemma had asked her to collect. The pharmacy near the mosque would definitely have the medication in stock, but they almost always had a lengthy queue and Safiyyah was already running late. She turned onto a square, relieved to see a green-painted cross on a sign above a shop: a pharmacy. It looked empty, so she entered, figuring it was worth a try to see if they had what she needed. The shop smelled of pear drops and hospitals, and the bespectacled pharmacist waited patiently as Safiyyah fumbled in her schoolbag for the prescription.

Just as she handed him the crumpled scrap of paper, a monstrous green truck pulled onto the kerb outside aggressively. The doors were flung open and two German soldiers leaped down at once. The taller one with blond hair didn't even close his door before charging towards the pharmacy. For a stomach-lurching moment, Safiyyah thought they were coming for *her*. Had they been the ones who had raided Monsieur Cassin's house? Had they known she had been there and was his friend? She watched, frozen to the spot as the shorter of the two called after the first, who had an almost maniacal look in his eyes as he charged towards them. The pharmacist was frozen too, staring in horror as the pair swung open the door to his shop, their lopsidedly parked vehicle blocking most of the sunlight from the room.

Safiyyah had shrunk into the corner against the shelves, almost knocking over a tinted glass bottle of cough syrup. The men charged straight to the counter, arguing loudly as they went. They hadn't even noticed Safiyyah, and clearly weren't there for her. The shorter man had a big leather bag on the crook of his right arm and was frantically offering a bottle of some sort of lotion to the other soldier with his left. Safiyyah couldn't make out a single word he was saying, but from the snappy tone that the taller one responded to him in, she knew they weren't getting along. The tall, angry one thrust his forearm in front of the pharmacist and, in broken French, demanded something to help it.

Safiyyah craned her neck to get a look. She had to hold in a gasp when she caught sight of the angry red blisters and welts that stretched from his palm up to his elbow. He undid the top button of his shirt, making a gesture as if to say he was overheating, and then held his head, presumably to signify a headache. The pharmacist asked how the blisters had appeared, and the shorter man began saying something in German and moved to open the leather bag he was holding, as if it held some sort of explanation. The taller soldier turned towards him, his face like thunder, and with one violent sweep pushed the other soldier back, swiping the bag and the bottle of lotion onto the floor.

The glass shattered, white lotion splashed onto the floorboards and the brown leather of the bag that now lay open on the floor. Safiyyah's heart thumped in her chest, she wanted to run out of the shop as fast as her legs would carry her. The soldiers' presence felt like a violent tornado, with the capacity to let loose and wreak havoc at any moment. They were now both leaning over the counter again, gesturing, trying to explain something to the pharmacist.

She couldn't shake the thought that these were the men who had broken Monsieur Cassin's heart just hours ago; they certainly seemed crazed and cruel enough. The man's arm and fever could have been caused by the poison ivy he'd touched. The final piece of the puzzle was solved when Safiyyah glanced down into the soiled leather bag on the floor just in front of her. There was a packet of cigarettes and a small green sheet of paper with a scrawly handwritten list of names on. Under them was a white, typewritten page with a hand-drawn graph at the top, and an illustration of a scarab beetle underneath.

Safiyyah could barely breathe. It had to be Monsieur Cassin's. She felt sick, here was his seized life's work literally at her feet, and she was powerless to do anything about it. She might be the last person to set eyes on the precious papers before they were burned to ashes and gone for ever. The shorter man's radio crackled at his belt, making Safiyyah jump. He left the shop to speak on it, pacing around the vehicle outside. The crazy soldier was now drawing something, presumably the poison ivy, onto a pad of paper. Safiyyah was barely breathing. The soldier outside was leaning against the truck and fiddling with his walkie-talkie, facing the street. The other soldier and the pharmacist were leaning intently over whatever was being drawn.

Safiyyah's body moved without permission from her brain. She opened her schoolbag, making as much noise as she could rustling through her books and papers. The tall soldier half glanced absentmindedly at her before turning back to the pharmacist. In one clean movement, she leaned forward and pulled out what she could of the manuscript from the soldier's leather bag.

The cigarettes and the list on the green paper fell back into place on the rest of Monsieur Cassin's manuscript, and Safiyyah tried to shove the papers she had taken into her open schoolbag. In horror, she realised that they wouldn't fit. She tried to fold the papers but the wad was so thick that they barely curved round enough for her to attempt squashing them in. She could see from the corner of her eye that the soldier outside was hooking his device back onto his belt, and turning to re-enter the shop. There was no way she could get the papers back into the soldiers' bag without them noticing. There was no going back. Safiyyah turned to face the shelf behind her, shoving the wad of papers up her school shirt. As the second soldier swung open the door of the shop, Safiyyah yanked her hair-tie out of her plait, pulling her curls over her neck and chest to hide any corners that might be showing through her shirt.

'Ahh, oui, oui!'

Safiyyah turned away from the shelf, keeping one hand clasped across her body so the papers didn't fall to the ground. The pharmacist had figured out what the soldier was trying to tell him and was about to begin perusing his shelf for some treatment. He paused, remembering Safiyyah's prescription and handed her the packet of medication she had come for.

'Mademoiselle. On your way now.'

He seemed keen for her to be out of there, and she was grateful. The soldiers' eyes bore into her, as if they were noticing her for the first time. She kept her eyes to the floor, doing her best to keep the papers still and subtle under her top while holding her schoolbag and Setti's medication in one hand *and* opening the door so she could leave.

Once round the corner and out of sight, Safiyyah yanked the papers out from under her shirt, not quite believing that she had just stolen from Nazi soldiers. Although what she stole had already been stolen, so it probably didn't count . . . Ethical technicalities aside, she knew she'd taken a major risk, and that she couldn't walk all the way back to the mosque with them stuffed up her shirt.

She removed the textbooks from her bag, tucking them under her arm and replacing them with Monsieur Cassin's papers, folded round on themselves as tightly as she could manage. Buckling up her schoolbag, she hoisted it onto her back and rushed home, replaying what had just happened in her mind in absolute disbelief. She knew she had probably only seized less than a third of the full manuscript, but it was still something. Something was better than nothing.

Safiyyah was approaching the mosque doors when the sight of a man and woman disorientated her. It took a moment, but the navy pleated skirt, striped cardigan and cropped haircut peppered with grey looked exactly like Madame Odette. The woman carried a black briefcase and as she walked briskly away from the mosque entrance, her distinctive gait made Safiyyah sure it was her. Walking just as briskly at her side was a tall, wiry man, whose unmistakable moustache was just visible to Safiyyah. Monsieur Claude! If the two hadn't been together, Safiyyah might have hesitated, but seeing them walking alongside like that, there was no mistaking them.

In a burst of excitement at seeing the librarians outside her home, Safiyyah called out, 'Madame! Madame Odette! Monsieur Claude!'

Madame Odette hesitated for a moment, turning her face an inch to the side, before continuing even faster away from Safiyyah down the street. Safiyyah was sure that Monsieur Claude had slowed down for a split second, but they were almost round the corner before she had a chance to run after them. There was no doubt that they had heard her, a man even further down the street had turned to look at Safiyyah. Perhaps it wasn't them after all ... A nagging feeling inside Safiyyah told her that it was, and hurt and confusion pricked her a little, though she quickly pushed the thoughts away and focused on getting back to Monsieur Cassin again.

Safiyyah shouted 'Salaam!' to Yemma in the kitchen, and handed Setti's medication to her with a quick hug. She ran off again to find Baba before Yemma could ask her any questions. Serendipitously, they bumped into each other on the steps to the courtyard from the offices. When Safiyyah first saw Baba, she felt apprehension, partly as the memory of seeing his shoes gone last night, and partly at the prospect of being in trouble for going to Monsieur Cassin's.

He gave her a quick hug, in a hurry as always nowadays.

'How was school today?' He was already walking past her as the words came out.

'Baba, Monsieur Cassin needs help. Now.'

He stopped walking and gave Safiyyah a strange, searching look.

'I-I-I stopped by after school. Soldiers stole his books and his manuscript.'

An expression that she couldn't make out flashed across her father's face. Something between fear, confusion and anger perhaps.

'I'll go now.'

'I'm coming with you, Baba!' Safiyyah needed to get him his papers back as soon as possible.

'It's better that you stay here, Safiyyah,' Baba said sternly.

'But, Baba, I promised him I would come back. Please, he'd want to see me, I know he would.'

Baba shook his head slightly, not looking her in the eye. Safiyyah took his silence as agreement, relief washing over her as she helped him put bread and savoury pastries into a paper bag for Monsieur Cassin. They walked quickly together in a tense silence, Safiyyah feeling grateful that Baba didn't interrogate her on why she hadn't come straight home.

18

Baba's eyes grew wide in disbelief and anger at the sight of Monsieur Cassin's hallway. Safiyyah tasted the sadness that hung low in the air again. But this time, Monsieur Cassin came to greet them, and she was relieved to see him on his feet, looking a little less lost and broken than he had earlier.

As they went with him to the living room, Baba scanned the chaos and shook his head over and over, lost for words. Safiyyah gasped when she entered the room, not at the mess this time but at the mass of big white butterflies that floated and twirled in the air. The sunlight from the window behind them streamed through their paper wings, illuminating them with a celestial glow. There must have been at least fifty, and the sight took Safiyyah's breath away. She looked at Monsieur Cassin, who gave her a weak smile. He had carried on making the butterflies after she'd left, and then threaded them up onto the curtain rail of the wide bay window.

Baba was the first to speak. 'I'm so terribly sorry. There really are no words to express it.'

He handed over the paper bag. 'I wish we could have

brought some mille-feuille with us, but as I'm sure you know, bread is a bit easier to come by these days. Safiyyah, will you please make a start on cleaning up the kitchen and hallway? I'll begin in here. Monsieur and I must chat a little now. Here, Monsieur, you must eat. Are you hurt?'

Safiyyah did as she was told, and began sweeping, wiping and tidying. She stacked cans and tins neatly in the cupboards, and scrubbed the surfaces until they shone and her fingers felt raw. She tried her best to listen to what the two men were talking about down the hallway, but their voices were low and she only picked up fragments of their conversation. At one point Baba seemed to be trying to persuade Monsieur Cassin to go somewhere. He mentioned *danger* many times, but Monsieur Cassin seemed to be resisting. Then their voices became even more hushed and Safiyyah had no choice but to focus on the sugar granules she was scooping up. Half an hour later, the kitchen was looking relatively normal and Safiyyah stepped out of the room to admire her hard work. Baba had done a good job too of sweeping up the living room and setting aright the pots and plants that could be rescued.

Safiyyah's schoolbag was sitting beside the stairs, and the sight of it set adrenaline rushing through her once again. When she re-entered the living room, Baba was placing rattan chairs and embroidered cushions back in their original positions, a big pile of soil and tangled roots swept into a corner. Monsieur Cassin was eating a piece of baguette, his hands trembling a little. She realised she wasn't going to be able to catch him alone without Baba being there, and so today there would be no ideal time to give him the papers. She was desperate to reunite Monsieur Cassin with his work, so she took a deep breath and unbuckled her bag. She sat beside Monsieur Cassin on the sofa and handed him the pile of papers.

'What's this?' he whispered, producing his reading glasses from a leather case in his trouser pocket. As he seated them onto the bridge of his nose, he gasped. Turning to Safiyyah, eyes wide in shock, he stuttered, 'I, how, I don't under— Safiyyah, *where?*'

Baba was watching them now, frowning in confusion. Safiyyah cowered under his gaze and felt her cheeks reddening.

'I was in the pharmacy when two soldiers came in, one had blisters all over his arm, from the poison ivy, you see. They dropped these on the floor so . . . I picked them up.'

Monsieur leafed through the pile, a look of sad amazement on his face.

Baba glared at Safiyyah, clearly not impressed. 'Two Nazi soldiers casually dropped Monsieur Cassin's manuscript on the floor of a pharmacy for you to take?'

'Well, they didn't drop it *for* me specifically, but they

didn't notice! They'd already stolen it anyway! And it's not the whole thing, it's not even a third. They were just going to burn it.'

Safiyyah's voice trailed off at the end as she saw that nothing she said seemed to redeem her in the slightest with Baba. He remained utterly furious. She knew he was just worried about her safety, but she'd hoped he might be a little impressed at her bravery at least . . .

It was Monsieur Cassin who broke the tense silence. 'Safiyyah, I really can't quite believe this . . . I can't quite believe that I'm holding chapters of my book again, honestly. Even a single chapter is precious, but this is beyond words. I'll be hiding this under the floorboards beneath my bed for sure. And who knows, perhaps once my hands decide that the kaleidoscope of butterflies is complete –' he gestured towards the threads hung at the window – 'maybe I'll write once again.'

Safiyyah smiled. It had all been worth it just to hear a tinge of hope in Monsieur Cassin's voice. Baba's expression was still serious, but she sensed a slight softening as he came to sit on the arm of the sofa beside Monsieur.

The old man continued, 'But you must know, my dear, that even more precious to me than words and pages, even those that my entire life has built up to, is you. You are one of the bravest, brightest, fiercest and most beautiful hearts I have ever had the privilege of meeting, and your safety and wellbeing is more important than anything else. You *must* be careful, our city is a changed place now.'

Baba was nodding in agreement. As Monsieur continued talking, he looked at Baba too. 'You cannot imagine the evils that the Nazis inflict on those who stand against them. You must all take great care.'

Safiyyah nodded sheepishly, and noticed that Baba was now looking at the floor.

Monsieur Cassin turned back to the papers on his lap. He ruffled through the stack and pulled a few to the front. He chuckled without smiling, passing a sheet to Baba to look at.

'My study of the plants that many people hate and call "weeds". I saw that everywhere from Asia to the Americas. Yet these so-called weeds often grow and repair broken ecosystems. They heal and protect the soil from the elements and can actually make way for other plants to grow. Bees and butterflies are attracted to them, building biodiversity. Flourishing forests and healthy valleys are pioneered by "weeds" . . .'

Baba looked out of the window, far away with these thoughts. He posed a question Safiyyah couldn't answer. 'Isn't it strange how humans decide what is and isn't desirable? What has the right to grow and take up space and what should be tugged out and cast aside, lifeless?'

'Indeed. Perhaps if we looked to nature more often

for guidance, we wouldn't be so lost. I certainly found far more harmony and respect in the wild than I ever have in so-called civilisation.'

They spent a few more moments together in silence, Baba reading through some of Monsieur's rescued pages, Safiyyah folding up another paper butterfly, before he announced that they must return home.

Safiyyah felt anxious at the prospect of leaving Monsieur alone again. 'But, Baba, can't we stay a little longer? What will Monsieur do?'

'I'll be fine, dear Safiyyah!'

Baba seemed stern again now. 'I'll come by again tomorrow. I'm sure I can organise for Madame Odette to get some books of Monsieur's choosing sent over soon too.'

Safiyyah was surprised to hear Baba speak casually of Madame Odette as if he knew her well. As far as she'd been aware, Baba only really knew of the librarian through Safiyyah's stories about her. Suspicion rose inside her as the image of the woman hurrying away from the mosque returned to Safiyyah's mind. She felt almost certain now that it had been her at the mosque earlier.

Safiyyah and her father walked a few streets in silence, before he turned to her, looking fit to burst, and hissed, 'I said nothing to you when you ran away from school the day of the bombing raid. If I had told your mother that you had left school without permission, you'd probably still be being punished at home now. I thought the stress of being caught up in the bombing would have been enough to teach you a lesson about disobeying your parents. I spoke to your school and Monsieur Cassin but decided to diffuse the situation by covering up your skiving for both you and your mother. She doesn't need any more worry on her shoulders and I figured you didn't need a scolding after the trauma you went through. How wrong I was though . . .'

Safiyyah felt mortified. She was flabbergasted at the fact Baba had known about the skiving the entire time. Embarrassment plus a sense of gratitude that he'd kept the secret overwhelmed her. She was lost for words.

Baba continued: 'I don't know where we went wrong with you, honestly. At what point did you start to think that it was acceptable to lie to your parents and teachers and gallivant around without a care? As if that wasn't bad enough, now you're sneaking about and *stealing* from Nazi soldiers. Soldiers who would happily shoot you without a second thought!'

'Baba, I came across them by chance and I didn't steal out of greed! It was because Monsieur Cassin's manuscript was right in front of me!'

'Safiyyah, you're missing the point! You've been deceitful more than once and that's that. You've lied and kept secrets from us, and I have a right to be angry about it.'

Safiyyah felt terribly misunderstood, and frustration simmered in her to the point that she thought she might cry. 'Baba, I am not a liar. I wanted to help Monsieur Cassin, that's all. You always taught me to help everyone in any way I can.' She paused, unsure of whether she should continue with what she felt like saying or not. Her emotions got the better of her. 'It's not me who secretly leaves the apartment at night and returns before morning like nothing is amiss. I'm not the one sneaking around or keeping secrets.'

Baba stopped walking and so did she. He glared at her across the pavement as if he was confused by her accusations but she'd seen the look of shock flash across his face as she'd spoken. So it was true. Her suspicions were correct, her father went somewhere in the middle of the night. She wondered if Yemma and Setti knew.

'I don't know what you're talking about, Safiyyah.' Baba's voice was low, but he'd never been a good liar. She could tell she'd caught him entirely off-guard. As he resumed walking at an even brisker pace than before, Safiyyah thought she'd try her luck.

'Why were Madame Odette and Monsieur Claude at the mosque today?'

He turned to look at Safiyyah again, his face clouded over with something more complicated than the anger that had been directed at her earlier. In fact, he seemed to have abandoned his previous accusations. He lowered his voice in case anyone heard.

'They came to meet us at the mosque today to discuss our library collection and how we might expand it.' He shrugged nonchalantly, as if to indicate that it was no big deal.

'Oh,' Safiyyah responded, thrown for a moment, surprised at how simple the explanation was. She jogged to catch up with her father, who was walking faster than she could manage. As they rounded the corner and the mosque's white walls came into view, Safiyyah pondered the fact that Madame Odette and Monsieur Claude were working with Baba and presumably Ammo Kader. It was a disorientating but exciting thought. Then all of a sudden she remembered how the pair had ignored her, and a familiar shadow fell over her once again. Baba's explanation was too good to be true. If they'd been there simply to discuss literature, why would they practically run down the street away from Safiyyah, ignoring her entirely? Perhaps if this had been the only mysterious occurrence, Safiyyah would have accepted it. But it wasn't. Too many things just didn't add up and she felt fed up with it all.

Much to her amazement and relief, Baba said nothing to Yemma of what had happened with Monsieur Cassin. He ate that evening in his office with Ammo Imam, and Yemma was busy chatting to Safiyyah's aunt, who visited for dinner. She brought a letter from Tarek, which excited everyone greatly. There was a deep sense of relief that they'd heard from him at last, and his mother seemed to glow a little, and talked with a trace of song in her voice. No one had said aloud what they'd feared for him since the Germans had driven back the Allies at Dunkirk. They all worried that Tarek had been amongst the thousands of soldiers who'd been killed on the beaches when the Nazis closed in on them, and dark shadows had loomed over his family since. Now their worst fears had been allayed, thanks to a small white envelope that had been delivered anonymously overnight.

Safiyyah's khala made a great fuss when anyone handled the letter, telling them to be careful so it didn't tear or crumple. The rest of the time she cried tears of relief and repeated 'All praise be to God' over and over. Khala made Safiyyah wash her hands before touching the letter in case she got stains on it from their couscous.

Yemma was eagerly reading the first page, and so Safiyyah read the second one in the meantime. She took in her cousin's words with relief, awe and admiration. He spoke of how horrendous the food had been, stodgy porridge and bland tinned beans, but once in a while someone would pass around a packet of sweets and it would feel like Eid or Christmas had come. She wrinkled her nose on reading that he hadn't been able to shower or wash properly since his departure. He'd been tasked with fixing anything broken for his regiment, and had successfully repaired everything from radios to tents, earning himself the odd piece of chewing gum or bite of chocolate.

Tarek's mother pointed proudly to the bit where he told how he'd head off into a field with his compass and pray his daily prayers. He described how those moments of solitary worship, away from the noise and stench of men, brought him calm. As his forehead pressed against cool grass, he knew that everything would somehow be all right in the end.

Safiyyah swapped pages with Yemma, and greedily read on, her eyes wide as Tarek described how his regiment had done everything they could to slow the Germans down. They had not been at Dunkirk when the Allies were cornered, and once the armistice had been signed between the French and German governments agreeing to a ceasefire, Tarek's regiment was disbanded. Most of them fled south into the Free Zone, which was still French territory.

As Safiyyah approached the final paragraphs, she slowed down to savour the words in her cousin's messy handwriting.

We are unbelievably fortunate to have made it here,
though it was a treacherous journey, as disbanded
troops are easy targets. I feel quite useless as a soldier
now that we cannot fight any more, but by God, we
are the lucky ones. So many others didn't get away
from the Germans and have been marched off, likely
to slave away on German or Polish farms as prisoners.
The Nazi hatred for soldiers from the colonies is
unrivalled though, particularly for anyone black. A
Senegalese soldier travelled south with us for a while,
his entire regiment was also African. He'd been
fetching water when the others were captured, and so
he made it away. The Germans shot every single one
of his fellow soldiers. Their white officers were kept
alive. He cried every night in his sleep. Please ask Setti
to say a prayer for him, his name is Moussa.

I've met a couple of Kabyle men where I am, one
of whom has business in Paris and will deliver this
letter to you, insha'Allah. Even if I can't fight in a
soldier's uniform any more, I swear I will resist the
Nazis in every way I can. I also promise to find my
way to you as soon as it is possible for me to try
crossing back into the Occupied Zone.

19

The long school summer holidays began, and Safiyyah busied herself in playing with and litter-training the kittens with Khala Najma, and occasionally Timothée too, when he stopped by. When he'd first visited to check on the animals, Setti had insisted he come upstairs and eat dinner with the family – of course, he couldn't refuse Setti! Everyone had taken a liking to him, and though Timothée had been shy and awkward to start with, by the time the mint tea was passed around, he'd relaxed.

Since then, he stopped by at the mosque often, and sometimes came upstairs for food too. Khala, Safiyyah and he had introduced Bonbon to the kittens again, and after another initial hiss and squabble, Bonbon took to them like a long-lost mother. Safiyyah taught Émeraude, who still refused to leave his cage despite the open door, to croak 'ISABELLE!'.

Safiyyah had heard the little click of the front door past midnight at least a dozen times now, but she didn't dare bring it up again with Baba. He seemed to be keeping her secret too after all. It still bothered Safiyyah though, and whether she was cuddling kittens by the roses in the courtyard or reading a book beside Setti in her room, her troubled mind drifted unfailingly back to her father.

The unsettled feeling about Madame Odette remained too, and it was around a month later that Safiyyah finally got her chance to investigate. Yemma asked her to pick up cleaning supplies, but their local shop was shut and boarded up. The next nearest one was very close to the library, and Safiyyah decided to run and see Madame Odette quickly. She was in luck. Madame was sitting beside her desk, reading letters through her half-moon glasses. Safiyyah's heart thumped as she approached, trying to look unfazed by what she was about to ask.

'Ah, bonjour! What a pleasant surprise, Safiyyah! How are you?'

'I'm well, thank you, Madame, and you? How is everything at the library?' Safiyyah shuffled on the spot anxiously.

'Oh, I'm fine, thank you. We've had a few interrogations by the Nazis but they don't seem too bothered by us for now.'

'That is a relief, long may it continue!'

'Amen!' Madame smiled warmly and at that moment, Safiyyah felt guilty for suspecting Madame of hiding something and ignoring her. She almost didn't ask what she came to ask, but ended up forcing the words out.

'So you've been helping the mosque library with their collection? How is it going? Will you be visiting soon?'

Safiyyah knew something was wrong before she even finished her questions. Madame's face fell, but she quickly pulled it back into composure. Her words tumbled out a little too fast. 'Oh, no, I'm not helping the mosque with anything. You must be mistaken. Far too much going on here for me to manage anything beyond these walls really!' Madame Odette glanced around the room awkwardly, her stiff smile betrayed by her eyes.

Safiyyah felt sick. She too forced a smile, which she was sure must have looked more like a grimace. 'Oh, all right, never mind. I must be off, or my mother will worry. Nice seeing you!'

'Au revoir, dear.'

Baba had confirmed that Madame Odette was at the mosque that day when Safiyyah saw her, but now Madame Odette plainly denied what Baba had claimed. One of them was lying. Perhaps both.

Safiyyah walked back home, furiously swinging the bag with cleaning bottles in, trying to figure out what she could do to get to the bottom of this horrible situation. A couple of streets away from the mosque, she was distracted from the turmoil inside her by shouting outside a shop. The front window of a jeweller's shop had been smashed; huge shards of glass lay on the floor. Clouds slowly drifted across one of the bigger jagged fragments as it reflected the sky above it, while other tiny pieces glinted in the sun like precious jewels.

A Nazi soldier was barking at the owners of the shop. The woman cowered behind her husband, an apron still tied around her waist. Another soldier brandished a black baton. Safiyyah wanted to snatch it from him and throw it into the river before he could smash anything else. The jeweller appeared to be pleading with the soldiers as he fumbled with papers. The barking soldier swiped the papers from the man's hands and they fluttered to the ground. She heard swearwords and 'Juif!' being spat at the couple. Safiyyah felt rage in the pit of her stomach. She forced her legs to carry her home before she did anything she might regret.

Baba was in the prayer hall, using his fingers to count prayers, instead of the beads that Setti preferred. Safiyyah sat down beside him, trying to steady her breathing as she whispered, 'Baba! Soldiers have smashed the window of a Jewish-owned shop a few streets away, and they were terrorising the owners. I saw it just now, you must do something!'

Baba inhaled sharply, the anger she felt now visible on his face too.

'What is the address?' He pulled out a tiny notebook and pencil from his pocket and waited for Safiyyah to reply. She was confused. Surely he should just go out there and help them, what would writing the details down do?!

'Ummm, it's a jeweller's, I don't know the address! If you go there now, you'll see for yourself.'

Baba's pen remained hovering above his notebook, he spoke quietly but sternly, 'Safiyyah. Where is it?'

'I think it's next door to a butcher, or maybe a grocer, on the big road as you approach the thirteenth arrondissement. Are you going to go?'

Baba ignored her question and asked another of his own. 'What colour is the door?'

Safiyyah could barely believe what she was hearing. She had always known her father to be a wise and logical man – what had happened? What ridiculous question would he ask next? What was their favourite gelato flavour? Did they have any pets? She gave him an exasperated look. 'Navy blue, I think, but, Baba, why does it matter? They need our help NOW!'

He wrote a few more notes and then tucked his book away, bowing his head once more in prayer.

Safiyyah's anger reached new heights. She waited until all the other men got up and left, having completed their congregational prayer. Once it was only the two of them, she moved to face him, fists clenched, her voice raised.

'How can you just sit there, Baba?! Why are you just doing nothing? People on our own doorstep are being treated like animals just for being Jewish and all you do is write about it in your notebook?!'

She stood up now, heat pulsing through her head. A man who had been putting his shoes on in the adjoining courtyard had stopped to watch her, but she didn't care in the slightest. 'You always said we should fight against injustice however we can! Why don't you care? You only care about yourself!'

Safiyyah stormed out of the hall, hot tears streaming down her face. Her eyes were so full of tears that she missed the ones falling from her father's eyes onto the carpet. She ran into the gardens, almost colliding with a circular pillar on the way. Grateful for the cool breeze on her skin, she sobbed until she was exhausted. She cried for Monsieur Cassin, for the man and woman and their broken shop. She cried for Hana and for Aharon and Remy. She cried for Isabelle, and Tarek. For frustration at her father's inaction, and for the lies she was being told by people she trusted.

When she could cry no longer, Safiyyah got up from where she had sat beneath an arch thick with intertwined grapevines. Her knees felt stiff from crouching on the stone floor, and her face puffy from weeping. She wound a curly vine around her finger, it was even thinner than the woollen yarn Setti knitted with. She couldn't continue like this; all of a sudden it felt like she didn't even know her father. It was as if there was a tangled knotty mess of yarn in her head and her heart, and she needed to unravel it. Safiyyah felt strangely calm, numb almost, as she unwound the delicate green frond from her hand. She headed up to the apartment, checking before she snuck in that Baba wasn't there. Yemma was feeding Fatima with Setti in the living room and Safiyyah greeted them quickly, handing her mother the cleaning bottles she'd asked for.

Sneaking into her parents' bedroom, Safiyyah opened the wardrobe as quietly as she could. Balancing precariously on a shelf, she reached into the uppermost section and felt about under piles of her mother's winter shawls and scarves until she found it. Safiyyah pulled out the wooden box with an intricate bone inlay design on the lid. She knew this was where Baba kept a spare key to their apartment, as well as much of Yemma's jewellery. She held her breath as she wriggled off the lid, which was stiffer than she'd expected. She heard a chair move in the living room and almost jumped down in panic, abandoning her mission. Under the bangles and chains that she would one day inherit, she found four keys. Moving the one she recognised as their apartment key to one side, she gathered the others together, before slipping them in her pocket and returning the box as quickly as she could. She'd made a mess of the shelf but could sense that she needed to get out of there fast. She made it into the hallway just seconds before Yemma did, feeling like her pocket was weighed down with lead.

'I'm going to see Khala Najma and the kittens, Yemma.'

Safiyyah felt horrible lying to her mother, but pushed the guilt away with the reassurance that very soon this would all be over with. Once she figured out what was going on with Baba, she never wanted to sneak around ever again, it was far too stressful!

'Sure, Safiyyah. Are you all right? You look a little upset.'

'I'm fine, Yemma. Where's Baba, by the way?'

'He had to visit someone's house, he was going there after he prayed. Do you need him?'

'No, no, I was just wondering. See you in a bit!'

Safiyyah feigned chirpiness, leaving the apartment as quickly as she could. She hurried down to Baba's office, checking that the coast was clear multiple times before pulling out the three keys she'd stashed away. Surely one of these must be a spare to Baba's office. She fumbled with the first, it had a pointy end and in her panic she couldn't angle it correctly. Forcing herself to breathe deeply, she steadied her hand. It didn't fit. The second key slid straight into the lock, but wouldn't turn either way. Safiyyah bit her lip as she tried the last one. *Third time lucky* was what Isabelle always said. Safiyyah barely believed it when it fitted, and then turned in the lock.

When the door clicked open, part of her wanted to run away. But she'd come this far, there was no use turning back. She didn't allow herself to worry about how she'd deal with anything she found. There was, of course, the possibility that she'd find nothing at all in the office, in which case she'd be back at square one. As she slowly opened the door, cringing as the hinge creaked loudly, she realised that wouldn't be the case.

On the floor beside Baba's desk was a pile of dirty-looking blankets and rags that Safiyyah didn't recognise. There was a general air of chaos, with bits and pieces strewn around. She'd certainly never seen anything of the sort in the office before, Baba was usually immaculate when it came to tidying and order.

She closed the door behind her gently, and went for a closer look at the pile of cloth. Poking out from under a grey blanket was the corner of a cushion she did recognise. White with black and orange patterns across its front, it was unmistakably one from Yemma's collection in their living room. Had Baba been coming to the office to sleep at night?! That made absolutely no sense.

She picked up a couple of the blankets gingerly, put off a little by their tattiness and faint staining. There were another couple of small cushions underneath. A deep red stain spread across one of them, almost dark brown in some places. Safiyyah recoiled at the sight of it, dropping the fabric she'd been clutching. The stain looked violent somehow, and she suddenly felt like she shouldn't be witnessing it. It was definitely blood, but whose could it be? There were two plates with crumbs on by the wall – sure enough, both from their kitchen.

Baffled, Safiyyah turned to Baba's desk. There were piles of papers strewn across its surface, a mug with rings of dried coffee inside. Safiyyah felt apprehensive at the prospect of rifling through her father's desk, somehow that felt like even more of an invasion of his privacy than sneaking the key had. As she sat down on the chair, she kicked something hard under the desk. Pulling back the black cloth cover, she saw Yemma's sewing machine.

From under the cloth, four small pieces of paper fluttered down to the floor. Each one had little numbers made from perforated holes across it. After a few moments of examining them closer, Safiyyah figured that the tiny holes might have been punched in by the needle of the sewing machine. Even more confused than she had been before entering the office, Safiyyah tucked the papers back carefully into the sewing machine cover, and opened Baba's bottom drawer, the largest one. The only thing she knew now with full certainty, was that there definitely *was* something going on.

Under stacks of normal-looking bills and receipts and the odd pencil or old toffee, was a glossy leather box. She tried to leave the remainder of the items in the drawer undisturbed as she did so, but it was nearly impossible. The box normally housed archived mosque records and other paperwork, and it looked as she expected it to. At the top was a statement of the mosque's bank balance at the end of last year, but Safiyyah noticed that the box seemed fuller than it had at any other time she'd seen it. In fact, it was positively brimming.

Instinct made her pull out the stack of papers, and sure enough, at the bottom was something unexpected. A brown-tinted apothecary bottle with a handwritten label on the front reading *Lactic Acid*. Beside it was a round carved rubber stamp with a wooden back. It looked official, with the words *République Française* circling its perimeter, but the rubber section was messily glued onto the wooden handle. Why on earth would Baba be in possession of something that looked like it belonged to a government official? Safiyyah knew that Baba and Ammo issued documents when babies were born to Muslim families to confirm their religious identity, but she'd seen that process before and it didn't involve dodgy stamps hidden at the bottom of drawers . . .

Other than a selection of blue and black fountain pens and a square ink pad, there was nothing else strange in the box. She placed it back as carefully as she could, assembling the stray pencils and sweets on top, before turning her attention to the other drawers. Nothing seemed amiss in any of them. As she was placing the last folder back into place in the last drawer she'd searched, her hand brushed against the inside of the wood under the tabletop. Instead of the rough, splintering wood that formed the inside of the desk, the surface felt smooth and cool against her knuckle. Like paper. She felt around further, until she found where the smoothness changed to the harsh grain of unpainted wood. Safiyyah gasped as she realised that there was a sheet of paper that had been taped to the underside of the desk. She kneeled on the floor, craning her neck upwards awkwardly to get a better look, but it was blank. At least it was on the side that was exposed. Carefully peeling away the two pieces of masking tape holding it in place, Safiyyah barely felt any pain as she scraped her hand against the drawer in the process. Baba's small, neat handwriting was all over the page; it looked like a list.

Some lines had been scribbled through, mostly ones at the top. Safiyyah began reading, eyes wide as dinnerplates as she desperately tried to take it all in. She'd been in the office for over ten minutes, and was feeling more and more anxious, knowing she shouldn't push her luck. But she was still no closer to understanding anything, and perhaps this mysterious list might be the missing piece of the puzzle . . .

At the top was a crossed-through name, beside it was written *Halima Ali,* and an address somewhere in the 18th arrondissement. Safiyyah wrinkled up her nose in even more confusion than she had already been feeling when she read the words:

Eye colour – brown

Height – 5 ft 4 inches

She was so engrossed in her reading that she didn't hear the quiet footsteps coming down the hallway. The office doorknob turned and the door swung open before she could even think about slamming the drawer shut and hiding. Safiyyah's mouth went dry with shock, the paper in her hand trembling behind her back. Baba stood in the doorway, looking like he'd seen a ghost. He glared at her with an intensity Safiyyah had never seen in him before in her whole life. After a couple of torturous moments, he clicked the door shut behind him, and walked towards her. Baba put his hand out and Safiyyah placed the piece of paper into it, shaking like a leaf.

20

Safiyyah had never seen her father look this way before. He was gripped by a wave of intense emotion and it seemed for a moment as if it might drown him. He perched on the edge of his desk, his head in his hands. Panic, anger and terror contorted his features as if he was in pain, his cheeks flushed pink above his beard. Safiyyah wanted the ground to open up and swallow her whole. She considered begging Baba for forgiveness, but her limbs were ice, frozen stiffly in place.

Despite still not being able to slot any of the pieces she'd uncovered together, she began to realise the scale of the secret she'd stumbled upon. Baba wiped his face with his hands, looking up towards the ceiling as if help might descend from the corners of the room. Whatever it was that he'd been hiding, it was far more serious than Safiyyah could have fathomed. She wished deeply that she'd never got tangled up in any of this in the first place. The silence was agonising, when would Baba say something?

Instead of speaking, Baba stood up suddenly, reaching to the top shelf of his bookcase. The wooden drum at the foot of the shelves fell onto its side as he knocked it off balance with his leg. Safiyyah jumped as it thudded onto the rug and rolled a little. Baba barely seemed to notice, and came towards Safiyyah with his Quran cradled in his arms. Even more confused than she had been before, Safiyyah stood up and took a step back, but Baba implored her to sit. He kneeled on the ground in front of her before untying the embroidered cloth adorning the book. The gold threads stitched in leaf designs through the fabric shimmered as Baba pulled out the Quran. He thrust the intricate green book onto Safiyyah's lap, and she gripped it tightly in surprise, imploring Baba with her eyes for an explanation.

He sighed deeply, breathing exhaustion out into the air in the room until a heavy fatigue enveloped Safiyyah too.

Eventually, he spoke sternly. 'You will swear secrecy on the Quran, Safiyyah. Everything I'm about to tell you has the capacity to destroy people's lives. Hundreds of lives. For ever. Irreversibly. In fact, let me just be clear now. People will die, Safiyyah, people will be *killed* if any of this information gets out. Anywhere. To anyone. Not only is my neck on the line, but Ammo Imam's, Ammo Kader's also, as well as innocent, desperate people all over our city.'

Safiyyah listened wide-eyed, stunned at the words coming out of her father's mouth. He wiped beads of sweat from his temple with a handkerchief.

'This isn't a weight I wanted you to have to bear, but clearly you wanted otherwise. We have entered very, very dark times. It is absolutely vital that ALL of this remains in this room. Do you hear me? You've proved incapable of listening and obeying any of my past instructions, but, Safiyyah, if you care even one iota about human life, you will keep your mouth *shut*. All right?'

Safiyyah gulped, her stomach turning and twisting at the prospect of what Baba might reveal. She nodded vigorously, hoping he could see her sincerity. He gestured towards the Quran. Safiyyah had never had to swear secrecy before in her life, nor had she ever seen anyone do it before either. This was a very, very big deal. She clutched at the holy book uncertainly, and thankfully Baba stepped in.

'I need you to swear that you will keep EVERYTHING I tell you to yourself. On God's perfect and sacred words, swear, Safiyyah, that you will keep this secret.'

Safiyyah's lip trembled, and the voice that left her mouth was at first shaky and thin. She cleared her throat and tried again: 'I-I swear on the Quran that I will keep everything you say a secret, Baba.'

'All right.' He took the book back, wrapping it and placing it carefully on the shelf. As he sat back down, he shook his head again, as if in disbelief that he was actually doing this. He opened his mouth to say something, but then closed it again. After another deep sigh, at last he began explaining the string of events that had changed the course of his life.

'Everything started months ago, when we first realised that Hitler's army had their boots on French soil. In fact, no, before that actually. Ammo Kader had been keeping his eye on Germany's movements before they actually invaded our country. The threat of their arrival here, as you already know from the bomb shelters and gas masks that appeared last year, has been very real for a long time now. The anxiety was everywhere, I'm sure you'll have noticed too . . . The looming prospect of bloodshed and violence, of loss and scarcity, seeped into every conversation. Slowly, slowly, I began to taste it in my food, smell it on the breezes that swept through the city, and even hear it in cries of gulls and swallows.'

Safiyyah realised how right her father was. She thought back to the last time she had truly been at ease, when the future had seemed vast and bright, like a clear, endless horizon.

'Initially after the invasion, it was dread and panic I felt. Ammo Kader and Ammo Imam, on the other hand, calmly got to work. It was as if the months of monitoring international affairs and preparing for the worst just flowed seamlessly into resisting the Germans. Ammo Kader quietly and quickly began liaising with people all over the city and country, people who, like us, detested what was happening. You know Ammo Kader, he knows absolutely everyone . . . From surgeons to hat makers, bakers to priests, librarians to doctors, there are hundreds, thousands maybe, of people who are secretly resisting in any way they can. Since the Vichy government fled, abandoning us to the Germans, the only thing opposing the Nazis in France *is* the Resistance. This work could not be more important.'

He caught her eye, raising his eyebrow for emphasis when he said the word *librarians*. Safiyyah felt something click inside her brain all of a sudden. So it *had* been Monsieur Claude and Madame Odette leaving the mosque that day after all. Safiyyah sensed that the shiftiness, the strange lies, stories not adding up, were all about to finally make sense. Baba gazed into the distance, a look of deep admiration sparkling in his eyes.

'Your mother and I felt anxious and unsure at first. It's dangerous, dangerous work, and we had you and Fatima to think of. But Ammo Imam reminded us of how God says that saving even one life is like saving the whole of humanity. He must feel the fear too, but he has never shown it. It is as if he can see his mission clearly laid out in front of him and all he has to do is tread the path.

'I still worry for you every single day, fear that I'm putting you at risk, but God poured strength into my heart. I feel I only have a trickle of the courage that Ammo Kader does, but even that is enough for me to know that what we are doing is right. How could we hope to sleep at night if we sat back and allowed the oppression of our neighbours, our brothers and sisters in humanity . . . ?'

Baba's fists were clenched by his side, his face flushed and his eyes aflame. Safiyyah perched at the edge of her seat now, lapping up every word he spoke and thirsty for more. In the pit of her stomach she felt horrified that she had accused her father of sitting back and doing nothing.

'So when the call came from our friend, Dr Somia, there was only one possible answer. A British soldier had been wounded in the north, then mercifully rescued by members of the Resistance in the countryside but was in a critical condition. One of the men who'd found him is Kabyle, and he contacted Dr Somia, who disobeyed the curfew and drove under the cover of night to help the soldier. He wanted him near his hospital to monitor and help him, so they brought him to Paris. It would be too dangerous for an obviously British soldier to be *in* the hospital, the Germans have spies everywhere. So Dr Somia asked if he could stay here instead.'

Safiyyah looked over at the stained blanket and cushions on the floor, astonished at what she was being told. Baba followed her gaze and nodded.

'The soldier stayed here for almost a fortnight. After praying upstairs, Dr Somia would visit multiple times a day, checking his progress and instructing me on how to help in the meantime. He joked that I'd become his nurse! By the grace of God, he recovered well. I have to give credit to Yemma's endless bowls of steaming soup that she brought down daily. Since then there have been two others.

'The last man left early this morning. He'd been parachuted into France as a spy, and got shot in his leg. He still had a painful limp but was stable and we decided it was best to get him out of here as soon as possible.'

'Why did you have to hide the soldiers? What would have happened if they had been found?'

'For the Nazis, the Allies are the enemy. If the Nazis found us helping someone British, we'd be in great trouble. They'd take the soldier prisoner for sure, and we'd be arrested and taken too. We've been hearing reports of an upcoming Nazi visit to the mosque soon, so we won't be able to hide any soldiers until they've been and gone.'

A chill spread through Safiyyah's spine, making her shudder a little. The weight of the danger her father faced began to sink in. As it did, her jaw tensed up and her shoulders stiffened. Memories flooded her mind of Baba over the recent months, how distant and stressed he'd seemed all the time. It was no wonder . . . She remembered when she'd had to stop attending Saturday morning meetings. The day she discovered his office was locked. How even when he *was* with them, his eyes would glaze over and it would seem like he was looking through her and Fatima, to somewhere far away. Suddenly it all began to make sense.

'Your beloved library is an important hub for the Resistance efforts,' Baba told her. 'Madame Odette has been liaising with others in the north, the south, and even in other countries, for a while now.'

For the first time in what felt like an age, a hint of humour passed across Baba's face and he chuckled, 'To be honest, I was surprised you hadn't spotted Monsieur Claude around the mosque before, he's been working with us so much lately that he's practically become part of the furniture!'

Safiyyah stared at Baba in shock. She felt she'd need days to take it all in properly. It was as if jagged pieces of a giant puzzle were slotting and clicking themselves into place in her mind. Some of the fragments remained floating around though, not yet ready to find their homes in the almost complete picture that was now forming for Safiyyah. Yemma's sewing machine, the hidden list, the strange things in her father's drawers . . .

Timidly, she asked, 'Why is all that stuff in your office? Yemma's machine, the bottle of acid . . . ?' She trailed off at the end of her sentence, seeing a new wave of anguish descend over her father. Perhaps he'd hoped she wouldn't have discovered all of that. He sighed loudly, looking sheepish and annoyed again all at once.

'To cut a very long story short, Safiyyah, we are providing Jews with fake identity documents. By giving them papers that say they're Muslim, we are protecting them from being treated like animals by the soldiers crawling our streets. Jews from all over the city have been disappearing already, and it's likely to only get worse.'

'*Disappearing*? I don't understand, Baba!'

'Of course no one just "disappears", the Germans are arresting them. Young men, mostly, but no one is safe. We've found out that many have been sent to prison camps, while there are others who we haven't been able to trace at all. If, by forging paperwork, we can keep Jews safe, I'll continue to do it all day and night long. Naturally, it was all Ammo Kader's courage and foresight. He is a central pillar in the Kabyle secret network, and he's ready to fight to his last breath for what is right.'

'What would happen if . . . if you were caught?'

'I'd be arrested too. It's always been illegal to forge official documents, and this time last year, I would never have dreamed of doing so! But everything is upside down now. If those in charge are more aligned with the devil than goodness and truth, then it becomes a duty to stand against them. How can I obediently follow a law that is so brutally unjust? Resistance is a duty upon all of us now. If it costs me my life or freedom, so be it. I'll be at peace knowing I did everything in my power to resist, to fight for what is right.'

Safiyyah's eyes welled with tears. She was overwhelmed with awe and respect for her father, as well as fear for his safety. He spoke faster now, as if a new energy pulsed through him.

'A kind man who used to work at a dry cleaner's spent a whole night teaching me the tricks of forgery. He knew all about the different types of chemicals and dyes, the subtleties of the business, and he uses his knowledge to help people who need it most. You should have heard him speak about it, as if it were magic! And I suppose in a sense, it is. It is quite literally saving people from terrible things. It's intricate, painstaking and terrifying work, but also the most important thing I've ever done in my life.

'Yemma let me borrow her sewing machine in order to make the tiny holes present on the official paperwork. The lactic acid removes stains wonderfully. That piece of paper on the underside of the drawer, the one I went to great lengths to *hide*, keeps a record of Jews to whom we need to give documents. The librarians have access to the names and addresses of thousands of Jews across the city, and by collaborating with them, we've given false Muslim identities to many already. The demand is increasing day upon day, I fear the worst is yet to come. "Struggle against sleep", the forger told me. That is what I must continue to do, we can't let anyone down.'

Safiyyah sat in astonished silence, unable to form words to match her racing thoughts. She pictured Baba hunched over his desk, concentrating intently on the documents as moonlight streamed in through the window. The times she had heard their apartment door click at night ran through her mind. Not finding Baba's shoes on the rack, the dark circles that seemed to dominate his face these days. Her cheeks flushed in mortification as she remembered the cruel things she had said to him earlier in the prayer hall. He'd been writing the details of the attack Safiyyah described in his notebook so he could help the Jewish couple, more powerfully than she could ever have imagined. Asking for the colour of their front door was not a frivolous question, but an important detail and precaution. Baba needed to ensure he had the exact place written down correctly in order to visit and provide them with fake identities.

She wanted to hug him tightly, but stayed in her seat. She still wasn't sure if he was terribly angry with her, and also felt a strange sense that she didn't fully know her father. She couldn't believe that such huge, dangerous and incredible secrets had been kept from her all this time. Of course, she understood why they had been, but she still felt a little odd. Most of all though, she felt proud. Proud to call the exhausted, haggard man with an overgrown beard who sat opposite her Baba.

*

Baba had been right about an imminent Nazi visit. Barely a week after their conversation, the ugly green uniforms that Safiyyah hated seeing in the streets were now polluting the mosque courtyard. As soon as the five soldiers and their commander had stepped through the engraved wooden door, it seemed as if the sun had dimmed. Bonbon had taken one look at the entourage and bolted back up towards the apartment (Safiyyah felt proud of her cat's excellent judgement). Baba had already buried all of his forgery tools and bottles under one of the flowerbeds beside the hammam, and returned Yemma's sewing machine and blankets to the apartment.

Safiyyah stood in a corner of the courtyard, scowling as Ammo Kader led the soldiers from room to room. He seemed mostly unfazed, though Safiyyah noticed a vein pulsing angrily in his forehead when he was close by. Every time she had seen him since the revelations from Baba, Safiyyah thought Ammo Kader resembled an angel. Today, he seemed to float across the tiles, his long white robe glowing as it reflected the sunlight, and he looked even more angelic than before.

If the visit had happened before she'd found out the truth, Safiyyah knew that she'd have been furious right now. Her blood would have been boiling at the sight of the Nazis polluting their sacred space and home, and she would have felt physically sick seeing Ammo chatting to them like this. Khala Najma brought out a tray of sugary biscuits and mint tea for the soldiers to take from. If Safiyyah didn't know what she now knew, she might have flung the tray onto the floor in her rage, but instead, she stood back calmly. It was all an illusion. She felt enveloped in a sense of serenity, the knowledge that this was all a front, and that Ammo was in reality fooling all these men, running a sophisticated ring of Resistance fighters. Safiyyah felt immeasurably proud of him, of Baba, and of everyone who was fighting in their own way, but she couldn't help but wish that she too could join them somehow. She felt helpless and small, and longed to be able to do more than simply give the Nazis daggers with her eyes.

Ammo was explaining that they could not enter the women's prayer section in order to protect the comfort and privacy of the female congregation. Safiyyah watched as a stout soldier with mean-looking beady eyes stuffed his face with the biscuits; he seemed to barely be paying attention to what Ammo was saying. Crumbs clung to his moustache and spilled down his shirt, and Safiyyah felt repulsed.

Setti came into sight from around the corner, and just as soon as she had passed the men and was out of their range of vision, she spat on the ground behind their boots. Safiyyah gasped, worried that one of them might have heard her, but thankfully they remained oblivious. Her grandmother was always endlessly elegant and refined, softly spoken with a tranquil air about her, and seeing her spit was a shock to Safiyyah's system.

Setti tiptoed over and joined Safiyyah, leaning against the wall. She spoke to Safiyyah under her breath. 'They aren't targeting us Muslims at the moment because they're scared of a Muslim uprising in Algeria, Tunisia and Morocco. The Germans are already fighting the Allies across our countries in North Africa. They are behaving civilly with us on the surface but I know they suspect something already. They mistrust Ammo Kader and your father, I can feel it.'

Safiyyah looked at Setti in horror: her grandmother's gut instinct was almost always correct. Setti knew when someone was hiding something or when something just wasn't right. Today, as Setti glared fiercely at the soldiers when they took their leave, Safiyyah prayed that this time her grandmother had got it wrong.

'Good riddance!' Setti hissed. 'Although something tells me this isn't the last time we'll be seeing them here.'

21

Some weeks later, Safiyyah was on her way home from the grocer's, swinging a cloth bag at her side as she walked. She'd only managed to buy four potatoes, a leek and two onions, after waiting in line for almost forty minutes, but it was better than nothing. They hadn't eaten meat for weeks, and Yemma's once-colourful table spreads had now dulled a lot. Where vibrant peppers, carrots and succulent chicken had once been sprinkled with citrusy coriander, bright parsley and wedges of lemon, now they often ate their couscous plain. Setti's freshly squeezed grapefruit, apple and of course orange juices had been replaced solely with water.

The price of food had shot up, and much of what was available in the city had been rerouted from ordinary shops to the bellies of Nazi soldiers. Almost everyone in Safiyyah's family had lost weight since there had been less food to go around.

Despite this, she knew that they were the lucky ones. It was so much harder for people like Timothée and his father. The last time Timothée had visited the mosque, about a week ago, he'd said his dad had a bad flu that he couldn't seem to shift. Setti normally gave oranges to anyone who was sick, she said they were little balls of vitamins and sunshine that could help you get back on your feet. Of course, she'd had no oranges to give Timothée and so she'd handed him her last jar of orange marmalade, in the hope that it might be some sort of substitute.

Safiyyah tried to recall the taste of the golden buttery pastries filled with spicy minced meat and peas that Khala Najma used to make for them in Ramadan. Her mouth had just started to water when her attention was pulled towards the small person sprinting up the street towards her. A young boy, with a grey cap on. Safiyyah could see that he was waving frantically. At her, it seemed . . .

It was Timothée. Safiyyah's heart sank when she saw his flushed cheeks and urgent, panicked expression; something was wrong. She walked straight past the door to the mosque, hurrying towards him. As she finally reached him, he bent down, placing his hands on his knees to catch his breath. She braced herself to hear that his father had deteriorated further.

'Safiyyah, your father, he's in trouble!'

Timothée paused, still panting, sweat dripping down the sides of his face. Safiyyah couldn't understand what he was saying.

'MY father?! Do you mean *your* father?'

'No, your baba has been arrested. He walked past me a few hours ago, he was visiting apartments in the fourth arrondissement, I think he was delivering . . . you know, *stuff*, to people. I reckon he was on his way back here when he passed me again, and I got up to say hi, but before I managed, I noticed a weird-looking fellow following behind him. The guy looked shifty, he was clearly keeping a distance, but he didn't take his eyes off your father. I tailed them both for a few streets, and then sure enough, the weird guy closed in on him and two other men in Nazi uniforms jumped out of a van and arrested him! I ran here straight away, someone needs to get him out of there!'

Safiyyah's heart was in her throat, and she began to feel like she might be sick. How could this be happening? She pushed the images of Baba being sent to a prison camp somewhere from her mind, and gestured to Timothée to follow her into the mosque. She told him to try to find Ammo Imam or Ammo Kader, before flying up the stairs two at a time to the apartment.

Setti was sitting just outside, quietly tending to four small saplings in terracotta plant pots. Safiyyah had helped her pick out, wash and germinate the seeds from the last couple of oranges they'd managed to get hold of months ago. She froze for a second and watched the old lady. She looked so peaceful, oblivious to what was happening to her son a few miles away. Safiyyah noticed how frail and gaunt she had become recently. Her cheeks seemed to have hollowed and the soft milky skin of her face hung slackly. Safiyyah desperately wished she didn't have to deliver the bad news to Setti, but she also didn't want to waste a single moment while her father was in the hands of the Germans.

She crouched down beside her, placing a hand on her back gently. 'Assalamu alaikum, Setti. Timothée saw Baba get arrested by the Germans. He's gone to find Ammo Imam and Ammo Kader for help.'

Shock, then horror, passed across her grandmother's face, but within moments, she was up on her feet calling for Yemma, prayer beads passing between her hands at lightning speed. By the time they all made it down the stairs, Ammo Imam and Ammo Kader were already heading out of the main door towards the police station. Yemma joined them, while Safiyyah, Setti and Timothée sat beside the cascading fountain in the courtyard, each lost in their own hearts. The gurgling of the fountain that was normally soothing, now agitated Safiyyah. She was grateful when Setti spoke.

'Don't worry, darling. He will be all right, insha'Allah.'

The tears that Safiyyah had been stifling finally overwhelmed her and spilled down her cheeks. Words wouldn't settle on her tongue and so she just nodded.

Timothée cleared his throat. 'I'm almost certain he was on his way back home, Safiyyah. Which means he won't have had anything on him that could get him into trouble. Your gran is right, he'll be back soon.'

Safiyyah was touched by Timothée's gentle tone, and felt reassured by his words. She nodded again, fresh salty tears surfacing. Setti had her eyes closed and was deeply engrossed in her whispered prayers. After a few moments, it clicked for Safiyyah that something was amiss with what Timothée had said. What had he meant about what Baba was carrying . . . ? Did he know about the false identity papers?

'Timothée,' Safiyyah whispered. 'What do you mean about my father not having anything on him that might get him into trouble? And when you say you think he was on his way back . . . On his way back from what, exactly?'

She tried to keep her tone steady, her voice nonchalant. Timothée stared at her for a moment, frowned incredulously and then said, 'C'mon, you must know what he does . . . Well, actually I don't know the details, but I know he's helping . . . y'know . . . people, people who need it. It's been months now, I've seen him at all times of day and night, different addresses. I don't know what he does exactly, but I assume he gives them something they need.'

He shrugged in response to Safiyyah's surprised look, before continuing, 'I know he's a good man. A very good man, in fact. I've helped the librarian guy out twice now, running errands and passing messages between the library and the Resistance in different parts of the city. Your dad works with them too, I saw him meeting them ages ago and I figured they were all on the same mission.'

Safiyyah couldn't believe what she was hearing. Timothée had known about Baba for longer than she had, and even more surprising than that was the fact that apparently he'd liaised with Monsieur Claude too! He didn't know *what* Baba was doing exactly, and perhaps it was best that way. She certainly wasn't going to spill any information after swearing secrecy. She tried to act casual.

'Yes, he is a good man. A brave, kind, incredible man. The best one I know.' She began to choke up again, and was more grateful than ever for Bonbon's warming arrival. The cat plopped herself onto Safiyyah's lap and nuzzled her face into her palms.

Two agonising hours later, Safiyyah's prayers were answered. Baba, Yemma, Ammo Kader and Ammo Imam came through the door. Her father looked more exhausted than normal, but his face moved into a wide smile when he saw her. She leaped up immediately and wrapped him in the tightest squeeze she could manage.

Baba had been questioned for over an hour by two soldiers, one Nazi, and one from the French Vichy government, who worked with the Germans. They'd threatened and blackmailed him, trying to make him admit to assisting Jews. They'd even accused him of issuing fake Muslim birth certificates to Jews. A chill swept through Safiyyah when she realised how closely they'd been monitoring Baba, and how near their suspicions were to the truth. It was a miracle that they hadn't found anything in his bag or pockets, otherwise things would have turned out very, very differently.

Timothée was right, Baba had already given out the papers he had left the mosque with, and so by the time the undercover spy began trailing him, there was no evidence with which to charge him. Despite this, the soldiers had continued to push and prod Baba in the hope that he would let something slip, and it was only upon Ammo Kader's arrival and firm intervention that they released him. Baba was out, but he was under no doubt that they weren't satisfied that he'd told the truth.

From Ammo Kader to Setti, everyone was shaken and haunted by what had happened, and one thing was certain: *les trois mousquetaires* would be watched by the Nazis like hawks from now on. It was no longer safe for Baba to hurry around the city handing out forged documents, nor for him or Ammo Kader to meet with the librarians or others from the Resistance, as they risked leading the Germans straight to them.

Timothée had returned to his own father after seeing that Baba was back safe and sound. Before he left, everyone had thanked him graciously, Setti and Yemma taking turns to give him huge hugs. Safiyyah handed him a comic book as a thank you.

It was late now, but she felt no tiredness. Safiyyah was sitting outside the closed living room door; she had been sent to bed after dinner so the adults could speak in private. Of course, she hadn't gone. Her joints ached from crouching in one spot, being careful not to move and let the floorboards creak. She overheard Baba say that the question was *how* on earth could they now get papers to those who needed them . . . Yemma offered to go instead of Baba, but they all agreed that it would still be very risky. Besides, Yemma didn't know her way around much past their arrondissement, and got terribly nervous with all the soldiers around.

Safiyyah had to stop herself from bursting into the room and presenting her idea to them. It seemed so blazingly obvious to her that she couldn't understand how none of them had thought of it yet. She and Timothée could do it! No one would suspect children of collaborating with the Resistance, surely. Safiyyah knew her way around much of the city like the back of her hand, and Timothée was an expert at moving around unnoticed. They'd be the ideal team.

She fidgeted with the tassels on the hallway carpet agitatedly as she waited for the adults to finish and get up. When she heard movement, she ducked back into her bedroom, and once Ammo Kader and Ammo Imam had left, she caught Baba. Before he could even ask her why she wasn't asleep, she launched into her proposal. She'd rehearsed it six times whilst crouching in the hallway, and felt confident that it was as persuasive as possible. Baba listened intently, shaking his head vigorously as soon as he realised what she was suggesting. She ignored him, and continued with her speech.

She knew she'd struck a chord with him when she said there was no alternative; they couldn't just let innocent Jews suffer when they had the power to help them. Baba looked away, clenching his jaw so tightly that his cheek rippled. When she finished, there was silence.

Yemma came into the room after brushing her teeth, looking alarmed at the tension between her husband and daughter.

'Safiyyah, I've heard what you have to say,' Baba said, 'and I appreciate your concern and courage. Let me think about it. We'll talk in the morning – you *really* must go to sleep now.'

As she settled into bed and pulled her blanket over her, Safiyyah knew somewhere deep inside her that things were about to change. She'd sensed from Baba's reaction that he knew he had no other choice but to allow her to help now. Her whole body prickled as she was filled with nerves, anticipation, and a touch of excitement to finally, finally be able to *do* something.

22

Safiyyah's first formal Resistance mission took place a week later. School was back on again after the summer holidays, which had been the strangest ones in Safiyyah's life. She wished she had someone to share everything with, a friend she could confide in. Of course she couldn't write anything down to tell Isabelle, and telling anyone else was far too risky. She'd actually started keeping a distance from Hafsa on purpose because of her big mouth – that was a dangerous trait in a time like this.

This morning, Safiyyah's thoughts were far away from the usual back-to-school nerves and excitement. She couldn't care less about not having new pens and pencils to swap with her friends. Instead, she was silently reciting prayers for safe passage while mapping out the routes she would need to take, for the thousandth time. She kissed Yemma goodbye, and told her not to worry. She knew her mother had been awake the entire night praying for her, and that she still wasn't speaking to Baba normally after he'd agreed to involve Safiyyah in his dangerous work.

She left the mosque three quarters of an hour earlier

than she normally would to get to school, and as she stepped onto the street, fought the anxiety that everyone who passed was staring at her accusingly. Timothée had visited the mosque the day before for a briefing by Baba and Ammo Kader, and after the surreal meeting, he'd given Safiyyah advice on not raising suspicions or getting caught. She ran through it now in her mind as she walked. If she kept her eyes on the ground too much, or looked about her shiftily, other people might sense something. She must act nonchalant and confident, as if absolutely nothing was amiss. Avoid eye contact with anyone, but look around as she normally would. Keep her body language natural and at ease, as if she truly were just on her way to school. Try to blend into crowds and groups of people. If she did find herself alone, she should walk close to building walls, sticking to shadows. If she kept her face turned towards the bricks, there was less chance of a spy or investigator snapping a clear photograph of her.

She arrived at the tailor's shop quicker than she had anticipated; she must have been walking faster than normal. Safiyyah made a mental note to consciously slow down for the next leg of her journey. Her stomach turned over and over as she pushed open the heavy glass door. Apart from the red-haired lady behind the till, the shop was empty. The shelves were chaotically laden with colourful spools of thread, pin cushions and long rolls of wool, felt and cotton fabrics. She walked nervously over to the woman, who was eyeing her sternly.

'Oui? How can I help you, mademoiselle?'

Safiyyah's trembling hands made it hard to unbuckle her schoolbag.

'My mother sent me to give you this skirt. She would like it to be hemmed by two inches please.'

Safiyyah handed over the emerald green skirt to the woman, feeling the folded piece of paper that Yemma had stitched into its lining crunch between her fingers. Safiyyah had no idea what it said, but knew it was an urgent message for the owner of the shop. Baba had told her to say the two sentences to the lady, and on having handed the skirt over, leave immediately. The woman said nothing as she folded the skirt and tucked it into a drawer beneath her desk. Safiyyah felt terribly awkward walking out just like that, but she did as she was told and was grateful to be back in the fresh air again. Phew. First part completed.

Next she headed to a large park, towards the west of the city. She had been here only once before with Isabelle years ago, and worried that she wouldn't remember the exact locations of the different parts of it. It was quieter than she had anticipated it being, she'd forgotten that all the other children in the city were returning to school today too ... The playgrounds were empty, only a handful of pedestrians and dog-walkers were present on the grass and paths.

Safiyyah tried to catch a glimpse of her watch without raising her arm and making it obvious that she was waiting for someone. She had four and a half minutes until Timothée was due. Not bad. She strolled around the bandstand and past the duck pond, counting down to his arrival. Baba had given him a watch especially for this task. She hoped his time-keeping was as good as his chameleon disguise skills, she didn't think she could cope with the stress of being kept waiting. Safiyyah carefully pulled out a newspaper from her bag. It was from the previous day, and had an envelope taped inside it. It contained a coded note from Baba, and Timothée was to deliver it before noon.

She was down to 'Twenty-five elephants, twenty-four elephants ...' when she saw a boy in a cap striding through the tree-lined path towards her. This was it. When he was about twenty paces away, she stopped beside a wooden bench. Pretending to notice something on her shoe, she put the newspaper onto the bench and bent down to adjust the strap a little. A second later, she stood up, hoisted her bag onto her back and, trying to act casual, walked straight past Timothée. She continued until she reached the gates of the park, praying that he'd picked up the newspaper as per the plan.

For the first time that morning, she breathed in and out deeply, releasing some of the tension lodged in her shoulders. She felt in awe of Timothée's confidence and composure in the face of such danger, despite him being over two years younger than her. What he lacked in age, he made up for in bravery.

As school drew to a close, Safiyyah began to tense up once again. She had guarded her bag so closely all day long that Amelie had asked what was in it. Safiyyah brushed the question off with a laugh, cringing inside as she dropped the bag onto the floor as if there was nothing of value in it. In truth, it contained what might be the difference between life and death for a family of three. Tucked and taped carefully into page fifty-two of one of her books were fake Muslim identity papers for a Jewish family who lived in the 5th arrondissement. By noon, Timothée should have delivered the message in the newspaper to them, alerting them of where Safiyyah would leave the book.

Behind the metal bin in the alley to the left of their apartment entrance.

She repeated this sentence to herself again and again as she walked towards the address. She hadn't been here before, they'd taken Timothée's word about the details of the street. He'd scoped it out two days ago, and Safiyyah felt endlessly panicked at the prospect of the bin not being there now, or soldiers being nearby. She breathed a sigh of relief when she saw it glinting in the sun, she'd never been so happy to see a bin before in her life!

Scanning the street for soldiers or anyone who might be looking at her, she crumpled up a scrap of paper she'd torn from her exercise book to look like litter, holding it out in plain sight in case anyone was watching. Heading down the alley and turning her body away from the street, she yanked the book from her bag and dropped it behind the bin. She chucked the crumpled ball of paper into the bin, and stood back to check that the book wasn't visible from the street. Her palms were sweating, and suddenly she could not shake the feeling that she was being watched. Flashbacks to the day of Baba's arrest threatened to overwhelm her, and as she tried to look around her slowly, as if casually taking in the street, she found her watcher.

Half-hidden behind a lacy net curtain, the eyes of a man a bit younger than Baba bored into her intensely. He stood at the window of the ground floor apartment she was walking past, the one the bin belonged to. He had dark curly hair that spilled down onto his forehead. His expression was so charged with emotion and his gaze so intent, that Safiyyah had to force herself not to stop dead in her tracks and stare back. She knew she wasn't supposed to make eye contact, but had felt something stir inside her chest when she noticed him.

Just before Safiyyah looked away, she saw him nod at her, his eyes still wistful and blazing with feeling, with gratitude. He bent to pick up a child from the floor, and

Safiyyah walked on by. The entire way home, the thing that had stirred inside Safiyyah's chest pulsed and fluttered. It hummed and swelled, and she knew then with utmost certainty that she must continue Baba's work at all costs.

23

Safiyyah and Isabelle had exchanged a handful of letters through the summer. Each time Safiyyah tore open an envelope with her best friend's neat handwriting on, her heart soared. She treasured the pressed pink, purple and yellow petals that would fall from the letter each time, and savoured every word. She loved hearing about Isabelle's pranks on the grumpy relative she was staying with, and of the shells and glass pebbles she found on the beach. Isabelle said she couldn't wait to meet Bonbon, Émeraude and the kittens, and Safiyyah daydreamed about the moment she finally would.

Yet when Isabelle's handwriting became loose and hurried-looking, she knew something was off. The letter had come one morning before Safiyyah left the apartment for school, and she wanted to scream by the time she reached the end of it. Isabelle's family were moving again, and she had no idea where they were headed to. Safiyyah had no way of contacting Isabelle now, and she worried that she might never find her again. As she cried over her bowl of porridge, Yemma reassured her that she would surely hear from Isabelle again. At the very least, the war had to end sometime and her family would be back in Paris then.

It was just a few days later that Safiyyah realised *why* Isabelle's family had relocated. The newsreader on Baba's secret wireless spoke with a gravelly voice and sombre tone. German bombs had rained down across London and beyond, killing over four hundred people in one dark, dark night. Safiyyah felt desperate as she prayed that Isabelle had made it to safety. Not being able to write to her felt like torture; Safiyyah felt like she had been abandoned to her fears. After ten minutes, she could bear to hear the updates no more. She turned Baba's radio off and ran to her room, where she penned a letter to Isabelle.

Safiyyah wrote through sobs that racked her body, tears smudging the ink as soon as it dried. She wrote knowing most of it was barely legible, and the rest might not even make much sense. She wrote and wrote until her fingers seized up and she felt that her heart had been laid bare on the paper in front of her. She wanted dearly to be able to write out the secrets that weighed heavily on her mind, but of course, left those out entirely. Once she signed it off, Safiyyah sat, staring at the three sheets of scrawled, smudged writing, wishing she could fold them up into paper aeroplanes and send them zooming across the waters of the Channel into Isabelle's hands.

A story she had read sprung into her mind all of a sudden, and Safiyyah leaped up and rummaged in the kitchen to find an old glass milk bottle. She tightly wound up the letter and pushed it through the neck of the bottle, before screwing the metal lid on. Without even tying her shoelaces properly, Safiyyah ran all the way to the banks of the River Seine, not scanning the streets for soldiers before she stepped onto them, nor caring who stared at her. If a soldier had approached and stopped her she'd felt like she could have knocked him over the head with the bottle and carried on running.

She hurled her message in a bottle into the river's choppy waters. It bobbed on the surface of the small waves, which carried it downstream. No telegram nor postman, pigeon nor loudspeaker could carry her message of love and concern to Isabelle, and so she turned to the seas. Setti said it is water that connects us all to each other, and now Safiyyah closed her eyes and allowed the lapping and gushing sounds of the river to calm her a little.

Britain was attacked every single night for another fifty-six nights. Once the sun set and the moon rose, deadly explosives poured down from Nazi planes onto the British Isles. They wreaked devastation and destruction everywhere they touched, from Glasgow to Plymouth. Safiyyah couldn't listen to the news reports any more, and chose to sit with Setti and say prayers instead. Isabelle was never far from Safiyyah's thoughts, and every day when she awoke from sleep, a familiar dullness descended on her within moments of opening her eyes. She directed all her energy towards what Baba tasked her with, grateful for the distraction and the sense of purpose they brought.

Over the weeks, the errands took her all across the city, and into the presence of all sorts of people. She delivered packages of pamphlets wrapped to look like sandwiches to hat makers. She handed coded notes stuffed inside stale loaves of bread to an old lady near the Eiffel Tower. She returned to the tailor, who gave her a bag full of yarns of wool to give to Baba.

She exchanged envelopes stashed in newspapers with Timothée in countless different parks, and visited the library many times. Each time she entered, she went straight to the children's section and pretended to browse the shelves. Then Monsieur Claude, Madame Odette, or one of the assistants would subtly pass her something for Baba. One day while she pretended to read a comic book in the children's section, wishing she could go to the World section instead, Madame Odette and another lady with olive-coloured skin in a blue dress approached her. Safiyyah didn't recognise the lady with Madame Odette, but she smiled warmly at Safiyyah as if she knew her well. Madame Odette offered Safiyyah a paper bag, which to her great surprise contained a couple of powdery bonbons! She hadn't eaten a sweet or chocolate for weeks, and she took one gratefully, melting into the sweet chewiness for a few moments.

'Madame! Where did you get these?!'

Madame Odette winked cheekily, 'Don't you worry about that, Safiyyah, just savour the taste!' She turned to whisper to the lady in the blue dress, who was still smiling at Safiyyah fondly.

'Madeleine, the pen is in my briefcase. Second pocket.'

The lady hurried off to fetch it, and it struck Safiyyah as strange that her name was Madeleine. She didn't *look* like a Madeleine, she had jet-black hair and dark eyes, and something about her reminded Safiyyah of Khala Najma. She looked like she might be from India or Iran. She returned a minute or so later and handed Safiyyah a shiny tortoiseshell fountain pen. 'For your father.' Her eyes twinkled as she smiled again at Safiyyah.

Safiyyah found out from Baba that stuck to the inside of the pen lid was a coded address. She never saw the lady again, but often remembered her and her smile that seemed to fill the room. Madame Odette told her later that Madeleine was an important undercover agent, and that she must never speak of having seen her.

Another time, Baba passed Safiyyah a packet of cigarettes. When he'd given her the box she had gasped and recoiled. Her father hated everything about smoking, and cigarettes weren't allowed in the mosque!

'Trust me, Safiyyah. Do as I say,' Baba addressed her sternly.

She handled the box as if it might infect her, but did as she was instructed and took it to a café beside the library. She needed to find an American man called Mr Bingham. Baba had described him accurately, and she saw him wearing a navy bowler hat, seated outside the café at a table on the street. To confirm that she had the right man, she asked, 'Sir, would you be able to tell me the time, please?'

His American accent was unmistakable, and so Safiyyah thanked him and made to walk past. She swiped her hand across his table and intentionally dropped the cigarette packet onto the floor from her other hand at the same time, trying to make it look like it had always been his. She apologised profusely, and bent to pick the box up, handing it to the man before making a quick exit. Baba had ingeniously hidden names of Jews who needed help on the inside of the cigarette papers before rolling them back up and sticking them together again.

Safiyyah returned home each day exhausted from the mental and physical energy it took to run around a city, defying its brutal occupiers. Constantly looking over your shoulder and keeping secrets was draining. Ultimately she just wished the war could be over, but what nourished and kept her going even when there was barely enough to eat, was the knowledge that she was doing something meaningful. Her city had been plunged into darkness, with evil lurking at every corner, but there was a pulsing, glowing secret network of light that ran through it like veins. Resisting. And Safiyyah was now a part of it.

24

Despite meeting new people on a weekly basis as she ran errands for her father, Safiyyah felt more alone than she ever had before. Even though she had only received and sent letters to Isabelle here and there, just knowing that she had no way of contacting her now gave Safiyyah a deep sense of loneliness. To top things off, Hana and two of the other girls that she enjoyed chatting to and being around were no longer at school.

Safiyyah knew that the other two girls had left the city with their families, they'd likely escaped the city and gone south to the Free Zone, but she wasn't sure about Hana. Amelie hadn't heard any news of her either, and Safiyyah felt a pang of alarm. She didn't even know where Hana lived to be able to go and check that things were all right. Safiyyah prayed that Hana and her family had simply fled south to the half of France that wasn't in Nazi hands, and had safely reached their destination.

Being Jewish in Paris was becoming harder by the day, now laws were changing to penalise them in every way. Monsieur Abrams and another Jewish teacher had been sacked from their jobs, simply because of who they were. Jews were no longer allowed to teach in schools or universities, nor work as journalists or for the civil service. Their businesses and properties could be seized and taken from them at any moment, and the arrests were increasing around the city each week. Just like in Germany, the Nazis wanted them gone, and for good. Jews were no longer allowed to ride the Métro carriages like everyone else, nor were they allowed to walk along the Champs-Élysées. The thing that disturbed Safiyyah the most though, was the yellow stars they were instructed to wear on their clothes at all times to identify them as Jews.

Rations had formally begun in the city, making bellies growl louder and fatigue feel sharper. Winter approached, shrinking daylight hours and causing the dark, chilly nights to stretch out longer and longer. The drop in temperature and increased daily errands that Safiyyah was running left her more desperate for food. Everyone had been given a ration book, and each month the little ration tickets were a different colour to prevent forgery. When someone from her family could get to the front of the hours-long queues before the shops ran out of food altogether, the stale bread, cubes of butter and the odd vegetables they'd come away with didn't go very far.

Yemma, Baba and Setti pushed more of their portions onto Safiyyah and Fatima's plates each day, but even so, she was always finished after two or three mouthfuls. Through the autumn, the two hens who lived in the back courtyard blessed them with nutritious eggs, and the families in the apartments would take turns to receive them. Once the cold set in and it became difficult to feed the chickens, they stopped laying eggs altogether, and eventually died.

On many occasions, Safiyyah worried she might faint from exhaustion and hunger as she walked across the city after school. It was almost impossible to come by halal meat, and Safiyyah barely remembered the taste of tender chicken or lamb. She began to dread the smell of tasteless swede stew or tapioca soup, and she and Yemma took to playing make believe with their food. As Yemma stirred the steaming pot on the stove, they came up with elaborate imaginary descriptions of what she was making. Bland artichoke and stale bread scraps could become succulent roasted lamb and fragrant saffron rice; watery soup might be sweet pavlova laden with juicy berries. They would share the descriptions with Baba and Setti, who would chuckle and add their own cravings to the dreamed-up table spread. Amelie said that her neighbours had taken to breeding rabbits they got from the countryside in their bathtub at home, and were selling the meat on illegally.

One rainy afternoon, Timothée ran into the mosque excitedly and called Safiyyah over in urgent tones. His cap was pulled low over his brow and his collar hid most of what remained of his face – it was risky for him to openly come to the mosque nowadays. His excitement was contagious, especially after long months of everything feeling dull and bleak. Safiyyah's eyes were wide as he pulled out a strip of pink bubblegum and a tiny square of white chocolate from his pocket.

She didn't know exactly where he'd got them from, but was aware it must have been through the black market somehow. He insisted that she share half of each sweet treasure with him and as she bit into the little piece of bubblegum, the sweetness exploded in her mouth. It was exquisite beyond words, and she and Timothée sat in silence in the prayer hall for a while, each reflecting on how the absence of something makes your appreciation of it a thousand times deeper.

It wasn't just things outside the mosque that were changing by the day. Safiyyah spent so much time running errands, that when she finally returned home she was so exhausted she would trudge upstairs with her eyes half-closed before collapsing onto the sofa. This meant that she hadn't noticed things changing under her nose within the mosque too. She hadn't seen Khala Najma taking trays of food to the unfamiliar people who'd been sleeping in the corners of the women's prayer hall, nor the ones huddled together in the hammam. She hadn't thought anything of the young Kabyle men milling in and out of the basement corridors in a hurry. Safiyyah had been sleeping so soundly that she hadn't heard her father leave their apartment every single night, returning with damp shoes and freezing bones.

The first time she realised something was going on was one morning after she woke for the pre-dawn prayer. The five daily prayers had become much dearer to Safiyyah in recent months than ever before; the moments of focus gave her a tranquillity she savoured. As she raised her hands to her head to enter into sacred conversation with God, it was as if she was pushing away all of the pain, chaos and horrors of life, and a precious stillness took hold of her.

This morning, before she jumped back into the warmth of her bed for a little more sleep, she was drawn to the window by noises beyond it. In the darkness, she could just about make out Ammo Kader's white woollen robe. He was walking through the courtyard towards the offices and basement, carrying a small lamp. It cast a yellow glow on two of the five people who were following close behind him. Two women in knee-length skirts and black woollen jackets and hats walked hurriedly, their heads bowed. Behind them was a taller, slender figure, a man, she reckoned, and based on the stout figure and slightly hunched back, there followed an old woman carrying a young child. Safiyyah felt disorientated, they didn't look like people from the mosque or congregation, and they looked to be in a great hurry.

Her intrigue had won over her desire for more sleep. She decided she would wait until they left the offices. There was only one entrance and perhaps the sun would be on its way up when they came out and she'd get a better look at them and be able to discover what was going on. It was the weekend thankfully, so there was no school to go to, but once an hour had passed with no sign of the group coming back out, Safiyyah decided to explore.

She slipped on her coat and shoes and went down towards the office buildings that she'd seen Ammo enter earlier. Safiyyah held her breath as she approached. Sneaking around had become second nature to her these days, but it felt very different when it was in her own home. She jumped as the door to the building swung open and Ammo appeared. Initially he looked startled by the daylight, which was odd, as it wasn't particularly bright. He was also surprised to see Safiyyah, but after a second smiled and greeted her.

'Assalamu alaikum, Safiyyah. Are you all right?'

'Wa alaikum assalam, I'm fine thanks!' She tried not to sound guilty as she craned her neck to look over his shoulder into the room he had come from. He noticed her looking and held the door open for her to enter, which confused her, but she went in anyway. He must have assumed that she had something to do in there for Baba. Of course Ammo knew about her involvement with their Resistance efforts. As she passed him, she noticed he had dark stains on his usually spotless robe. It was noticeably marked now on the shoulder and at its hem.

Safiyyah entered the rooms tentatively, expecting to see the people she had seen earlier, but they were all entirely empty. Next she went down the steps to the basement. No one. Had she entirely imagined the group following Ammo this morning? Surely not! She looked around for another door, but there wasn't anything, other than a broom cupboard at the back of the basement. No one could have left through that, as it would only have led into the earth anyway. Baffled, Safiyyah locked the office doors behind her and went in search of Yemma or Baba for an explanation.

She found Yemma back in the apartment, she was lying on her stomach in the living room playing a game with Fatima and her dolls.

'Yemma, I saw Ammo Kader take a group of people who didn't look like Muslims down to the offices this morning. He came out just now but the people have vanished and left no trace! I'm so confused. Who were they and where did they go?'

Yemma looked at Safiyyah strangely, almost as if trying to figure out if Safiyyah actually had no idea what was going on. Safiyyah realised at that moment that she did in fact have an idea of who they might be. Ammo had been busy helping Jews in any way he could for months and months . . .

'They're Jews, aren't they?'

Yemma nodded.

'But why are they in the mosque? Isn't that too risky? And where did Ammo take them? Where are they now?'

Yemma sat up properly and turned her full attention to her elder daughter.

'Of course it's risky, but it's a risk worth taking, Safiyyah.'

'But . . . but we're delivering their papers to them, why did he bring them here?'

'Times are changing, darling. The Nazis are already suspicious of us, and giving false identities out. That on its own just isn't enough any more. Jews need to leave here as quickly as they can while they're free. It's just not safe at all for them, and things are only going to get worse.'

Safiyyah's thoughts turned to Monsieur Cassin. She'd last visited him a few weeks ago and he seemed terribly anxious and frail. She hoped he'd eaten the soup she had given him.

'We have hunger and exhaustion to deal with, while in every Jewish household, they have that, plus terror for their lives and freedom. Ammo was receiving so many requests for help from desperate Jewish families. As if violently taking their businesses and livelihoods wasn't enough, the Germans are taking their right to human dignity away from them left, right and centre. The Nazis talk about them as if they are beasts. We are helping them get out of the city, Safiyyah.'

Safiyyah was astounded. How had she missed this? Perhaps the door in the basement didn't lead to a broom cupboard after all . . .

'How, Yemma? How do they get out of the city? Where did they go from the basement? And who is "we"?'

'I don't know how much I should tell you, Safiyyah, perhaps I should leave it to your father to explain. I suppose it's not my secret to give away . . .'

'Please, Yemma, I'm already sworn to secrecy on so much stuff, I swear I won't let this out, ever!'

Her mother looked weary, but continued anyway: 'The souterrain. The underground passages that run beneath our entire city. Ammo Kader and Baba are working with some of the wine merchants who ship barrels of wine across the Seine.'

Safiyyah looked at her mother quizzically, even more confused than she had been before. 'What *about* the souterrain and the wine barrels, Yemma?!'

'Be patient and I'll get there! We have secret access from the mosque into the tunnels, and your father and Ammo Kader know the route to the port from which the wine barges leave on the Seine. It's not far from here. Jews come to the mosque and hide in the hammam or women's section. Those are the safest places because if any Nazis did try to search the mosque, we could tell the Germans that men simply aren't allowed access in order to protect the privacy and comfort of our women.

'Once Baba or Ammo get word from the wine merchants that there is space in wine barrels on a barge, they take the Jews there underground, usually under the cover of night. They hide in the barrels and are transported to safety. We try to keep people moving as quickly as we can,' Yemma went on, 'to minimise the risk of discovery. The longest anyone has stayed at the mosque so far is four nights. That was because there was an incident at the port so Baba didn't receive word from the sailor for a while.'

Safiyyah's mind was blown. It was genius. She reckoned she might actually have brought a message to Baba from a wine merchant last week without knowing it! She'd met the man close to the riverbank and he'd had sailor's boots on. This explained the stains on Ammo's clothes too. She'd heard of the souterrain before, as well as the catacombs: underground burial chambers. She knew they were linked together by tunnels, but had never given them much thought. All of a sudden she felt fascinated by this mysterious maze, and wanted to know more. She wondered if there might be maps of it anywhere that she could get her hands on . . .

25

It turned out Safiyyah would have found out about the Jews being helped to safety soon anyway. The very next day, a young Kabyle delivery man on a bicycle puffed and panted as he pedalled his way up the street towards the mosque. He had a big green messenger's box attached to the front of his bicycle, and he strenuously dragged his vehicle up the step and through the mosque entrance. He wheeled it into a side room, and Ammo Kader arrived shortly afterwards, closing the door behind him.

Safiyyah hovered, trying to catch snippets of what sounded like a frantic, hushed conversation in the room. Eventually, Ammo emerged with two young boys in tow. They looked a little older than Fatima and were definitely brothers, with the same thick black hair and grey eyes. The older of the two looked lost, and the younger like he might burst into tears at any point. Both were wearing blue pyjamas with yellow moons printed on them. Ammo held their hands and took them gently through the courtyard, as the other man left the room with his bicycle. He wheeled it now effortlessly, as if it weighed nothing at all, and mounted it on the steps before cycling away again.

Safiyyah found out later that the man was part of the Resistance and had been on his way to deliver papers and financial help to a Jewish couple. They'd been trying to travel to safety in America with the help of the American man with the bowler hat who Safiyyah had met weeks before. The Germans had got word though, and beat the Kabyle messenger to the apartment. The couple had been arrested before he'd got a chance to give them anything. The two boys were their children. Luckily they'd been at the neighbours' house when the raid happened, and the neighbours had kept them hidden.

Ammo took them upstairs to his apartment and settled them in with his own young children as best he could. Safiyyah's heart went out to the boys, she couldn't bear to imagine what they were experiencing. She asked Yemma if she could visit to take them some toys to help settle them in. Yemma told her to wait, so as not to overwhelm their little souls as they were already going through so much loss and change.

That night, the youngest boy's screams were audible across the neighbouring apartments in the mosque. No matter how tightly Ammo's wife hugged him, no matter how softly she rocked him from side to side in her arms, the broken-hearted child's cries persisted. Safiyyah barely slept, and the next morning, she fetched Crème and Croissant from downstairs. The kittens were almost fully grown now, and had lovely affectionate temperaments.

She left Chien behind because he still behaved very much like a puppy and she figured calmer cuddles might be better than chaos.

She knocked gingerly on Ammo Kader's apartment door and his wife, Khala Rabiah, welcomed her in with a tired smile. Dark shadows ringed her eyes, her long, usually luscious hair now hung limply around her face. Their own three children were playing with toy cars and leafing through comic books in the living room, and they all leaped up excitedly on seeing the kittens in Safiyyah's arms. She let them each have a quick stroke before following their mother to where the two boys were in the children's bedroom. Khala nodded at the elder of the two and whispered to Safiyyah, 'Levi,' and then at the little one, 'Noah.'

Levi was tucked under the blanket on one of the beds, staring at a piece of stale toast on a patterned plate in front of him. Safiyyah perched tentatively at the edge of the bed, placing Croissant down beside the boy. His collarbone stuck out jaggedly, his wrists were like sticks. He had avoided making eye contact when Safiyyah entered, but she saw his gaze lift as soon as Croissant's paws touched the blanket. He sat up a little straighter in the bed and stretched out a little hand, which the kitten pawed at playfully. Safiyyah thought she saw a hint of a tiny smile at one corner of the boy's mouth.

Next she turned to Noah. He was lying curled in a

ball in the corner of the room underneath the window. His thumb was firmly lodged in his mouth, and his eyes blinked slowly as if he was fighting a battle with impending sleep.

'Noah,' Safiyyah whispered softly, letting Crème jump down onto the floor near him. Safiyyah petted Crème, who began to purr loudly. She remembered the day she had met Bonbon and how instantly comforting her presence was; she was desperate for Crème to have the same effect now.

Khala looked at Noah tenderly and sadly, shaking her head. 'He hasn't let anyone near him since last night. He only stopped screaming because he was too exhausted to work his voice. He's dozed off a few times but it seems like he's scared to fall asleep. Poor, poor thing . . .'

She trailed off at the end of her sentence because both she and Safiyyah had turned to look at Crème. He had slowly wandered over to Noah. The kitten gently nudged the boy's clenched fist with her furry head, and Noah seemed to wake up a little from his daze. He stirred and altered his position slightly, so that his eyes were in line with the kitten's face. Safiyyah's heart melted a little when Crème tilted her head to look at Noah, before settling herself into the crook of his neck. Noah placed a shaky hand on the kitten's back, and within a few minutes, had finally succumbed to slumber.

Safiyyah stopped by later that evening again, delighted to see Noah sitting up now, with Crème purring on his lap as he ran a toy car along the carpet. Levi was napping peacefully this time, with Croissant guarding him from the foot of the bed. It was as if the cats knew how badly the boys needed them. Khala Rabiah mouthed *Thank you* to Safiyyah from across the room.

She asked Khala, 'What will happen to them now? Can they stay with you for ever?'

'I don't think so, Safiyyah. We could give them papers to say they are our children, but their lighter eyes and complexion would give it away. I'm not sure what will happen, most likely Ammo will wait until there are others passing through who would be capable and willing to take them onto safety elsewhere.'

Safiyyah watched Levi's chest rise and fall slowly to the rhythm of sleep, feeling her heart pound inside her own.

26

Christmas approached and passed, but this year there were no carol singers in merry throngs in the streets, nor pretty lights strung up across the city. Normally at school the children would chatter excitedly about their activities over the holidays, their Christmas tree decorations and the feasts they ate to celebrate, but this year, most of the remaining children barely had enough energy to talk at all. The city was endless grey, the sky was endless grey, and even the dazzling turquoise tiles in the mosque courtyard seemed to have lost their sparkle.

It was a particularly icy, overcast day, the type on which it felt like the sun never rose at all. Safiyyah was helping Setti to knit scarves for the refugees. They had already sent a bag full of brightly coloured hats and scarves to the community centre that Timothée and his father were staying in.

Setti's orange saplings had been dying off one by one as the temperature dropped, and she had been visibly upset when the final plant dropped its leaves and wilted. Yemma had bought her as many yarns of wool as she could afford, in the hope that knitting to help people in need would give her a new sense of purpose. It seemed to be working, although Safiyyah noticed her grandmother seemed lost in her thoughts more and more these days. Safiyyah knew it wasn't the orange trees themselves that meant so much to Setti, it was everything they represented.

Barely anyone had enough coal to adequately heat their homes now, and they slept in as many layers of clothes as they could. Last night Safiyyah had resorted to four pairs of socks and three jumpers, and it still took ages to fall asleep. Now, she rubbed her hands together quickly to try and generate some heat. She'd been finding it increasingly hard to move the knitting needles against each other with her frozen fingers. Setti told her to put her hands in her underarms and keep them there for a while to warm up. It was just beginning to work when they heard the apartment door burst open.

Baba stood just inside the doorway, delicate snowflakes still intact on his hat and jumper sleeves, like he'd been dusted with powdered sugar. Safiyyah noticed he wasn't wearing his coat – it was snowing outside and yet he was only wearing a jumper? He unwrapped the black scarf he had wound around his neck and face, and frantically called Yemma to come out. Safiyyah felt panic rise: what terrible thing had happened now?

Yemma ran out of the apartment, still in her slippers, and they closed the door behind them. Safiyyah heard Yemma gasp and then whisper a prayer, and the panic intensified within her. She and Setti could hear Yemma and Baba whispering to each other in urgent tones, and just as Safiyyah could bear it no more and was about to open the front door, Baba appeared. He looked terribly anxious as he addressed his daughter and mother quietly.

'We have a guest. We must look after her well.'

He moved further into the apartment, allowing Yemma and a smaller figure to come into view. The child was about Safiyyah's height, and was almost swallowed up by Baba's black duffel coat, which reached down to their ankles. Their hands were hidden by the long sleeves, and the child's face half-concealed by the collar. There was a scruffy woollen hat pulled down almost to their eyebrows, and the little bit of skin that was visible was dirty. Their eyes were lowered to the carpet the entire time, and as Yemma ushered them in, their shuffling footsteps seemed strained and weary. Something in the lowered eyes made Safiyyah think it was a girl, but she couldn't be sure. Setti ushered Safiyyah into her bedroom to give Yemma and the child some space, but Safiyyah peeked her head back round the doorframe.

It felt strange watching her mother tend so gently to the child. They appeared to flinch when Yemma took Baba's coat off. The child was wearing a dress underneath that looked as if it was once a shade of green. So it was a girl. Yemma removed the hat, and a straggly mop of dark brown hair fell down to her shoulders. It looked knotted and filthy, as if it had not been washed in weeks. Yemma put her hand on the girl's shoulder, who stood shivering with her back to Safiyyah.

'I'll get you fixed with a warm bath and a hot drink, sweetheart. Come and sit with Setti while I get everything sorted.'

Safiyyah leaped back out of sight into her bedroom before her mother passed, her arm around the girl. Craning her neck, Safiyyah could just about see a sliver of the living room. Setti stood to welcome her, placing her hand on her chest and introducing herself, before offering her a spot on the sofa with a blanket. Before the girl turned to sit down, Yemma called Safiyyah out to fetch towels, clothes and a bucket. Safiyyah had still only caught a glimpse of the girl. Her matted hair obscured most of her face, but Safiyyah had felt a flash of familiarity that she couldn't make sense of.

She brought out the softest towels she could find, as well as her favourite warm pyjamas, ones that Setti had brought her from Algeria. Grabbing a cardigan and two pairs of socks from her drawer, Safiyyah felt sick thinking about what the poor girl had been through to have arrived in such a state. Where were her family? Where had she been staying? Safiyyah ran back into her room for a comb, she would definitely be needing that too.

Yemma had hot water ready in the bathroom, and

Safiyyah laid out the clothes and towels neatly on the shelf beside the bath. She felt desperate to make the girl comfortable.

'Go and fetch her, Safiyyah, please,' Yemma asked as she mixed hot water with cold water from a jug and checked the temperature with her hand. Safiyyah felt nervous at the prospect of speaking to the strange girl, and walked into the living room shyly. When she laid eyes on the girl's face, Safiyyah gasped, her mouth falling open. The words she'd prepared simply would not come. Setti looked at Safiyyah in alarm, glaring at her as if to say, *Compose yourself!* Safiyyah could not believe what she was seeing, and she felt her heart skip two beats as she tried to comprehend it.

It was Hana. Her eyes were still lowered to the ground, and her face looked mottled and grey, but now, sitting right in front of Safiyyah, there was no mistaking her. She desperately wanted to hug her tightly and never let go. Instead, she stood, frozen to the spot, opening her mouth and closing it again.

Setti broke the silence, frowning at Safiyyah in confusion. 'This is my granddaughter, Safiyyah. She is eleven years old and she loves cats and maps.'

Safiyyah came to her senses and sat shyly beside Hana on the sofa. Up close she could see a purplish bruise on Hana's left cheek, and her entire face seemed drawn and gaunt. Her dark eyes were distant and glazed, the passionate sparkle that Safiyyah had always so admired was nowhere to be found.

'Hana, it's me, Safiyyah! You're going to be all right.'

At first, Safiyyah thought perhaps she hadn't heard her properly because she didn't react. After an agonising moment, Hana glanced up quickly at Safiyyah. For a split second their gazes locked and then Hana turned her eyes away from Safiyyah, and her head a little too. Safiyyah felt hurt and confused; it was impossible for Hana to have forgotten her, they'd been in the same class for years now at school. Safiyyah considered them to be friends . . .

Yemma entered the room, raising her palms as she spoke: 'Safiyyah, I sent you in here ages ago! The water is getting cold and I won't be able to heat any more after this.'

She walked towards Hana, and beckoned her up from the sofa and towards the bathroom. Once the two of them had left the room, Safiyyah explained to Setti that the girls were classmates. More than that, they had been friends.

'Why did she turn away from me like that, Setti? As if she doesn't know me. Have I done something wrong?'

'No, darling, you've done nothing bad. I don't think her reaction was about you, I think it was about *her.* We have no idea yet what the poor child has been through, what pain she is living with. It seems like she might have lost everything. Perhaps she feels embarrassed in front of you at the condition she is in. Dignity is important for everybody.'

'But I'd never judge her, I only want to help her . . .'

'I know that, but it might take time for Hana to realise it too. Time and care are two of the most important things we can give her now.'

Baba moved Fatima's cot and things into Setti's room, and made up a small bed for Hana in Fatima's room. Hana emerged from the bathroom looking clean, but absolutely exhausted. Her eyelids seemed to be drooping as she trudged in Safiyyah's pyjamas into Fatima's room. Safiyyah sat on the floor outside as Yemma gently rubbed argan oil into the ends of Hana's hair. She could see that Yemma had had to cut bits of hair out, presumably where knots simply would not budge.

Before the war, Yemma was always meticulous about caring for her and her daughters' hair. She insisted on applying strange concoctions of egg, yoghurt and lemon juice to their heads before they bathed, to soften and condition. Of course this had ended a long time ago. Safiyyah felt nostalgic watching her massage Hana's scalp.

She wondered what might have happened to Hana's parents, though in her gut she knew. Hana's eyes were almost closing as Yemma wiped the oil off her hands and stood to fetch food. Did Hana's mother used to care for her daughter's hair like this too? Was Hana thinking about her right now? Safiyyah wiped the tears from her eyes as she stood to help Yemma carry a cup of tea and a bowl of soup to Hana where she sat in bed. By the time they had placed the food beside her, she was already fast asleep.

Safiyyah sat with the adults that evening. Baba told them that he had been returning from collecting rations when he was tipped off that someone needed help. He had found Hana alone in the attic of a dilapidated building. She responded when he told her he could take her to safety at the mosque, and that there were other Jews there too. She didn't want to speak at all at first, but he coaxed her into sharing some details with him so that he could help her properly.

Her parents had been arrested on their way back from a secret Resistance meeting around two weeks earlier. A family friend had stopped by to tell Hana the bad news, but couldn't help her as they'd made arrangements to escape the city in a truck and there was no room for an extra person with them. She had stayed in their apartment for a week by herself after the arrest, hoping for her parents to somehow come home, but they never did.

Terrified that there might be a raid, she spent most of the time hiding and sleeping in a cupboard, living off the little food in the kitchen. One day she'd heard German soldiers in a neighbouring apartment, and had moved to a disused building just a street down from her home. The attic seemed like the warmest part and so she'd stayed there since. From the window in the attic, she could look out and see her apartment block and so she spent all day keeping an eye out in case her parents returned.

At night she would sneak out to find scraps to eat, most of the time returning with an empty belly. A Roma refugee who Baba was in touch with had seen Hana leave and enter the crumbling building and figured she needed help. Baba had asked Hana more questions that might help him locate her parents, but she could no longer speak. She hadn't said another word since, it had all just been too much for her.

Setti, Yemma, Baba and Safiyyah sat in silent disbelief and sorrow for a while.

'It's a miracle she made it here alive,' Yemma muttered.

'Between the Nazis, starvation and hypothermia . . . Truly a miracle,' Baba agreed, shaking his head.

'What will happen now?' Safiyyah whispered.

'I've put out the word to see if we can track down her parents. The priority is nursing her back to health, strength and spirit. Then we should think about getting her out of Paris as quickly as we can. I will make her papers to say that she is our child, though I fear some of the Nazi officials who know of me, know that I only have two children.'

Safiyyah barely slept that night. All she could think about was what Hana was going through, and what she might be able to do to help.

27

The next day, after helping Yemma prepare Hana some breakfast, Safiyyah brought Bonbon into Hana's room. Hana barely looked up from where she was fiddling with the edge of the blanket she was sitting under. Safiyyah placed Bonbon down on the bed and stroked her head, hoping Hana might follow suit. Instead, Hana sniffed and closed her eyes, resting her head on the wall behind her. Safiyyah was surprised, she knew Hana liked animals, and had hoped Bonbon's charm would work like the kittens had with Levi and Noah. She waited for another ten minutes in the room with Bonbon before accepting that this wasn't going to be as easy as she'd hoped.

A few hours later, Safiyyah tore out pages and pages of lined paper from the back of one of her school exercise books, and knocked gently on Hana's door. There was no answer, so she peered round the edge of the door: Hana was still sitting in bed, tugging at the tassels on the bedspread anxiously. Safiyyah laid out the sheets of paper on the floor beside the bed, seating herself on the ground cross-legged in front of them. Nervously, she picked up a sheet and began to slowly fold and press it.

Taking care to hold it so Hana could see what she was doing, and making each action clear, she created a little origami butterfly, just as Isabelle had taught her.

Hana was watching her out of the corner of her eye, but showed no change of expression when Safiyyah held the paper creature up to show her. Nor did she move an inch when Safiyyah put a fresh piece of paper near her hands. Safiyyah folded the rest of the butterflies, leaving a couple of sheets flat in case Hana wanted to try later on.

When Safiyyah returned the next morning though, they lay untouched, just as she'd left them. Hana still avoided eye contact, wearing the same forlorn, dejected look on her face as the first day she had arrived. Safiyyah longed to hear just one word from her, to see just one movement or expression that signalled that the old Hana was in there somewhere.

Next, she carried in piles of her favourite books and comics. She stacked them into two piles within Hana's reach, and positioned *The Wonders of the World* and *Desert Treasure Quest* at the top. She figured a fascinating fact book and an exciting adventure story might be appealing, so it'd be good to have them in sight.

'I can read to you if you'd like – just call me.'

Safiyyah cringed as she said this, she was beginning to feel like she might just be annoying Hana.

After taking in some soup for Hana's lunch and seeing the books lying there undisturbed, she decided to try one final thing. She snipped off a handful of lengths of colourful wool from Setti's balls of yarn, and grabbed a bowl of little beads. She put half of them next to Hana, and began weaving her half into a bracelet. She knotted and twisted the threads, creating a stripy zig-zag design down its length, interspersed with coloured beads. Hana watched her weave but made no move to begin her own. By the time Safiyyah had finished, Hana's eyes were glazed over as she stared into space. Safiyyah felt a wave of hopelessness wash over her. She quietly placed the bracelet down and stepped out of the room with a lump in her throat.

She let tears spill out until the tightness in her chest began to settle. Setti appeared in the doorway of Safiyyah's room, as she so often did when Safiyyah needed her warmth the most. Setti gave her a comforting squeeze.

'Setti, I don't know what to do for Hana. I hate to see her like this. You don't understand, you haven't seen what she's usually like. She's an amazing debater and writer, she's the smartest person in our class! She's bold and brave and funny, she's just brilliant! It's like only her shadow is sitting there . . . I tried giving her Bonbon to cuddle, books to read, things to do with her hands that might ease her nerves a little, but she won't even look at me!'

Safiyyah threw her palms up in despair, and Setti clasped them in her own soft hands.

'My dear, I believe all of those things about Hana, I can sense great beauty in her. I'm proud of you for trying so hard to help her feel better. None of your efforts have gone to waste, trust me. But patience is key. When you plant a seed in soil, just because it hasn't sprouted in a few days, or a week, you don't dig it up in frustration. You wait and water it, water it and wait, in full certainty that it *is* growing and preparing to bloom, even though you can't physically see *anything* happening. You anticipate that beautiful green sprout surfacing because you know that miracles are occurring under the soil.

'If you were to look at bare soil after a few days of sunshine and watering, give up hope and walk away, it would be tragic! Each time you're kind and patient and giving with Hana, you are watering and shining light on a seed. Have faith that miracles are happening, slowly but surely, even though you might not be able to see them. She has lost her parents, everything she has ever known and loved. She is traumatised, and the road to healing is a long and often messy one. But the journey has begun, and that is what matters.'

Safiyyah nodded slowly, allowing her grandmother's wisdom to sink in. She breathed in and out deeply, feeling calm all of a sudden, along with a renewed sense of hope.

28

Within a week, traces of colour had returned to Hana's cheeks, and she would sometimes walk to the living room and eat dinner with everyone else. She still hadn't breathed a word. Whenever Safiyyah thought about the horrible things that had happened to her friend, her own chest would tighten up. When she thought of what it might be like to have your entire world disappear in an afternoon, she understood why Hana couldn't speak any more. When Safiyyah imagined the loneliness, fear and desperation Hana must have felt in the two weeks that followed her parents' arrest, she decided that she would be there for her for ever. Perhaps Hana had so much pain inside her that she feared if she were to open her mouth to speak, she would scream so loudly that her bones might shatter.

Safiyyah grew comfortable with her silence, and she didn't allow the lack of response to stop her from smiling at Hana warmly, or placing a hand on hers gently from time to time. When Safiyyah did feel odd or rejected, she imagined the seed under the soil, changing imperceptibly, just like a heart in the darkness of its chest.

Fatima still played in her old room, perhaps out of habit, perhaps because she sensed that Hana liked the wordless company. Yemma brushed Hana's hair every evening, humming as she smoothed and plaited it afterwards. Baba had forged identity papers for Hana, and this made everyone feel a little more at ease with her staying in the apartment.

Word came that empty barrels on a barge had been organised for a middle-aged Jewish couple who had slept last night in the hammam. Plans had been made for them to be smuggled out of the city at dawn the next morning, and Baba announced that Levi and Noah would be going with them.

Safiyyah's heart lurched when she heard that the two boys were going away. She had grown fond of them.

She set her alarm earlier than the normal time for Fajr prayer, and dropped into Ammo Kader's apartment to say goodbye. Khala Rabiah had already woken the children up and dressed them in hats and coats. Levi was teasing Croissant with a piece of string, and Noah was on his knees, playing quietly with toy trucks with Ammo's youngest son. Khala had prepared tiny cloth sacks for each of them to take, with a couple of toys and some bread inside. Safiyyah gave them both a hug, wishing she could give them the kittens to take wherever it was they were going.

After about ten minutes, Baba knocked on the door

and took the boys downstairs, Noah crying in his arms. He could sense that something was changing again and he didn't like it. Khala Rabiah was tearful too, and as soon as they closed the door she sank down onto her prayer mat and raised her hands in supplication.

Crème jumped up onto Safiyyah's lap, meowing loudly again and again. It was only a few moments later that she realised that Croissant was nowhere in the apartment. She checked under tables and beds and in every cupboard, but he was gone. Perhaps Crème had been trying to alert her to his absence.

'Oh dear, he might have followed the boys downstairs!' Khala Rabiah said in dismay.

'Don't worry, I'll find him!' Safiyyah was out of Ammo's apartment in a flash, running all the way downstairs towards the basement. She called out for the kitten in the courtyards and hallways, but felt sure that he'd have loyally followed the boys wherever they went. She found him clawing at the closed door at the back of the basement mournfully. Thank goodness he hadn't got through into the tunnels with Baba and the boys, he might never have found his way out! Safiyyah leaned against the door handle as she bent down to pick the cat up, and was surprised to feel the door move a little. Surely Baba would have locked it from the inside when he left? As she pushed, it swung open a little more ... Apparently not. She glimpsed the wooden steps leading down into darkness. He must have forgotten in his hurry, he'd seemed anxious about getting them to the river on time.

Butterflies fluttered in Safiyyah's stomach as she realised what she was about to do. Grabbing Croissant, she calmed him with a cuddle and placed him down in one of the office rooms nearby, before rummaging madly in the drawers for a torch. She found a tiny one, and ran back down to the basement.

Curiosity had got the better of her; it seemed too good an opportunity to miss to finally get to see the souterrain for herself. She had been fascinated by the concept of the underground maze ever since she'd heard about it, and figured she'd never have access to it again. She'd tried asking Baba for more information about it a few times, but he barely breathed a word on the topic. She hadn't been able to explore a map for months and months now, what better than a real-life exploration? It was now or never. She'd have a quick look around, then she'd come back home. It would be fine.

She flicked the torch on as she shut the basement door behind her, its tiny beam of light seeming a little pathetic now that her surroundings were pitch black. The first thing she noticed was the cold. It hadn't seemed possible for anywhere to be colder than the night-time chill above ground, but underground was positively freezing. Her breath formed little vapour clouds in front of her. The adrenaline coursing through her body took the edge off the temperature, and she looked around in awe. The torch cast a yellowy glow onto the sandstone that the tunnel had been carved from. The space was rough-looking, reaching up higher than she'd expected.

Baba, the couple and the boys were not in sight or earshot, which made sense seeing as they had probably set off a good five minutes before Safiyyah had. The tunnel stretched right and left, and Safiyyah realised she had no clue which way the river was. She decided to walk a little in each direction to see if things became any clearer, but it all looked exactly the same both ways. She knew she couldn't risk getting lost down here, it was entirely possible to never emerge again, considering the expansiveness of the souterrain.

Feeling defeated and foolish, she was about to climb back up the steps when she noticed something on the ground on the right. It was a tiny brown glove. It must have been Levi or Noah's! She set off confidently down the right-hand tunnel, grateful for the clue and also hoping that the boy's hand wasn't too cold right now.

She walked quickly, planning to explore a little and get safely back to the mosque before Baba returned and told her off. The tunnel began to veer to the right, and its ceiling became lower and lower, until she could jump up and touch the damp stone. She imagined Baba having to stoop until his knees hurt. The ground was jagged in places, and she nearly tripped on ledges that jutted out.

After about ten minutes of walking quickly, Safiyyah began to tire, the biting cold was chilling her to the bones and making her feel short of breath. Deciding she'd seen enough, she turned around and began to walk back in the direction she'd come.

After a few paces, she stopped in confusion. Ahead of her was a fork, two tunnels veered off in slightly different directions, their pitch-black openings like an angry pair of eyes. She had no idea that there was a tunnel running almost parallel to the one she'd been walking through, nor that it had converged with hers without her noticing. She stared at the black eyes glaring at her, and began feeling considerably less courageous than she had just moments ago. She had no clue which one she had come from. If she chose the wrong one now, she might end up hopelessly lost. Safiyyah tried to look for her footprints on the ground, but it was no use.

If she chose the wrong route and Baba was to return to the mosque while she was down there, he would lock the door behind him. Even if she did find her way back, she'd be trapped and probably freeze to death. She was already struggling to hold the torch with her numb fingers, and began to feel a little panicked. It seemed best to continue on the path she had been, assuming she would catch up with Baba. Even if he'd turned back already, hopefully he'd take the same route home. She couldn't bear to think of what would happen if not . . .

In the distance it seemed like the tunnel opened up a fair bit, the space between the walls was widening. Safiyyah wondered if she might be approaching the river already. Just before she got near a part that felt like an underground clearing, her torch's light went out. Everything was darker than she knew was possible. She spun around in every direction, straining her eyes, desperate to see something other than black. This had all been a mistake. Why had she even wanted to see this place? She switched the torch on and off again and again, but nothing.

Safiyyah shuffled with tiny steps and reached her arm out until she felt something solid. It would be easier to walk using the wall as a guide at least. She pushed thoughts of being stuck down there for ever away from her mind, forcing herself to take deep breaths. As she began to grope her way along the wall, she recoiled at the feel of something smooth, cold and rounded. That wasn't sandstone . . . As her fingers moved along the surface again, she felt curved hollows, dips and grooves, and suddenly, she knew what it was. Safiyyah cried out, leaping away from the wall of human bones. It was a catacomb. An underground burial chamber. She felt like she was in an awful nightmare.

In her panic she remembered her cousin Tarek

sometimes hitting electronic devices to make them work. She hit the torch hard against her hand, praying for it to turn back on. On the third attempt, it flickered back to life and, as she'd feared, Safiyyah found herself surrounded by stacks of skulls and bones. Hundreds and hundreds of them. Horrible images of skeletons coming to life all around her began to flit through her mind.

She wanted to pinch herself and wake up in her bed, but instead gritted her teeth and walked as quickly as she could through the catacomb, grateful when it narrowed into a sandstone tunnel once again. She prayed with each step she took, practically running when a stretch was straight. After another few minutes, Safiyyah heard something. Footsteps. Then the swinging light from Baba's lantern appeared on the wall. When Baba saw her running towards him, he stopped in shock. He was still disorientated when she wrapped her arms around his waist, sobbing.

'I'm sorry, Baba, the kitten followed Noah and Levi down to the basement and I went to get him but then I saw the door was open and I wanted to see the souterrain and then I didn't realise there was a fork in the path and then I touched skulls in a catacomb and, and . . . I'm sorry!'

Her father struggled to take in the frenzied, barely comprehensible explanation, but comforted her anyway.

'Safiyyah, you've done well to keep yourself out of

trouble over the last few months, but *really* . . . Following me blindly into the souterrain with not even a slight understanding of where the tunnels lead? You could have ended up at the edge of the city and never made it back, God forbid!' He shook his head as they began to walk back. 'What will we do with you, Safiyyah?!'

'Sorry . . .' Safiyyah felt exhausted, like she could collapse into a heap on the floor there and then. Her thoughts turned to the group Baba had just helped board a wine barge. 'Were the boys all right?'

'Yes, thanks be to God, they seemed at ease with the couple who'll be looking after them. They'd told the children they were going on a grand adventure on the boat, which calmed their nerves while they went through these awful tunnels. We got to the river just in time, ten minutes later and I fear the boat might have sailed!'

'Is the river far from here, Baba?'

'No, just another few minutes' walk from where you found me, the path branches in two. It's right and then a left and you arrive at the steps that take you up near Halle aux Vins.'

The entire walk back, Safiyyah quietly took in the twisty route to the mosque. On the way out she had been nervous and jittery, barely able to pay attention to her surroundings, but now she was with Baba, her usual instinct of mapping out paths returned. By the time they reached the mosque basement, Safiyyah could see a detailed bird's eye view of the route to the river in her mind. The mapping soothed her, though she was still spooked by the catacomb and wanted to never ever see the souterrain again. She fell asleep as soon as her head hit the pillow, dreaming of the eerie sandstone passages deep beneath her.

29

Two weeks later, Safiyyah returned to the apartment after running errands, desperate for a bowl of soup to warm her hands around. It was so icy outside, and not that much better inside, she didn't even care if it was pebble soup, she just wanted heat. As she approached, she had to double-take at the sight she beheld. Hana was crouching with Setti in front of the door, tending to plant pots in which Setti was trying to grow parsnips and leeks. She looked up sideways at Safiyyah, who thought she glimpsed a flicker of a smile across her friend's lips. It was enough to make Safiyyah's heart glow, and she joined the pair in moving the plants from smaller pots to larger ones, patting soil around the roots.

As she sat across from Hana, she noticed a burst of colour peeking through from under her sleeve. It was the woollen friendship bracelet Safiyyah had woven and left in her room! Safiyyah had to stop herself from grinning like an idiot, but she knew something had finally shifted. Some small part of Hana's broken heart had begun to heal.

That night, instead of saying salaam when it came to

bedtime, Setti handed them both blankets and coats, and gestured for them to follow her out of the apartment.

Safiyyah donned an extra jumper, coat, and swung the blankets over her arm, intrigued at what was happening. As soon as she realised the route that Setti was taking, Safiyyah knew they were heading somewhere high up. She had never been allowed up to the sections of the mosque above the apartments, and they definitely weren't going in the direction of the towering minaret. When the trio emerged from a door out into open air, she realised they were on some sort of rooftop pathway! The moon hung like a brilliant white lamp overhead, casting an ethereal glow across the courtyard and fountains that lay far below them.

Safiyyah had no idea that this spot existed, and seeing the mosque from this angle she felt as if she'd discovered somewhere entirely new. The thin cypress trees in the gardens looked like little quills standing to attention, the steps and flower pots and doorways seemed like something from Fatima's miniature playsets. What really took Safiyyah's breath away though was the vast inky expanse above them. Entirely unobscured by buildings or streetlights, the night sky stretched endlessly, punctuated only by dots of twinkling light. Safiyyah had never seen so many stars before in her life.

In her awe, she hadn't noticed that Setti had laid down three cushions for them to sit on. Hana sat close to

Setti, they both had blankets draped over them and pulled up to their faces to keep the warmth in. Hana had clearly become more comfortable in Setti's presence over the last few weeks. Safiyyah joined them, warming herself under the covers Setti had given her, before lying back to take in the sky again. Somehow up here, everything that had been troubling her felt smaller. The presence of the brilliant moon in the pin-drop silence was endlessly calming, and she found herself wanting to gulp the stillness and serenity in to save it for later.

Safiyyah realised that Setti was watching her, smiling.

'Isn't it wonderful? I used to spend time with the sky every night back in Algeria. The stars were much brighter there though. God put secrets in the natural world that you're only let in on when you truly become companions. Most of us don't sit and stare for long enough. We've forgotten how to hear the secrets.'

Safiyyah wondered what Hana was thinking of Setti's riddle, feeling a little embarrassed. She glanced over at Hana and realised she needn't have worried. She was gazing up with wide eyes, looking rapt, as if searching for the secrets.

Setti continued. 'You have to surrender yourself to the wonders. Once you embrace the silence fully, the most beautiful songs begin.'

They sat for a while in companionable silence, until Safiyyah spotted a bear shape in the stars and pointed it out. Setti chuckled and said she could see an orange tree constellation. Hana said nothing but Safiyyah saw her tracing shapes with her finger on the blanket as she gazed heavenward.

The peace was broken by the harsh sound of an angry man's voice somewhere in a street nearby. There was a bang and a crash afterwards, and Safiyyah felt Hana flinch beside her. Setti put her arm around Hana. The mood had shifted back to the reality of the war they were in.

'May all this be over soon,' Setti prayed sadly.

'Arghh,' said Safiyyah. 'I wish I could go and actually *fight*. I want to really, TRULY battle against the Germans. I hate them! If I were a boy, I'd find a way to go to the front line and fight. It's just not fair!' Safiyyah voiced the thing that had been frustrating her for weeks now.

Running errands and passing messages and papers back and forth for the Resistance was one thing, but there was a war raging out there. When Tarek had signed up to the army all those months ago, Safiyyah had been distraught at the prospect of it. But now that life in Paris felt so bleak, and the war showed no sign of ending, Safiyyah felt helpless stuck in the city.

Setti looked at her oddly. 'Safiyyah Maryam.' No one called Safiyyah by her middle name, other than Yemma when she was very angry with her. It felt strange hearing Setti calmly address her by it now.

'Maryam. Safiyyah Maryam.' Safiyyah was puzzled as to why Setti was repeating her names, as if she had only just learned them . . . Setti said her middle name slowly, rolling it on her tongue as if she could taste it. 'Your name is Maryam. I remember someone once telling me that in ancient Hebrew, Maryam means *worth two men*. Just because men might be physically stronger or bigger, and they are allowed to fight for their country in wars, doesn't mean they are any better or more powerful than us. Everyone has their unique part to play. It may look different but it is no more important overall. Lives are saved and battles are fought all around us, some louder than others.'

Hana had sat up a little, and was looking at Setti intently now as she continued.

'Your time will come, Safiyyah. Perhaps you will do something that no man can. Just remember the maps that lead to light through darkness. The maps that you hold in here.' Setti pointed to her heart, before shrugging mysteriously and turning back to the moon above.

'My mother's name is Miriam.' Hana's voice was small but unmistakable. Both Safiyyah and Setti tried to hide their overjoyed surprise at hearing Hana speak. Hana cleared her throat and coughed a little, as if blasting away rust that had formed in her mouth during her silence. 'She is definitely worth two men. My grandfather said another meaning of the name is *rebellion*. That suits my mother well – she and my father were arrested while returning from a meeting of rebellion against the Nazis.'

Safiyyah was astounded and relieved. It was like seeing a glimpse of the old Hana after worrying that she was lost for ever. Setti smiled warmly before replying, 'A wonderful name for a wonderful woman. She sounds like an inspiration for us all, Hana.'

Safiyyah was about to speak in agreement, when Hana began to cry. Setti spoke instead, and Safiyyah was grateful.

'Dear child, I know all you wish for right now is to feel the warmth of your beautiful mother's embrace. Might I ask you, though, to turn your gaze skywards once more?'

Hana turned her face towards the black expanse above them, her tears glinting in the moonlight.

'Your mother and father are missing you right this very moment. As they do in all their moments. No matter where they are, it is the same moon that glows above them, the same stars that twinkle and glimmer when they raise their eyes upwards, as the ones you see right now. Whenever you want to feel close to them, just look and know that your gaze and hearts are meeting up there. They'll be looking at the bright crescent right this minute, thinking of you too.'

Tears now poured down Hana's cheeks like rapid little streams as she nodded. Safiyyah's cheeks were wet too.

Setti continued, 'The darkest part of every night is just before the sun rises. The bleakest point in winter is just before we turn into spring. Don't lose hope of reunion, Hana, if God split the vast sea in two for Moses, what isn't possible for you?'

Now Setti's eyes brimmed with tears too. The three of them sat in silence for a while longer, bathed in the light of the moon, gazes fixed fiercely on the heavens.

30

Hana still rarely spoke, but what she did say was enough for Safiyyah's heart to feel full, and for their friendship to bloom again. Hana still had her dark days of course, when clouds descended around her and she couldn't see through their thick damp shadows, but then they'd shift, and Safiyyah made sure she was right there when they did.

The girls read books together and told their own stories before bed. Hana had opened up a little here and there about her parents and their life together before the war. They looked through a book about constellations and begged Setti to take them back up to the roof, and played hide-and-seek with Fatima, much to the little girl's delight.

The day the letter came, it felt like the rug had been pulled from beneath Safiyyah's feet once again. Safiyyah's auntie, Baba's sister, had been under the weather for a week or so, and Safiyyah, Setti and Yemma went round to visit. Many people all around the city were suffering with tuberculosis, and the family had been praying that Khala didn't have it.

Yemma and Setti were making soup from vegetable scraps in the kitchen, while Safiyyah, Sumayyah and Fatima kept Khala company under her blankets in the living room. Ibrahim was keen to help in the kitchen; he hadn't had any interesting ingredients to cook with for ages and so new people's presence felt like a big treat. But first, he had been sent downstairs by his mother to check for post.

Sumayyah whispered to Safiyyah: 'Yemma sends him down sometimes twice or three times a day. She's so anxious about Tarek all the time. We have no idea where he might be, so to be honest, we're all worried.'

Safiyyah felt terrible for not having been there for Sumayyah recently. Since Hana had arrived, Safiyyah had barely spoken to anyone outside of her apartment. She stayed quiet most of the time with Amelie at school because she needed to guard the secret of Hana. At home, everyone had been wrapped up in trying to take care of Hana and so they hadn't visited their cousins for weeks.

Ibrahim burst back into the room, his apron tails flailing behind him as he ran. He handed the white envelope to his mother, who immediately regained some energy and began tearing it open. She paused for a moment, turning it back round again to look at the writing on the front. From the look on her auntie's face, Safiyyah knew something wasn't right. Her already pale face was now as white as a sheet. Sumayyah sensed the same thing and sat beside her mother on the sofa. The letter wasn't from Tarek.

Within seconds of starting to read the letter, Sumayyah clapped a hand to her mouth, tears filling her eyes. A few moments later, her mother dropped the piece of paper to the floor and cried out in anguish, 'Allah! My boy!'

Yemma and Setti rushed into the room. Setti began comforting Khala, and Yemma picked up the letter and began to read. Halfway through, she gasped, 'Tarek has been taken prisoner, God have mercy!'

Safiyyah's stomach twisted into a heavy knot as she stood up to put her arms around Sumayyah and squeeze her tightly. She felt glad that Tarek was still alive, but also wasn't sure if being taken prisoner by the Nazis was preferable or not . . . His mother was inconsolable, and Safiyyah's family stayed by her side until Tarek's father came home.

They had to get back to the mosque before the curfew began, and it was on the way there that Setti clutched her hands to her chest and, through her tears, said she was in pain. They just about made it up the stairs with Setti leaning heavily on Safiyyah and Yemma for support before she practically collapsed. They laid her down on her bed and brought her water. Hana stayed by her side as she recited passages from the Quran to comfort herself. When they gave the bad news about Tarek to Baba, he was distraught and went to his office for the rest of the night. After pouring her heart out in prostration, Safiyyah did the only thing she knew could comfort her and went up to the rooftop in search of the moon.

Setti's pain didn't improve the next day, or the day after that. She stayed in bed mostly, passing her prayer beads through her fingers, or praying quietly. Safiyyah had never seen her grandmother like this before. It was as if the news of Tarek had drained the life from her body, she seemed to be getting thinner and weaker by the day. After a week, she was barely eating anything at all and spent most of her time sleeping.

Safiyyah opened her curtains as soon as the sun came up, keen to get a tiny bit of winter light to her at least. She'd read from the Quran to comfort her when she was awake for short periods, until her eyes would grow drowsy again. Hana sat with Setti in bed, passing her a glass to take sips of water and massaged Setti's aching arms and legs. Without Setti's wisdom, warm hugs and even warmer laughter, Safiyyah's world felt grey.

One evening Safiyyah asked Baba, 'What can be done to help her? I worry she's wasting away. We need to do something!'

She wanted her father to disagree with her, to tell her she was overreacting and that Setti was going to be just fine, but instead he said, 'I know, darling. I think her heart has shattered into pieces. She has been so strong over so many years, through so many difficulties. I'm not sure what can be done now . . . We must just be there for her.'

Safiyyah ran into her room, feeling angry that Baba seemed to be giving up. She didn't want to believe that there was nothing that could pull Setti out of her pain.

A few days later Baba's friend Dr Somia came to see Setti. The moment he left Setti's room and closed the door behind him, Safiyyah's heart sank lower than she knew was possible. The downcast look on his face and slow shake of his head as he looked to Yemma and Baba spoke volumes. It was bad news. Later, Yemma sat Safiyyah down gently and told her that she should prepare to say her goodbyes to Setti.

It felt as if a cruel fist had tightened itself around Safiyyah's heart. She snuck into Setti's room, hot tears streaming down her cheeks, and perched at the end of the bed. Setti didn't even stir. Safiyyah stifled sobs as images of her life without Setti swirled through her mind. Losing Setti would be like the sun disappearing from the world. To be plunged into an endless, icy darkness. Safiyyah had so much to say to Setti, she couldn't slip away just like this.

Safiyyah was startled by a hand on her shoulder. Hana had sat down beside her on the bed, her cheeks streaked with lines of salty tears too. 'Is there something we could bring to Setti that might give her comfort, Safiyyah? Or perhaps something you could sing to her?'

Safiyyah gasped, turning her full body to Hana, tears no longer flowing. Suddenly, she realised what she needed to do.

Safiyyah knew about the black market in Paris. You could get everything from chocolate to tobacco, hunks of meat to banned magazines, if you were willing to pay the right price. Apparently a block of cheese could cost as much as a goat, coffee as much as caviar.

She and Amelie had overheard Henri talking about a gang that ran much of the black market in neighbourhoods across the city. Apparently the leader had broken criminals out of a local prison in order to form the gang, and between them they ruthlessly ran the undercover trading show.

She was bundled up in her coat, hat and scarf, which she'd pulled over her mouth and nose, hoping to disguise herself. A thin layer of snow had settled on the ground and the sky was bright white as more fragile snowflakes floated to the ground. It made a nice change from grey at least, Safiyyah thought as she approached the railway bridge arches that supposedly hosted the market once a week in the early morning. She'd learned the location from one of the men in the Resistance to whom she delivered a pack of pamphlets two weeks ago, and of course, remembered it.

Her hand was firmly clamped around a little black box in her coat pocket, which contained the silver locket Isabelle had given her the day she left. That morning Safiyyah had carefully removed the pressed flowers from inside and put them between the pages of a book for safe-keeping. Safiyyah felt terrible about it, but in her heart she knew that Isabelle would want her to.

Her heart sank when she arrived at the tall brick archways beside the Seine, to find nothing but a handful of people milling around. There was no market in sight. She was beginning to think it might have been called off, or that she'd got the location wrong, when a white van pulled up loudly, its brakes screeching as it reversed into the arch. Suddenly, Safiyyah felt vulnerable. She didn't want to deal with criminals, let alone cruel, jail-breaking ones, but before she could think about running off, the back doors of the van were flung open.

A man with a balaclava and gloves on jumped out onto the ground, and another began throwing cardboard boxes to him. The people who had been hovering nearby swarmed over to where the stack of boxes was growing, and Safiyyah found herself following them. The first man jumped down too and began opening the boxes, showing their contents and shouting prices into the cold air.

There were jars of what looked like honey, packets of biscuits and bottles of wine. In another box were packs of cigarettes, blocks of butter and cheese, and a few slabs of chocolate. Safiyyah had forgotten what most of this stuff looked like, it seemed to have come from another time, another life altogether.

People had begun haggling, shouting offers over one another and, as the only child there, Safiyyah began to feel overwhelmed. In an attempt to take a wad of cash for a jar of olives from a lady in a fur coat, one of the traders knocked a box from its pile and it fell to the floor, splitting open as it did so. Six vibrant oranges and four lemons burst out, rolling towards her on the light snow. They seemed to glow on the stark white of the ground. A man in a stripy scarf grabbed three oranges and ran away with them as quickly as he could, the balaclava man shouting after him.

A lady with blonde hair and a leather jacket moved to pick up some of the brightly coloured fruit. Safiyyah, fearing that she would miss her chance, dived down over two of the oranges, landing with a thud onto the hard ground. The woman stared at her in surprise, and picked up the last orange and a couple of lemons before pulling out a thick pile of notes for the man as payment.

One of the traders shouted at Safiyyah to get up and pay for what she wanted. She barely heard the price he yelled over her rising anxiety that the worth of the locket would not be enough. Passing the box to him, she prayed it would buy her at least one orange. She didn't breathe as he weighed the silver in his hand, asking her if it was real and where it was from. He seemed satisfied with her answers, and gestured that she could take two oranges with her.

Relieved and excited, Safiyyah hid one in each pocket and ran the entire way home. She arrived out of breath, but smiling ear to ear. As she pulled the fruit from her coat, she beckoned Hana to come with her into the kitchen. 'Yemma, Baba! Look!' The oranges seemed to glow here in their kitchen too. Both her parents' eyes were wide as they took in the strange sight of juicy ripe fruit in their home after months of barely anything but stale bread and potatoes. It could have been the Koh-i-Noor diamond that she'd brought home if their reactions were anything to go by.

'Did you STEAL these, Safiyyah?!'

'How . . . what . . . where?!'

Her parents bombarded her with questions. She began feeling a little sheepish at the prospect of needing to explain herself to them. She'd hoped to simply cut an orange into pieces and let Setti taste it without any of the talking. Now in hindsight she figured that was a little naïve . . .

'Of course I didn't steal them, Yemma! I found a man who was selling them, so I bought them. Let's not waste time, let's get some to Setti right away!'

Her attempt at changing the subject didn't work. Baba looked at her through narrowed eyes: 'You bought these oranges with what money exactly, Safiyyah? They must have cost a fortune!'

Safiyyah felt her cheeks burn. 'I-I-I sold the locket Isabelle gave me, I'm sorry. It's not that I didn't value it, it's just that I value Setti over everything I own. Please just give me a chance at giving her a little joy, Yemma, and then I can be in trouble or whatever you decide!'

Her parents looked at each other for a long moment, as if they were passing messages with their eyes. Safiyyah could see that Baba had softened, and breathed a big sigh of relief when Yemma shook her head but pulled out a knife and a plate from the cupboard anyway. Hana helped Safiyyah arrange juicy orange segments onto a plate, grinning at her in nervous excitement. The girls licked the unbelievably sweet juice from their fingers, and took the plate to Setti's bed.

Yemma and Baba watched from the doorway, looking anxious again now. Safiyyah had brought the second uncut orange with her and as she gently woke Setti up, she placed it inside her grandmother's hand. Setti stirred a little but then drifted back into slumber. Safiyyah looked to Hana nervously. Perhaps this had all been a foolish mistake after all . . . Why was Safiyyah so convinced that a little piece of fruit could help restore some of her grandmother's spirit? There was a war on, for goodness' sake, her grandson was the Nazis' prisoner and the poor woman was exhausted from struggling for most of her life. Her heart was failing by the day. Safiyyah looked to the floor, feeling ridiculous.

'Safiyyah! Look!' Hana whispered urgently. Setti had opened her eyes and was peering at the piece of fruit in her hand as if it were an object from another universe. She turned it over and over in her trembling palm, before looking up to Safiyyah, then Hana, baffled. Hana whispered to Safiyyah again, 'She thinks she's dreaming! Get the plate!'

Safiyyah brought the plate of fruit closer to Setti, and sat down gently beside her on the bed.

'Setti, we brought you oranges. Here, taste one.' Safiyyah felt anxious as she helped her grandmother raise a segment to her lips, holding the plate underneath to catch any drips. Setti slurped and sucked at the fruit, her eyes widening as the zesty tang hit her tastebuds. Safiyyah glanced at Yemma, who was whispering something to Baba, smiling tearily in disbelief.

Safiyyah lowered the fruit onto the plate, and let Setti lean back and rest again. The old lady closed her eyes as a wide smile spread out across her face. At first, Safiyyah thought Setti was about to cough, but she quickly realised that she was laughing instead. Everyone glanced at each other in amazement as Setti's chuckle turned into a giggle. How they had missed her! She opened her eyes and gazed around at her family lovingly. She looked absolutely exhausted again, but something in her eyes had changed.

'Tlemcen!' she whispered, gripping the orange in her hand. 'Algeria.' Safiyyah felt a wave of gratitude surge within her. Not only had Setti enjoyed the taste of the orange after months of missing it, but she'd tasted the soil and the sun by which it was grown. The tiny segment of fruit had given her a glimpse of home, of joy, of normality, and Safiyyah felt honoured to have brought it to her. It was the first time that anyone had heard her speak for over a week, let alone laugh! Yemma and Baba came fully into the room, looking visibly relieved.

Baba smiled at Safiyyah as he held Setti's hand in his, his eyes glistening with tears. One by one, each of them sat beside Setti, who was alert now, and told them how much they loved her. Baba kissed her hand again and again, Yemma stroked Setti's hair and reminisced about times gone by. Before Yemma stood to let Hana sit down, Setti whispered something in her ear. Setti looked from the oranges on the plate to Hana as she spoke urgently to Yemma, who nodded in response. Safiyyah couldn't hear what Setti had said, but she heard her mother respond with, 'I promise.'

Safiyyah's turn came last, and by then the others had quietly left the room. She offered Setti another slice of orange, which she slurped on gladly. Before Setti closed her eyes again, she whispered, 'Thank you, Safiyyah.'

Safiyyah felt overwhelmed with emotion. She wondered how her grandmother knew that it had been her who bought them. 'Anything for you, Setti.' She paused, not knowing where to start now that Setti was awake and listening to her. Safiyyah cleared her throat, swallowing back the lump there that threatened to overwhelm her.

'Setti, my Setti.' It was too much, Safiyyah's voice cracked and the tears flowed once again. 'Please, Setti, please don't leave me! I don't want to live without you, I can't!'

Safiyyah's face was red now, her shoulders racked by heaving sobs and she was all too grateful when Setti gently pulled her down to cry on her shoulder.

'My Safiyyah, my brave, courageous, adventurous, kind Safiyyah. My time has come, just as everyone's must. I am tired of this world, I'm ready now to be reunited with those I have spent years missing. I'm excited to see my dear husband again! My brothers and my sister, my parents. Oh, it has been so long! How much we have to catch up on, imagine! I'll tell them all about you.'

Safiyyah had never considered that Setti might be looking forward to seeing her other loved ones. Now that she thought about it, she imagined sadly how lonely Setti might have felt over the years, how much she must have yearned for these other members of her family.

It was a strange thought, but in this moment, their meeting again comforted Safiyyah.

'You see, my darling, for me, passing onto the next life is a journey of reunion. A journey of love.' Setti's eyes seemed to light up and glitter as if she was gazing at a sky full of stars. 'Oh, oh, to be blessed with the presence of our beloved Prophet, peace be upon him. Safiyyah my dear, I cannot wait.'

Safiyyah was so moved by Setti's sudden energy and words, she was speechless. It was as if her grandmother was a young girl again, with an unquenchable thirst for life, an eagerness for wonders. Except the thirst was for a life that Safiyyah couldn't experience with her. Her eyes filled with tears again at this realisation.

'Safiyyah, Safiyyah, what is that thing you and Isabelle always say to each other when you're leaving? *This isn't goodbye . . .*'

Safiyyah choked, 'It's *see you later?*'

'Exactly! I'm just going ahead a little. I'm beating you to it!' Setti winked weakly. 'My work here is done, my dear, yours is just beginning. But we will be together again.' She touched Safiyyah's chest gently. 'And of course, until that day, I'll always be with you in here. Promise me you'll always be true to the light, and to *your* light, Safiyyah?'

Safiyyah didn't fully understand what Setti meant by her question, but she nodded vigorously anyway and embraced her grandmother tightly, her shirt and hair soaked now with her own tears. Setti closed her eyes, the excitement had exhausted her.

Safiyyah planted a kiss on Setti's forehead, before quietly leaving the room. She joined Yemma and Baba on the sofa. She felt lighter than she had done just hours before, and judging by the atmosphere in the room, so did her parents.

'It was an excellent idea, Safiyyah. Well done. But next time, please just tell us what you're thinking. We can't have you buying illegal goods on the black market!'

'Baba, you send me out to do illegal things every single week, this was hardly any worse . . .'

Baba shook his head. Yemma rolled her eyes.

'Even if I were a great queen, I would gladly sell all of my gold and silver and diamonds just for a single smile from Setti,' Safiyyah replied, before running off to find Hana.

31

Two days later, Setti was gone. All the neighbours knew the exact moment in which she had passed because Safiyyah screamed out in devastation. Unable to suppress the pain she felt after her grandmother breathed her last breath, the cry that escaped Safiyyah's lips was so loud that it woke the children sleeping next door.

Setti's body was wrapped and shrouded in bright white cloth fragranced with some musk that Ammo Kader had brought back from the holy land of Makkah. As they prayed the funeral prayer behind Ammo Imam, Safiyyah found her mind drifting to images of Setti greeting her parents joyfully and embracing her husband, Safiyyah's grandfather, tightly.

Back in the apartment, Baba restrung Setti's favourite prayer beads onto two separate threads, so that he and Yemma could each have a set. Safiyyah wrapped herself in Setti's biscuit-coloured shawl and lay in bed, breathing in her warm fragrance lingering on its threads.

The day passed in a blur of sympathetic visitors and tears, of the gentle murmur of voices reading from the holy Quran throughout the apartment. That evening, once friends and neighbours who had visited to pay condolences had left, Safiyyah sat with Yemma, Baba and Hana. Setti's absence felt like a gaping void that threatened to swallow them all into its darkness. Safiyyah shared what Setti had said to her the other day, and by the time she finished, both of her parents were smiling through the tears that soaked their faces.

Baba looked at Setti's prayer beads that he now held in his hands and spoke, barely audibly, 'Setti spent every waking moment calling to and praising God, seeking His presence. Now she is finally fully in it.'

Safiyyah felt completely overwhelmed. 'Baba, I miss her so much and it hasn't even been a day. How can I go on like this?'

'I know, my love, it is so, so hard. It almost feels impossible. But you'll be given the strength you need to get through it. Trust me. Just take it one moment at a time. Be patient with your heart. Any time you're missing Setti deeply, why not send her soul a gift?'

Safiyyah was confused 'A gift? What do you mean, Baba?'

'Any time you say a prayer for Setti, it will reach her soul like a beautiful gift. And any time you do something good that she taught you, she will receive light and peace because of it. So if she taught you how to pray, every time you pray, Setti will be given unimaginable gifts.'

Safiyyah's heart lit up at the prospect of being able to

give gifts to Setti. 'So, if Setti taught me to be brave, she'll get amazing gifts whenever I'm brave?!'

'Exactly. We're still connected to her so powerfully. Don't ever forget that. It makes the loneliness much more bearable knowing that as soon as your heart whispers a prayer for her, it is delivered instantly.'

Safiyyah spent most of the night sending gifts through prayers to Setti. Baba had been right, it was a great comfort knowing that Setti's soul was receiving light and peace and all sorts of wonders because of Safiyyah. She drifted off to sleep dreaming of Setti unwrapping the most exquisite, glowing presents, and slept peacefully until the morning.

32

Snowdrops peeked their little white heads shyly out of soil all around the city, and frosts became less persistent. The sun seemed to have more vigour and warmth in its rays as the days stretched longer, and it summoned bare branches to bud. Glimpses of blue skies and daffodils energised Safiyyah a little, after what had been the longest, darkest winter of her life. She had taken to pressing flowers as they began to adorn the cold soil, it made her feel a little closer to Isabelle, whom she prayed for every single day.

The mosque was busier than ever now; almost every other day Baba or Ammo would take a group of desperate Jews through the souterrain to the hope of safety on a wine barge. The basement and hammam sometimes hid around ten people at a time. Suspicion from the Nazis had increased with each passing day, but through Ammo's ingenuity, everything had run smoothly so far. He had a bell installed under his desk in his office, which connected to various different rooms around the mosque. If Nazis arrived unannounced, Ammo would ring the bell and any Jews in the mosque would hear the alarm, and quickly move down to the women's prayer hall. By the time the Nazis had unlaced and removed their big bulky boots, which Ammo insisted they do to enter the mosque, everyone was out of sight. Ammo told the Nazis strictly that no men were allowed in the women's prayer space, and so far, they had obliged.

Adults would stay downstairs until safe passage could be arranged, while children were sent up to the apartments. Ayah and Hafsa's families had hosted young children over the months, though none had stayed as long as Hana. Four times now, Baba had suggested that he take Hana out of the city via the wine market. He had found kind adults who were willing to escort her out of Paris and look after her from thereon, but Hana had begged him to let her stay for longer. Hana just wasn't ready for another difficult uprooting yet, and Safiyyah was so glad she felt like that. Of course, Safiyyah wanted Hana to be safe more than anything, but she also couldn't bear the thought of letting her go. She couldn't imagine what life would be like without her any more. Baba had relented reluctantly, and it was now coming up to three months that Hana had been with them.

Yemma knew that April would be bringing the Jewish festival of Passover with it, and quietly suggested to Safiyyah and Baba one day that they do something to help Hana mark it. Her family was a religious one, and each year her parents hosted a big Seder dinner. Their friends would come round and together they would tell the historic story of the exodus of Jews from slavery to freedom. Safiyyah agreed enthusiastically, knowing how much the Muslim celebrations of Eid meant to her and how important it was to do this for her friend.

The table would normally be laid with unleavened bread, bitter herbs, a mixture of fruit, nuts and wine, boiled eggs and a lamb shank bone, amongst other things. Each item held special symbolic meaning, but Yemma had no way of getting hold of any of it. She consulted an elderly Jewish lady who was staying in the women's section for advice. The lady told her how to bake the special matzo bread using wheat flour, and advised her to mix up some salt water for the table too. Normally the boiled eggs would be dipped into it, but in the absence of eggs, at least there'd be something more from the traditional menu.

They didn't mention anything to Hana, wanting to keep their plans a surprise. Safiyyah picked crocuses, daisies, irises and daffodils from the gardens to put in a little vase on the table. She selected all the brightest colours she could find – it was a celebration of freedom after all. Baba spoke to a Jewish family and two young men who were also staying in the mosque on the day of the Seder meal, and they were overjoyed to hear of the plan.

Baba took a small table down to the basement and

Yemma draped her finest tablecloth across it. She lit a couple of candles and arranged Safiyyah's flowers in the centre. The Jewish adults helped to lay plates and cups out, and once they had settled themselves around the table, Safiyyah went to fetch Hana, telling her that she needed her help moving some things for Khala Najma.

Just before they left the apartment, a thought occurred to Safiyyah. She opened her wardrobe and pulled out her smartest dress. It was made from dark blue satiny material that reminded Safiyyah of the night sky, and reached knee-length with a bow tied around the waist. Safiyyah draped it out on her bed, remembering last Eid when she had worn it to the mosque party. Calling Hana in and ignoring her baffled look, she told her to put it on quickly. Safiyyah shut the door behind her, pretending not to hear Hana's questions. She stifled her excitement as she heard Hana unzip the dress. Hana emerged looking elegant, and as she followed her friend out of the apartment, Safiyyah handed her a silver hairband to put on.

'Safiyyah?! I don't understand! Why the outfit? What things are we moving for Khala Najma and why are you being weird?'

'Just come with me!'

'What on earth?! Why did I just put your dress on?'

Safiyyah ignored Hana's barrage and raced ahead of her down to the basement, knowing she would follow.

'Where is Khala Najma?' Hana asked when they got to the basement door, slightly out of breath.

'Go on in,' Safiyyah whispered, opening the door for Hana. She was silent for a moment, as she took in the makeshift Seder table spread, the warm smiles on the people seated around it. Their faces were gently illuminated by the golden yellow light of the candles. The elderly Jewish lady beckoned Hana over, and when she turned to sit down, Safiyyah saw that her eyes were filled with tears. For a moment, she worried that perhaps this would be too much for her friend, too painful a reminder of everything she had lost, but then she saw Hana smile a little as the lady put her arm around her. Yemma had been right when she said that Hana needed to do this, to honour this part of her.

They recited prayers and sang songs late into the night, remembering how Moses and his people were saved from oppression and slavery. Safiyyah watched in quiet wonder as Hana's voice emerged fuller and stronger than it had been since her arrival at the mosque. As they recounted the ancient stories, there was a conviction in Hana, a sense of firmness and passion. She was sparkling again, Safiyyah thought.

33

The days began to warm up, and Safiyyah and Hana spent the longer afternoons in the mosque gardens, chatting or reading. They taught Émeraude new words and sat with him to keep him company; the bird had still not left his cage once since arriving. The girls had tried tempting him into the courtyard with food and toys, but nothing made a difference. They played with Bonbon and picked flowers from the garden to brighten up the prayer rooms. Sometimes the girls spoke about their dreams for the future. They always involved finding and rescuing Hana's parents first. After that they ranged from building a farm filled with beautiful horses, to opening a café in which maps were served alongside tea. Hana's mother had always wanted to see lions and elephants in Kenya, and so the girls made plans to travel there together.

Sometimes, Hana would suddenly become quiet, her eyes distant and sad. Safiyyah knew to give her a hug, and sit with her in her silence, until the storm clouds passed. Most of the time that they were together, the girls inhabited a bubble that was sheltered from the war raging beyond the walls of the mosque. It restored their hearts which were weary from living through it.

Safiyyah was on her way home from school one afternoon, looking forward to telling Hana about what she had read in geography about Kenyan savannahs, when she heard them. Rowdy, harsh voices that belonged to a group of three German soldiers who were standing at the end of the street. Safiyyah's last Resistance errand had been yesterday, and so she wasn't concerned about having anything incriminating on her.

She'd grown more and more used to seeing the soldiers around and generally, keeping her head down and walking past worked just fine. She'd only been stopped and asked for her papers once before, and though her heart was in her throat while the soldier had studied them, he'd let her go with no further questions asked. Today she sensed that there was something off about the trio ahead of her, but figured that if she were to turn around in the street, she'd draw more attention to herself than if she continued, eyes to the ground.

As she neared, she could tell from their voices and stances that at least two of them were drunk. A young woman walked past and one of the men jeered at her horribly, making her flinch. The others laughed as she walked away quickly, pulling her jacket collar up around her neck as if to hide herself from their ugly ogling. Safiyyah wished she could punch each one of the soldiers, but her anger turned to terror as soon as she realised that they were now looking at her. She felt their eyes boring through her like hot metal, and felt the urge to sprint as fast as she could. That would only create a suspicious scene though, and so she walked steadily, trying to show confidence.

'Papers! STOP!' Two of the men lunged towards her as she approached, one of them stumbling a little. Trembling, Safiyyah fumbled for her papers, wishing she had not left the mosque at all today. One of the soldiers snatched them from her viciously, before holding them by her face and squinting from her to the photo and back again. He showed it to the man next to him, who shook his head.

Safiyyah's heart sank, her palms were sweaty. Why were they doing this? It was obviously a picture of her.

The second soldier shouted at her in German, making her jump. The only word she recognised was 'Jew'. He gestured for her to empty her schoolbag, and as she did so, tears stung her eyes. One of them grabbed a book from her, before tearing pages out aggressively. The shrieking sound of the paper made Safiyyah cower, and before she could help it, she was crying.

The soldier shouted at her again, only this time, she had no idea what he was saying. Another of the men gestured for her to follow them, his hand wrapped around his rifle. Grabbing her scattered pencils and books from the pavement and shoving them back into her bag, Safiyyah walked with the men in the direction they were pushing her in. One of them shoved her from behind, and in that moment, she felt smaller and more powerless than ever before in her life. Was she being arrested? What had she done? Did they know about her errands for the Resistance?

Then an even louder voice boomed from behind them. German again. All three of the men turned around instantly. It was another soldier, perhaps higher in rank. He was frowning at the others and shouting aggressively as he marched towards them. He didn't seem interested in Safiyyah at all.

As soon as Safiyyah sensed their fear of the fourth man, she ran for her life. She could hear the angry German voice behind her, but she didn't look back once.

It was only when she locked the door of her apartment behind her that she felt she could breathe again. Sinking to the floor, sweating with terror, Safiyyah sobbed.

Yemma was furious, and swore that she should never have let her daughter out alone. Hana comforted Safiyyah as best as she could, and even though Safiyyah knew she was safe inside the mosque now, somehow the anxiety didn't subside.

Safiyyah struggled to sleep, and struggled to focus on anything. She stayed at home from school for a week, and felt nervous even going near the outer boundaries of the mosque. She found herself replaying the incident in her mind again and again, and every time she did so her chest would tighten as if someone was squeezing her lungs. It felt like there was not enough air for her to catch her breath all of a sudden, and the panic that followed was crippling.

Safiyyah hated the intense fear that she was feeling every day and night. Her old self, who wandered around the city passing messages and packages, now seemed alien and distant, almost like a dream. More than anything, she wanted Setti's guidance and warmth. Her absence tinged every shape and colour of Safiyyah's world, but the sadness had seemed like it was becoming manageable. After what happened with the soldiers though, it had come back with edges sharper than ever.

She was perched on the steps just outside the men's prayer hall one drizzly afternoon, her mind drifting back to the awful soldiers again. The familiar terror gripped her heart and began making its way through her body. Her breathing became shallower and a lump rose in her throat, but before the tears fell this time, she was distracted by something. Her attention was brought back to the here and now by a little white butterfly, floating around the roses beside her. Unbothered by the drizzle, it flapped towards her slowly, appearing to glow against the grey of the concrete on the ground. It fluttered around her face, making her duck a little, before landing on her knee. It was a thing of beauty, and as Safiyyah examined its delicate legs and antennae and paper-thin wings, she couldn't help but smile a little.

Just as quickly as it had arrived, it flapped away. The beginnings of the call to prayer began floating through the mosque melodiously. The muezzin's soulful, rippling voice rang through the courtyard, echoing around Safiyyah and warming her up inside. She paid attention to it like she hadn't ever before, lingering on every drawn-out word of the adhan. Having felt like a stranger in her own body lately, somehow hearing it felt like truly coming home.

34

Sumayyah visited later that afternoon, and she had brought a cloth bag with what looked like fabric inside it. The girls talked a little about Tarek, and how he was never far from their hearts and prayers. Sumayyah had always been firm in her conviction that he would come back to them. Her faith was unwavering and Safiyyah loved that about her.

After a while, Sumayya said, 'Your mother mentioned that you had a horrible experience with some soldiers last week. I'm so sorry. How are you now?'

Safiyyah wasn't sure that she wanted to have this conversation, after all it occupied most of her waking and sleeping consciousness nowadays already.

Hesitantly, she replied, 'I'm all right. Well, I guess not that great, really. I haven't left the mosque since, I feel terrible that errands are being missed, but I just can't bring myself to go. The thought of it makes me feel panicked and awful all over again.'

'I can imagine. Be gentle on yourself. I'm here if you need me, all right?' Sumayyah paused, fingering the satiny fabric of the hijab draped around her head. She had started wearing it a year ago, and always looked immaculate in flowy fabrics and colours that complemented her complexion. 'I had a thought: generally the soldiers stay away from Muslims, you know, because of their fears of a rebellion in North Africa. If you wore a hijab when you went outside the mosque, it would be clear that you're a Muslim. That might protect you and also make you feel safer?'

It hadn't occurred to Safiyyah, but it made perfect sense now that she thought about it. Safiyyah liked to wear a hijab sometimes here and there, but didn't wear it consistently. She nodded slowly.

'In case you did want to try, I brought a few different colours with me that you might like.' She picked up the bag she'd brought with her and gestured for Safiyyah to follow her into Safiyyah's parents' room where there was a mirror. Sumayyah tipped out a shimmery blue scarf the colour of a pale sky, a deep olive green one and a peachy pink scarf onto the bed.

'I like how you wear yours, can you show me how you wrap it?' Safiyyah picked up the green one and handed it to her cousin. She tied up her own hair and turned around in front of the mirror for Sumayyah to begin.

Sumayyah spoke passionately as she began roughly measuring and folding the cloth. 'The Nazis have been controlling everything we do, from the scraps we eat to the coal we have to heat our homes, what we read to where we go. Can you believe they've imposed fashion rules too?! Despite their restrictions on the amount of cloth that can be used by people for garments and hats, people are finding ways round it. My friend told me a hat maker she knows is making statement hats for women out of newspaper, wood shavings and fabric scraps! I've definitely noticed Parisian women donning hats and skirts that go against the Nazi dress code. Garments have now become a form of resistance too.'

'Now you say that, I've been seeing lots of women wearing big turbans wrapped around their heads! I didn't notice that before the war.'

'Exactly, that's them defying the Germans in one way that they can.'

'A rebellion of headgear!' Safiyyah admired how Sumayyah was draping and tucking the scarf to frame her face.

'It seems absurd that an army is so threatened by and concerned with what women wear on their heads, doesn't it?! I suppose the Germans realise that hats and headwear allow expression. They can inspire loyalty, dignity and a sense of belonging, as well as represent rebellion. There is a unique kind of power in headwear . . . Which is why oppressors fear it.'

Sumayyah pinned the last stretch of cloth at the side of Safiyyah's face, adjusting the folds and pulling it gently around her neck. She pointed at the hijab: 'We've always known that this is a sacred act of obedience to God that allows us to choose who sees which parts of us, right? We've all been taught that it empowers us and honours us, but now, Safiyyah, in occupied Paris, I've realised it has a whole new meaning. Just like the hundreds of women who are defying the Nazis with their hats and turbans, signifying their resentment, this is resistance. This is power.'

Safiyyah was moved and impressed by Sumayyah's thoughts, and also immediately felt comforted and embraced by the fabric that covered her head. She turned to hug Sumayyah tightly. 'Thank you! Truly. I know exactly what I'll wear as my hijab when I do go out.'

Safiyyah pulled Setti's biscuit-coloured shawl from her bed and hugged it, inhaling the jasmine scent, before passing it to Sumayyah to do the same.

That night, Safiyyah dreamed that she was seated at a grand, long table, laid with delicate crystal glasses and all sorts of delicious-looking foods. The things she noticed first were the oranges. Huge, bright, succulent and unlike any oranges Safiyyah had ever seen in real life. They were piled high at the centre of the spread, on a gold platter. Suddenly, she became aware of the presence of another person seated opposite her. Setti. She looked young and happy. Her eyes sparkled as she looked at Safiyyah intensely. The white butterfly from earlier in the day landed silently on Safiyyah's knee again. Setti picked up an orange from the pile and winked at her granddaughter cheekily.

Then, the butterfly became an angular origami butterfly amongst hundreds of others, maybe thousands. They were strung up in front of Monsieur Cassin's living room window from thread, and they spun and glowed in the light from outside. Suddenly, they took flight. Slowly at first, then faster and faster, wings began to flap and flutter and a mass of white floated upwards. They filled the space around Safiyyah and Setti, ascending slowly. It was like a beautiful blizzard, and the pair watched, mesmerised, as the creatures drifted up into a vast, endlessly bright sky above them.

Safiyyah woke up gasping, the vivid image still blazing white in her mind, her grandmother's presence pulsing through the room.

35

Word reached Ammo Kader that the Germans were stepping up their plans to eradicate Jews from the country. More and more arrests were taking place, and attacks on Jewish properties were becoming more openly vicious by the day. Ammo and Baba were still taking a steady stream of Jews to the river via the underground tunnels each week, but when Ammo Kader received intelligence that a new chapter of horror was about to unfold, he knew he needed to step up his own plans too.

A mass arrest was being covertly planned across the city. The Germans were instructing French police to capture and round up as many Jews as they could, before removing them from the city. No one knew exactly where they would be sent, but it would most likely be to prison camps. Obviously the Germans didn't want civilians to know of the plans, and had increased guards at checkpoints at the edge of the city to prevent people escaping. They were aiming for tens of thousands of Jews to be removed from Paris over a short space of time, using the register of Jewish families and individuals that the police had been building for months. Thanks to the librarians, Ammo had access to his own Jewish register of sorts.

From Madame Odette and Monsieur Claude to the Kabyle delivery boys, from tailors to bakers, Ammo Kader's contacts in the Resistance network went into overdrive. For days, word was secretly spread as widely as possible to Jews across Paris that they could get safe passage with the wine merchants at the river via the mosque. Khala Najma disguised messages as rubbish, which she left outside the mosque's back entrance for Timothée to collect discreetly.

Safiyyah borrowed Ibrahim's bicycle and cycled around the city, distributing information and papers to families. She had begun to love wrapping her hijab before leaving the mosque; those few moments spent folding and tucking soothed her a little. She reminded herself of her conversation with Sumayyah, and felt strong and much safer with it on. Somehow, it felt like she was wearing armour. Though whenever she'd cycle past a soldier, her nerves would kick back in. Sometimes a lump would start to form in her throat, but as long as she remembered to breathe deeply, she got by.

As the suspected date of the round-up approached, more Jews began arriving than ever before. Tensions were high inside the mosque – everyone was vulnerable with people trickling in constantly through the hammam and back entrance.

Yemma had become so anxious that she'd taken to hovering around the mosque entrance, pretending to sweep the street in order to keep watch for any approaching Germans. She said she'd seen two in particular who patrolled the area and looked like they were snooping around the mosque walls a few times. In the messages that were sent around the city, Jews who wanted to escape had been instructed to make their way to the mosque with as few bags as possible and to take detours en route, so as not to give away the operation.

Hana had become more and more nervous and tense too. Baba had told her that she had no choice but to leave the mosque imminently, it was far too dangerous for her to stay any longer. The German suspicions about the mosque's activity were growing by the day, and it was getting harder and harder to keep them at bay. It was only a matter of time before they would come and raid every inch, and Baba couldn't risk her life like that.

Safiyyah wanted to cry whenever she thought of Hana making the journey through the dark tunnels, onto an unknown destination. It had been over a year since the Germans set their boots in Paris, and Safiyyah hated every aspect of war and what it brought with it, except Hana. The war had brought Hana into Safiyyah's life like a sister. Somehow to Safiyyah she felt *closer* than a sister. She felt lonely even just thinking about Hana's departure and so she focussed on pedalling her bicycle around the city, one errand at a time.

Ammo Kader was hearing conflicting reports and rumours about how and when the mass arrests would take place, but knew it was imminent. He wanted to allow for as many Jews as possible to arrive at the mosque, but also didn't want to run the risk of anyone getting caught in the process. Baba and Ammo Kader were the only ones who knew the route through the souterrain and so there was immense pressure on the pair of them to keep leading groups of Jews to safety.

When she glimpsed him here and there, it seemed to Safiyyah that Baba hadn't slept in days. He practically looked as if he had black eyes, and he seemed jittery all the time. The frenzied messages secretly put out days before were working, and as more and more Jews arrived, Baba, Ammo Kader and Ammo Imam met to discuss what to do. They couldn't keep up with the number of arrivals and so despite Baba and Ammo Kader leading groups into the basement back-to-back, many people were accumulating in the mosque buildings in between.

In order to create a cover for the extra bodies present in the mosque, Ammo Imam called for a gathering of song and prayer in the big hall. It would also act as a distraction if, in the worst-case scenario, any suspicious German soldiers did arrive and wanted to look around. The Nazis could be shown into the prayer hall while

Baba or Ammo Kader quietly and quickly led whichever group of Jews was already in the mosque to safety through the basement. It was agreed upon, and arrangements began to be made for the gathering early that evening, so it would be over before the curfew kicked in. Safiyyah was sent to invite local Muslim families to make the event convincing.

Baba had been trying to persuade Monsieur Cassin to flee ever since the day his home was raided all those months ago, but Monsieur Cassin had been adamant that he wouldn't. Sometimes he'd blamed his knees, sometimes his age. Mostly, he'd said he couldn't leave his plants.

This week, Safiyyah had been so worried for him that she had drawn a picture of a Rose of Jericho plant and dropped it in the bag with his medication. It was a plant that he had studied for much of his life. It could go without water for years and appear completely dead, but with just a few drops of water it would spring back to life. It seemed to defy science and was truly a miracle in nature. He had once told her that it was seen as a symbol of hope against all odds. Safiyyah felt sure that he would have understood her secret message to him.

He had, and after all those months, something had finally changed in his heart. Monsieur Cassin had sent coded word to Baba that he finally felt ready to leave Paris.

Once Safiyyah had dropped by several other households and spread the word, she set off on her bicycle to the 4th arrondissement. As she rode through the familiar streets with pillared houses, iron railings and huge old trees, butterflies flapped in her stomach relentlessly. She began to wonder, after today, would Monsieur Cassin's beautiful home lie empty? What would happen to his plants? She felt terribly sad at the prospect of never seeing him again. Losing Hana was bad enough, but losing Monsieur Cassin as well made her feel sick. Telling herself that she should be grateful that she would get to say goodbye, she pedalled onto his street.

Timothée had already delivered word to Monsieur Cassin the day before about getting to the mosque safely, and now Safiyyah was to leave a package disguised as rubbish behind his bins. Inside it was a white robe, a camel-coloured wool cloak for him to put over it, and a traditional chechia felt hat with tassels on. He was to don the Kabyle men's attire and be ready to leave by five o'clock. It was definitely not safe for him to be seen entering the mosque without a convincing disguise. Safiyyah had felt terribly worried about someone suspecting him with his blue eyes and fair skin, and had also packed some black kohl eyeliner for him to smear round his eyes, as North African men often did.

She and Baba had discussed options for getting him to the mosque, and while a taxi would have been ideal, they couldn't risk the driver not suspecting something and turning him in. Instead, a Kabyle man who worked with Baba and Ammo was to meet him at five and escort him on the Métro to the mosque, acting like he was his elderly father.

Safiyyah stopped for a moment in front of Monsieur's bay windows, feeling wistful and a sense of nostalgia that was closer to pain than pleasure. She threw the package behind his bins in the alleyway beside his house and said a prayer for his safe deliverance. She hadn't been to sit with him in his house for weeks, so as to avoid any suspicions about him being involved with the mosque. Timothée had even taken over delivering his medication. How she longed for time to turn back, for her to knock on the door and be invited in by his warm smile and the smell of freshly baked mille-feuille. Instead, she pushed her bike onto the road and set off back towards home. There was no time to waste.

36

Preparations for the gathering were underway. Khala Najma was arranging cups on trays to be served later. Safiyyah brought her the small amount of mint she could find in the mosque garden and so Khala began chopping up the leaves into tiny pieces to make them go further.

As she passed through the prayer hall, Safiyyah was surprised to see Baba's drum, amongst others, had been brought through from his office and was sitting beside the wooden steps to the imam's podium. It hadn't been moved from his office for years and years. She assumed it had stayed there ever since he stopped singing after the Great War. Ammo must have asked for all the drums to be brought in, he had said they needed to be able to make as much noise as possible at the gathering.

Safiyyah's footsteps were laboured as she approached the apartment. She hated goodbyes. She found Yemma packing a little cloth sack for Hana to take with her. Her mother had tears in her eyes as she placed a piece of bread and a slab of butter wrapped in paper inside. Safiyyah ran to fetch a small comic book and a lightweight cotton dress of hers that could easily fit inside for Hana to change into in a few days. When she returned to Yemma, she was wriggling one of her gold bangles off her wrist. She wrapped it inside a handkerchief carefully, before tying the sack up tightly. Safiyyah took a deep breath, and went to find Hana.

She was sitting on the sofa with Fatima on her lap. Safiyyah's sister's little arms were thrown around Hana's neck, she could clearly sense that something was happening. As soon as Hana looked up at Safiyyah, her chin wobbled and her eyes welled up. Safiyyah couldn't help but mirror her friend, and ran over to join Fatima in embracing her.

'Your baba said I need to go to the basement with the others in the next half an hour.'

'Half an hour?!' Safiyyah's stomach lurched when she realised how soon Hana would need to leave.

'Yes,' Hana said sadly. 'He needs everyone out of sight either in the basement or the women's prayer area by then. He was getting very anxious when he stopped by a little while ago.'

Safiyyah had so much to say, but struggled to find a single word. After another hug, she managed, 'We will all miss you SO much, Hana.'

'Me too. I don't know how to thank you for everything you've done for me . . .'

Safiyyah was horrified. 'Thank us?! You don't need to

thank us! You're part of our family and you always will be, Hana.'

Hana smiled weakly and nodded, looking exhausted. Safiyyah continued, 'When I'm an explorer, we'll go away together. Us two and your parents. Mine can come too if they want! Yes, all of us!'

Hana interjected, 'And Fatima of course.'

'Of course! We'll see the monkeys and giraffes, the gazelles leaping through the savannah grasses.'

Hana smiled again, before her eyes filled with tears.

'Hana, you will find your parents, insha'Allah. Remember the miracles of Moses. Anything is possible. Find my friend Monsieur Cassin in the basement, he'll be here soon. He will look after you until then, he's a wonderful man. Please remember that you are brave and brilliant. The most inspiring, intelligent and incredible girl I know.' Safiyyah was crying now too. 'Please don't forget me, Hana!'

Hana pulled a brightly coloured woven bracelet from her pocket. She pulled back her own sleeve, revealing the one that Safiyyah had made for her all those months ago. She had worn it ever since. Now she took Safiyyah's wrist and tied the one that she had woven from Setti's yarn around it. When the knot was tight, she looked Safiyyah in the eye, 'Never.'

Yemma came gently through the door, a look of

sympathy on her face. 'Hana,' she whispered, 'you must make your way down now, Baba wants you to be in his group, the first one that will leave. People are getting seated for the gathering, while almost all the Jews are now on standby to go. Khala Najma is at the entrance, sending down any last-minute arrivals.'

Hana stood up, raising her head and taking a deep breath in. Safiyyah marvelled at her bravery and composure. Yemma squeezed Hana tightly, handing her the sack she had packed. She pressed a tiny packet into Hana's hand. Hana looked closely at the little paper envelope. As soon as Safiyyah heard something inside it rattle, like tiny stones, she knew what it was.

'Setti instructed me to save these for you, my dear. Seeds from the only oranges we've seen in a year. Plant them in your new home, I know you'll find fertile soil soon. May they bear fruit for your tongue and your heart always.'

Safiyyah, Yemma and Fatima walked Hana down to the courtyard before one last heartfelt hug. They parted ways, Hana heading for the basement and the sisters to the prayer hall, where they were supposed to stay for the duration of the gathering. Yemma hurried to the entrance of the mosque where she had become accustomed to standing guard.

Ammo had told them to say they were gathering for a holy Islamic occasion if asked by anyone from outside, and that everyone should participate as they normally would. Safiyyah and Fatima sat down close to the front next to Khala Rabiah, where Ammo Imam and two older men who were usually tasked with singing were seated. She felt oddly numb as she took in the men, women and children from the local Muslim community who had come to the mosque. She'd been hoping to see Monsieur Cassin, but everything had been a bit of a whirlwind, and it didn't look possible now. The thought of him leaving with no goodbye left her feeling gutted and hollow.

One of the munshids picked up a small drum and tested it with a couple of beats. Out of the corner of her eye, Safiyyah saw someone sprint past the entrance of the prayer hall, and her heart began pounding. She stood up when she heard what she was sure was Yemma shrieking. A couple of the women in the hall heard it too, and looked about them in alarm. Khala Najma walked in, looking flustered and called out, 'Assalamu alaikum, everyone, thank you for joining us tonight. There is nothing to be alarmed at, we just had an issue in the kitchen. Please stay seated and we will begin the prayers in a moment or two.' She nodded at Ammo Imam to begin reciting from the Quran.

Safiyyah wasn't convinced by Khala Najma's explanation and, leaving Fatima with Khala Rabiah, she put her shoes on, and went to investigate. She ran in the direction that the person had sprinted in, towards the offices and basement.

She saw Yemma, red-faced and visibly panicked, striding back towards the prayer hall alongside Ammo Kader and Baba, who also looked horrified.

'Safiyyah, get back inside the prayer hall, RIGHT now. Do NOT move from there, do you hear me? There are two soldiers who will be here any minute now,' her mother hissed, and her tone chilled Safiyyah to the bone.

She followed them back into the courtyard where Ammo Imam's voice could be heard reading the opening chapter from the Quran. Yemma and Baba entered the prayer hall together, while Ammo Kader hurried off towards the main door, presumably to see the soldiers. It looked like Yemma's anxious 'sweeping' of the street to keep guard had paid off. Safiyyah prayed desperately that the soldiers would be satisfied with whatever Ammo Kader said to them and wouldn't come in further than the entryway.

Ammo Imam had begun some group prayers, which everyone was participating in by the time her fear was realised. She spotted Ammo Kader walking through the main courtyard with two Nazi soldiers behind him. He wore an expression on his face that she had never in her life seen before. A mixture of shock and intense fear, perhaps. When the congregation spotted the soldiers, a hushed and horrified whisper rippled through the room. Ammo Imam's voice rose as he tried to encourage the group to focus on prayer once again.

Safiyyah was just close enough to hear Ammo Kader speak to the soldiers, 'We are honoured that you will be witnessing our gathering today. Please remove your boots as this is a sacred space. If you'd like, I will explain the meanings of the prayers and songs as we go through? I would be happy to share these parts of our faith with you! Come, come sit at the front over here, you are our guests of honour.'

He feigned enthusiasm, and Safiyyah hoped they would not be able to identify his fake smile as the grimace that it actually was. The soldiers were seated just opposite her, Baba, Ammo Imam and the munshids. She felt sick to the core being in such close proximity to them, and the familiar tightening in her chest began. With a lurch in her stomach, she recognised the shorter soldier as the one who had been stuffing his face with biscuits the day of the tour all those months ago. That meant he probably knew his way around the mosque relatively well.

She glanced at Baba, who was staring down at his hands as he recited the prayers. She thought of Hana, of Monsieur Cassin, of the countless others who were in the basement waiting for Baba, and shuddered. Hopefully he would be able to slip away soon while Ammo sat with the soldiers. The taller soldier started fidgeting after a few minutes, and seemed entirely uninterested in Ammo Kader's commentary of what was being recited. He interrupted Ammo's explanation rudely: 'We need to look around the mosque, we don't have time to partake in prayers. Shall we go?'

Ammo responded immediately, 'Oh, but the songs haven't yet begun! Those are really quite mesmerising, you haven't yet experienced this part of our culture, have you? It would really mean a lot to us if you sat a while, you won't regret it! The first one will be in praise of our beloved Prophet, peace be upon him, whose beauty was like the full moon.'

Ammo called to Khala Najma, who was walking in to distribute cups of tea. Ammo took the tray from her and instructed her to bring something for the soldiers to eat. On the mention of food, the shorter soldier's eyes lit up, and he said something to his colleague in German. The second soldier rolled his eyes, but settled down a little. Ammo noticed the exchange between the men and continued, 'We have an excellent chef, you see, she really is brilliant. Of course, we don't have much in the way of ingredients, but she will still work her magic!'

One of the old men began singing in Arabic, tapping a simple beat on his drum. Baba made to stand up, nodding courteously at the soldiers, 'I must tend to a couple of things down the road, I will be back shortly.' Safiyyah's breath of relief at her father leaving was cut short when the taller soldier pulled out his rifle, pointing it straight at Baba's head.

Everyone stopped singing and looked on in horror at the soldier. Baba put his hands up in the air immediately, feigning confusion and surprise. The soldier with the gun spoke firmly, 'You will go nowhere. Sit back down.'

He looked around the room before continuing, 'In fact, no man will leave this room. If we are to stay and witness your religious celebration, nobody moves. Once your chef returns with food, she too will stay seated.' He grinned sinisterly and Safiyyah wanted to punch him.

'There are soldiers watching at every entrance to the mosque. If you have nothing to hide then everything will be just fine, won't it?'

He looked pointedly at Ammo Kader, who composed his face as best he could and nodded. 'Of course, sir. What would we have to hide?! Come now, let's resume the songs, shall we?'

Safiyyah couldn't breathe. Baba was staring into space. She noticed he had sat on his hands, presumably to stop them trembling. Ammo Kader glanced at Baba, a vein pulsing in his forehead. Safiyyah felt so hot and sick all of a sudden, she thought she might faint.

What was to happen? Baba should have been almost at the river with the first big group by now, Ammo would have been preparing the second half to follow. But both men were utterly stuck. Had they been betrayed? Safiyyah realised it didn't even matter now. She covered her mouth with the back of her hand when she thought of Hana and the others, shivering in the basement, waiting in earnest for her father. It was all she could do to stop herself from sobbing.

She thought back to the day when she had followed the kitten down there, how dark and cold and terrifying the souterrain was. All of a sudden, a thought occurred to Safiyyah. The soldier had said no *man* could leave the room. She was pretty sure that he wouldn't let any women out either if they tried. But what about a child?

She was the only person other than Ammo Kader and Baba in the building, maybe even in the city, who stood a chance of finding her way through the souterrain to the river. If she sat and did nothing, it was just a matter of time before the soldiers finished their food, lost patience and searched the mosque. They'd find everyone in hiding and ship them off to a prison camp. Ammo, Baba and so many others would also be shipped off with them. She realised that she had nothing to lose.

Safiyyah swallowed her panic as best as she could, and pretended to suddenly remember something. She put on her very best little girl voice, trying to make herself seem younger and more naïve than she was. Clapping her hand over her mouth and then speaking just loud enough for the soldiers to hear over the singing, she called across to her mother, 'Oh! Oh no, Yemma! My cat! The poor thing is shut outside and she hasn't had anything to eat since the morning! I must let Bonbon into the apartment!'

Yemma caught her eye for a split second, then waved her away impatiently, telling her to keep her voice down during the singing: 'Yes, yes, go and let the cat in and make sure it hasn't made a mess outside!'

Safiyyah could feel the soldiers watching her as she stood up to go. She knew they'd heard her and all she could do was hope that Yemma's act was enough to fool them. She glanced briefly at Baba before she turned to face the door. He was staring at her intensely, unblinkingly. She desperately wanted to nod at him, to communicate her intention in some small way, but it was too risky. And besides, in that split second of eye contact, she knew that he knew. His gaze was heavy with a thousand emotions, but she turned away before anyone could notice their locked eyes. Adding a little skip in her step for childish effect as she walked towards the door, Safiyyah cringed.

Just a few paces away from the entrance, a sound stopped her in her tracks. A deep voice rose in song, spreading goose bumps across her arms. It was so familiar and yet so unfamiliar all at once. She was truly hearing her father's voice for the first time in her life. She turned her head to the side slightly to catch a glimpse of him while she bent to put her shoes on. His eyes were closed, his palms facing the skies in prayer as he sang. Setti had been right, the war hadn't stolen his voice, it just buried it. He invoked God's sacred names, begging for mercy and help from the heavens, his voice rising and falling, rippling and flowing around the room and into the courtyard like shimmering water. It was beguiling. Somehow as Safiyyah ran, she felt calmer, more focused. Her mind felt clear. Her heart no longer quivered like a leaf in the wind as it had moments ago.

37

As soon as she was out of sight of the soldiers, she sprinted down to check if there was anyone in the women's section. Two Jewish ladies were crouched in the corner beside the shelf with Qurans on. Safiyyah beckoned them silently and urgently to follow her. Thanking God that the side door of the men's hall was closed, she led them down to the basement as quickly as she could. There was nobody at all in the basement.

Safiyyah panicked for a moment, but then opened the secret door leading to the steps down into the tunnels. Grabbing the lantern that Baba must have left on the table when Yemma came running to fetch him, Safiyyah climbed down about ten steps to check if there was anyone down there. A sea of faces came into view. Some of them shielded their eyes from the light of her lamp, others squinted up at her with desperate expressions. Safiyyah tried to see how far the line of people trailed back, but there were too many of them to make out from where she stood. She could see that the people closest to the bottom of the steps were shivering.

A grey-haired woman called up to her, 'Where is your

father? He was supposed to take the first group to the river a while ago? We brought everyone down here just in case.'

Safiyyah had no idea what to say. Seeing so many people in the tunnel stunned her, freezing all the courage she had felt moments ago. She couldn't possibly tell them that their only hopes of escaping the city were currently being held hostage by Nazis just upstairs . . .

The woman's expression became more anguished. 'Is there a problem? Where is he?!'

A wave of doubt and terror engulfed Safiyyah. Why did she think she could do this?

'One minute,' she replied to the lady, before scrambling back up the steps as quickly as she could. She sent the two ladies from the women's prayer hall down to join the others, and sat down on the floor of the basement for a moment. Her chest was tightening and all of a sudden it seemed like she was running out of air.

Baba had told her that there were holes in the souterrain that a person could easily fall into and never be able to get out of. The tunnels twisted for hundreds of miles under the city, people had got lost in the past and died down there. Some parts flooded sometimes, whole stretches of tunnels were submerged in cold, murky water. Baba had been trying to discourage her from wandering down there again, and it had worked a treat. It wasn't even herself she was worried about right now, it was the weight of the responsibility for so many people. She had no idea how many people were down there.

What if she got them all lost? Somehow all her courage had fallen away. Safiyyah, who memorised a map by looking at it, who never forgot a route once she'd travelled it. How was that same girl now trembling here?

She pulled the folds of Setti's shawl up over her mouth and nose, comforted by the warmth as she breathed slowly through the soft fabric. Setti's voice entered her mind. What was it that she had once said about choosing the path of light? Safiyyah placed her hand on her chest as Setti had once done and realised *the most important map is in here.* She thought of Hana down there, of Monsieur Cassin, of the poor lady who'd asked her questions. She thought of the sea of anxious faces, the crowd of broken hearts that stood petrified in the dark. Safiyyah stood up and climbed down the steps, closing the door behind her.

All eyes were on her, she could sense people's confusion and worry as they parted to let her step onto the ground. The lady called out again, 'Where is your father?'

Safiyyah steadied her voice, 'I will be taking you to the river.'

A collective gasp fanned out through the crowd. She heard whispers of 'No,' and 'Surely not?' Safiyyah ignored them, and made her way through the group. It seemed to stretch on for ever, she guessed there were more than fifty people in total.

She felt a hand grasp hers. 'Safiyyah!' Hana's presence and touch instantly warmed her, and Safiyyah pulled her through the crowd with her.

Just before they reached the end of the group, a man's voice rang out: 'How can we trust a child to navigate the souterrain?!'

Before Safiyyah could think of something to respond with to set his mind at ease, another voice got there first: 'If there's any child that can lead us there, trust me, it's her.'

'Monsieur Cassin!' The crowd parted and on seeing him nearby, Safiyyah threw her arms around his waist. He was a sight to behold in his Kabyle outfit. He even had the kohl around his eyes! 'Dear child! What is going on?'

Hana looked at Safiyyah questioningly too, and she mouthed to them both: 'Baba got stuck. We must leave immediately. There's no time to waste. I've been here before, follow me.'

Hana kept a firm grip on Safiyyah's hand, providing great comfort to them both.

'Is your baba all right, Safiyyah?' Hana whispered.

'I hope so. Two soldiers came and wouldn't let him or Ammo leave. I made an excuse and ran. I reckon Khala Najma will be bringing food out for them now. Hopefully they'll take their time eating. Our only hope is that they don't find the basement back door, I've no way of locking it . . .'

There was no key in the door and so Safiyyah couldn't secure it as Baba and Ammo usually would. This alarmed her but she pushed on anyway; it wasn't like she had a choice. It was easier to see where she was going with Baba's lantern compared to the tiny torch she had the last time, and the path was comfortingly familiar. She hadn't lost her ability to navigate after all, the twists and turns of the tunnel had absorbed just as well into her mind as sunny streets and alleyways did.

She called back to warn the group whenever there was a ledge jutting out of the sandstone, or a dip in the floor. She slowed down her pace on purpose to allow everyone to catch up when the ceiling sank lower and they had to duck. Safiyyah warned Hana before they approached the catacomb, and now that she wasn't alone going through it, it didn't seem quite as terrifying.

A couple of times, Monsieur Cassin or one of the other older members of the group needed to stop to catch their breath. In those moments, Safiyyah tried desperately to recall Baba's description of the remainder of the route that she hadn't seen. She was certain that he said the road branched in two, and she had a strong feeling it was right and then a left, but that nagging doubt kept creeping in and panicking her.

Just out of the catacomb, an old lady began to struggle.

Her son offered to put her on his back, but the ceiling was too low for that. She was leaning against the wall, finding it difficult to breathe. 'My limbs have had enough, go on without me,' she panted. Monsieur Cassin looked at her helplessly.

Safiyyah called to her, 'Don't worry, we can wait until you feel better. I promise there isn't long to go now!'

It was no use, even five minutes later, her legs would not move. Hana left Safiyyah's side and pushed her way through to the old lady. Taking her hand, Hana began to sing softly in Hebrew. Within moments, others joined her in song. After a minute or so, the old lady's face had softened, something inside her had stirred. She found it within her to continue walking, with a lot of support from her son by her side.

Hana joined Safiyyah at the front again, still singing softly. Some voices were hearty, some barely whispers, some were deep and others lilting, but they wove together and reverberated through the tunnel, stirring their weary hearts.

When they reached the branch that Baba had described, Safiyyah closed her eyes and called upon God in the most sincere and desperate way in her life. *Oh, Light of all lights. Oh, Guide of all guides, show me the way.* Right and then left, right and then left. She went with her gut. Within five minutes, she could make out steps leading up. Praying desperately that they were at the right place, she leaped up the steps. Before she'd even hauled the door aside, she could smell seaweed! She inhaled the fishy smell in relief as if it was a beautiful fragrance, and felt like crying out for joy. She grinned at Hana and gestured to her to wait until she'd found the right boat.

The sun was low in the sky now, and Safiyyah could see a faint moon beyond the bridge above them. There were four or five barges, merchants shouted and dragged barrels of wine onto them roughly. She had no idea which was the one they needed, or if there was more than one. She felt frightened again, they were so close to safety now, but suddenly it felt so far. Any of the men around her could be collaborating with the Nazis and it was impossible to tell. Her thoughts were interrupted by a gruff voice.

'*Pssst*, hey!'

She turned to see a tall man in sailor's boots and a rain jacket pulled up past his chin. Something about him was familiar, but Safiyyah couldn't tell if this was a good or bad thing . . . She walked over to him, determined not to give anything away until she had a sure enough sign.

'What's a little girl doing at our wine market port?' He snorted a little. 'A *Muslim* girl especially?'

'I-I came for a walk, Monsieur.'

He eyed her again strangely, as if trying to read something written across her face. 'Oh, really? Ten minutes before curfew begins you came out for a little stroll? On an evening like tonight, when there are soldiers raiding buildings on every corner . . .'

Safiyyah couldn't figure out where this was going. She knew that if he was the man who was waiting for the Jews, he wouldn't just tell any old stranger that, he'd be waiting for Baba. But he could also be working with the Germans, the city was crawling with Nazi sympathisers now.

'Yes. I did.'

'Which way did you come here?' His eyes were narrowed as he studied her reaction carefully.

'A-along the river.'

'From what direction?'

'From the fifth . . .'

His eyes lit up. 'Ahh. So you have come from the mosque?'

She felt vulnerable, but figured this might be her hint.

'Yes, I came from near the mosque.'

His eyes narrowed again. 'So you *didn't* come along the river, or you'd have known that soldiers have blocked the roads there while they make arrests.' He raised his eyebrows, smirking a little.

Safiyyah panicked, but she needn't have. He continued, looking around them, 'Where are they all? Why are you here? What happened to the men who were bringing them? In fact, never mind that, we don't have time. Are there many people tonight?'

She was almost convinced that he was her man, after all, who else would be interrogating her like this? He was clearly anticipating them, but she wanted to do her own little check for peace of mind.

'What men are you talking about? Who are they?'

He chuckled a little, as if impressed by her tactic. 'Mosque rector, white robe and a taller man, short curly hair, deaf in one ear. I usually meet them at the tunnel door so they don't become visible to anyone, but you're later than we'd agreed. I was about to give up, to be honest.'

Safiyyah smiled. This was it. 'There are quite a few people. I don't know how many.'

'Right, you hang back, send five people at a time. Wait about two minutes in between dispatches. This needs to be smooth, there could be Nazis here any moment.'

He ran over to the nearest barge and started shifting a barrel, and Safiyyah ran back to the door. She whispered down the steps, 'Five people at a time to come up, please. I'll tell you when to walk over to the barge.'

Despite Hana and Monsieur Cassin being at the front, they hung back, and Safiyyah was glad. The first five, an old couple and three teenage boys, made their way quickly onto hiding places amidst the barrels, the barge rocking as each person stepped onto it. After ten people had boarded, the sailor moved the next group onto the second boat. And then the third.

Safiyyah placed her hand on her chest and nodded at each person as they passed her. Some mirrored her action, others mouthed *'Thank you'* with anxious expressions. A young couple held each other's hands tightly, hopeful smiles on their faces as they stepped into the late sunshine. The old lady was still humming Hana's song to herself as she hobbled across the cobbles with her son's help. The lady who had questioned Safiyyah at the beginning kissed her cheek as she passed, her eyes glossy with tears.

Monsieur Cassin, Hana and another man around Baba's age were the last three to come up. Safiyyah walked with them over to their barge. She decided that it was not the time for more tears. 'Hana, meet Monsieur Cassin, Monsieur Cassin, meet Hana.' They smiled at each other, and shook hands jokingly.

Safiyyah gave Hana a final hug. 'Hana, please look after Monsieur's knees, listen to his incredible stories, oh, and find him some mille-feuille!' Hana stepped onto the barge, the small, watery distance between her and Safiyyah already feeling like an ocean. 'I will come and find you, Hana, I promise.'

Safiyyah swallowed, pushing the lump in her throat as far down as she could. She turned to Monsieur Cassin, who was being helped on by the sailor.

'Monsieur, please take care of Hana, she's going to find her parents. She has orange trees you could help her to plant – grow an orchard together!'

He nodded, waving at Safiyyah with a wink before being helped inside a barrel by the sailor. The barges began to slowly move away from the harbour, and just before Hana crouched entirely out of view, she pointed at something. Safiyyah looked up, confused. The moon. Pale and almost translucent, Safiyyah gazed at the perfect disk hanging low on the horizon, knowing that Hana was doing the same.

She watched the barges grow smaller and smaller on the river, until they were the size of toy boats. Safiyyah felt elation, grief, and relief all at once. Exhaustion hit her hard, and she felt as if she could have lain down on the cold cobbles and slept right there.

Suddenly remembering the Nazis in the mosque, the way their eyes had fixed on Baba and Ammo accusingly, Safiyyah quickly stepped down into the tunnel and began the long walk back through the souterrain. Now that she was alone again, it seemed darker and colder, and emotion began to overwhelm her.

She could barely see the sandstone walls through her tears, but wiped them away quickly when she heard what sounded like footsteps ahead of her. She froze. The sound was definitely footsteps. More than one person's, and they were getting louder and louder. The soldiers. Had they found the basement door?

Safiyyah turned down her lantern quickly and crouched on the floor, the damp wall cold against her back. She was considering running as fast as she could back towards the river, away from whoever was approaching, but she was frozen to the spot. She barely dared to breath. She couldn't tell if the cold feeling spreading through her body was terror or the icy dampness from the wall she was pressed against.

Then she heard her name. A familiar voice echoing through the darkness.

Baba, Ammo Kader. They were all right. They were here. Safiyyah's knees buckled when they embraced her tightly. All three of their tears fell fast now, salty water joining the puddles on the damp earth of the tunnel.

It was Yemma and Khala Rabiah's turn to sob in overwhelming relief when they saw Ammo and Baba return to the mosque basement with Safiyyah. Yemma squeezed her so tightly that Safiyyah could barely breathe, she'd never seen her mother this emotional in her life. Prayers of gratitude were the only words that anyone could manage to whisper as they walked together slowly back up to the courtyard. The weight of everything that had unfolded that evening hung low in the near twilight air.

The soldiers were all gone now, nothing at all had been discovered. The congregation had gone home and Safiyyah was glad that it was just their family and neighbours left at the mosque. She needed quiet.

She sat in her mother's arms beside the fountain.

Yemma spoke softly. 'You are ever so brave, Safiyyah. I am so proud of you.'

Unable to muster words, Safiyyah squeezed Yemma's hand.

Her thoughts drifted to Setti, who had taught her to be brave. The sun was setting now, casting an intense golden glow across the turquoise tiles. Where was Hana's boat? The shadows of the cypress trees and the fountain stretched along the courtyard as the glow began to fade, the night winning over day. A wave of exhaustion swept across Safiyyah, and she rested her head on Yemma's shoulder. Beside the minaret, an almost perfectly round moon was rising high against the sunset.

Ammo Imam's voice rang clear and melodious through the courtyard with the call to prayer.

Khala Najma saw Safiyyah and ran to hug her tightly, tears streaming down her cheeks. 'Safiyyah, look,' Khala whispered excitedly, pointing across at one of the cypress trees in the corner. A small shape of vibrant green was perching amongst the leaves. Émeraude had finally flown his cage.

Ten years later

Safiyyah opened her chocolate-coloured leather journal, its pages flapping about wildly in the sea breeze. Its cover was soft and luxurious, a thoughtful present from Tarek and Sumayyah for her travels. Leaning it carefully against the ship's metal railings, she uncapped her new ornate fountain pen. It had her initials engraved delicately along its lid, *S.M.* She chuckled when she remembered Isabelle's strict instructions *not* to press too hard when she gifted it at Safiyyah's farewell party. Delighting in the velvety flow of ink along the page, she wrote:

Date: 25ᵗʰ July 1951

Destination: Where oranges grow.

The ship's engine roared and groaned, and began slowly slicing through the water below. Safiyyah inhaled the salty sea smell, anticipation filling her entirely. She looked down at the rolling waves pulling away from the edge of the boat, crashing into the glimmering expanse. The frothy white wave caps danced and bubbled endlessly as the water rose and fell. Foamy white spray leaped into the air in all directions. To Safiyyah, it looked like a thousand white butterflies.

Historical Note

Yesterday at dawn, the Jews of Paris were arrested. The elderly, the women, and the children. In exile like ourselves, workers like ourselves. They are our brothers, their children are like our own children. Anyone who encounters one of his children must give that child shelter and protection for as long as misfortune – or sorrow – lasts. Oh man of my country, your heart is generous.

This note was recently discovered in a stack of old papers in a Tunisian owned café in Paris. Dating from World War Two and written in the Kabyle language, it would have been secretly read out and passed among the North African Muslim community at the time. It is a heartfelt testament to incredible Resistance efforts that have largely been forgotten.

When I first began researching the role of the Grand Mosque of Paris in saving Jews in World War Two, I was absolutely blown away. I was moved to tears by their remarkable courage and commitment to humanity, and awed by the sophistication and resilience of their activities. For far too long, this story has remained in the shadows, absent from the pages of history books, almost erased from the World War Two narrative. I feel incredibly grateful to have the opportunity to write this story, and intend for it to be a humanising, unifying force in an all too often bitterly divided world. My hope is that the time has now come for these forgotten heroes to be honoured, for their stories to be told and celebrated.

The heart of the mosque's Resistance activities was the inspirational rector, Sidi Abdel-Qadir Ben Ghabrit (also referred to as Si Kaddour Benghabrit), whose diplomatic and political skills and visionary influence made the operations possible. In this novel he is referred to as Ammo Kader (a phonetic spelling of his name). The soul of the mosque's Resistance activities was an incredible imam and spiritual leader whose name is no longer known. His bravery and persistence in the face of grave danger saved countless lives. Together, the imam and Ben Ghabrit worked tirelessly, along with many others from the Parisian Muslim community and beyond, risking their lives for the sake of humanity. The estimated number of Jews who were saved through forged identity documents, hiding in the mosque, and being escorted through the catacombs underneath it, range from 500 to 1,700. Jews of all ethnic backgrounds were assisted. European Jews couldn't stay for as long in the mosque as it was easier for Germans to distinguish them from the Muslims, and so their passage out of the city was prioritised.

While researching the book, I spent time at the Grand Mosque of Paris. I drank mint tea in its tiled courtyards, listened to the melodious recitation from the Imam as I prayed in the carpeted grand hall, and watched the moon rise from the gardens. I spoke to kind staff at the mosque about its remarkable history, and spent hours walking and cycling around the neighbouring streets and areas. I learned so much from the brilliant picture book *The Grand Mosque of Paris* by Karen Gray Ruelle and Deborah Durland DeSaix, the vital work of Derri Berkani, who originally brought the story of the mosque to light, and Ismaël Ferroukhi's excellent film *Les Hommes Libres*, as well as the scholarly work of Annette Herskovits and Nadjia Bouzeghrane.

Various other characters throughout the book pay homage to real life heroes. Madeleine in chapter 23 is a nod to Noor Inayat Khan, Indian aristocrat-turned-British spy and the first female wireless operator sent into France during World War Two, who provided important information to the Resistance. The kind man who taught Baba the tricks of forgery is Adolfo Kaminsky, a genius forger who saved thousands of lives with false passports and certificates. Mr Bingham is Hiram 'Harry' Bingham, an American diplomat who used his position to give visas to help Jews and refugees escape France. Dr Ahmed Somia was a Tunisian doctor who found a way to send Jewish children away from Paris by pretending they needed treatment in clinics, where they would be safe. He also worked alongside fellow doctors to covertly treat injured Allied soldiers and pilots. Madame Odette and Monsieur Claude are inspired by the librarians in Paris who secretly delivered books to Jews when they were no longer allowed to use libraries under the Nazis.

The Resistance activities of the mosque in the story are true to life, from the underground passages and use of wine barrels as hiding places, to the bell warning system which told Jews a raid was imminent. Many details in the book have been taken from archive accounts: the flocks of frenzied pigeons during the bombing of Paris, the yellow ribbon tying siblings' hands together as their families fled conflict, the hat makers' movement of 'rebellious headgear', to name a few. The horrific mass arrests that the Nazis carried out are represented in the penultimate chapter of this story. The gathering in the mosque organised in the same chapter reflects a tradition that takes place across the Muslim world, to commemorate the birth and life of the Prophet Mohammed (peace be upon him), whose teachings inspired and committed the rector and imam to risking their own lives to save others.

In order to bring the story to life, artistic liberties have been taken with some timelines and details. Jews in France were not legally required to wear yellow stars on their garments until 1942, and Noor Inayat Khan landed in France in 1943. The festival of Eid-ul-Fitr runs according to the Islamic lunar calendar and fell in November in 1940.

Although Safiyyah and her family are fictional characters, there were ten apartments within the mosque complex inhabited by staff and their families. Ben Ghabrit's family sheltered Jewish children among their own, as did others, while adults were hidden elsewhere in the mosque. All those living in the mosque would have been involved in the Resistance activities in some way, no matter how small their efforts may have seemed. Safiyyah represents all the unlikely heroes, whose names aren't memorialised and whose stories aren't sung and praised, but whose courage and actions change our world forever.

Both Jewish and Muslim tradition share the saying; *For whoever saves a single life, it is as if they have saved all of humanity.*

Acknowledgements

Infinite, heartfelt thanks go to editor extraordinaire Eloise Wilson, thank you for trusting me with this story. The book simply wouldn't be what it is without your clear eyes, wit, warmth and wisdom. Thank you for your patience, creativity and nurturing. I'm endlessly grateful. From sweet mint tea under the Parisian sun, to pizzas in London drizzle, and everything in between, it has truly been a dream.

Thanks to Chloe Sackur for your sharp mind and invaluable fine-tooth combing of the text. All my gratitude to everyone at Andersen Press who made this book happen and are taking it out into the wide world; Charlie Sheppard, Rob Farrimond, Sarah Kimmelman, Paul Black, Liz White, Elena Battista, Kim Singh-Sall and the Walker Books sales team. Kaja Kajfež, thank you for working your magic on the beautiful cover illustration, and to art directors Kate Grove and Jack Noel, I just love it!

Thanks to super agents Megan Carroll and Laetitia Rutherford for all your belief and hard work, and for making my author dreams come true.

To Nani and Nana, for all your love and generosity and the great gift of grandparents.

To my very early author hero readers, Katya Balen, Aisha Bushby, A M Dassu, Anna Fargher, Nizrana Farook, Radiya Hafiza, A M Howell, Kiran Millwood Hargrave, Rashmi Sirdeshpande and A F Steadman your kind words of praise brought me to tears and I'm forever grateful for your support.

To Maryam, Yusuf, Safi, and Adam, thank you for being full of wonder and for being wonderful, and for letting me use your names in this book!

To my family and in-laws, for surprise parties, for cheering me on, and nourishment.

To the dear friends who have encouraged and celebrated my work, I'm grateful to know such lovely humans, thank you!

To Yasmine, for introducing me to your rich Kabyle heritage a decade ago, your pride in your culture, and your (late-night!) guidance with this book.

To Anum, for your inspiring, loving, healing, earth presence that I can't do without.

This book is about compassion, hope and healing. Thanks to all the souls who have shown me kindness, given me hope, and helped me to heal through my own dark time last year. Appa. Sara. Sana. Zainab. Sadia. Samia. And the others, you know who you are. In the wisdom of Winnie, 'Sometimes it's the smallest things that take up the most room in your heart.'

To my dad, for the daily fresh green juices to energise

me while I wrote this story and the Michael and Oliver bedtime stories all those years ago. For pep talks, change curves, and abundant book vouchers!

Hamza, thanks for your enthusiasm and for letting me use your laptop, without which this book wouldn't have been finished.

Thank you, Mochi and Sultan for your moral support and profound wisdom.

To my mum, for teaching me about maps of light, helping me to heal, to be brave and to never lose hope, and for always being kind. For cutting up endless orange peels and being on hand to discuss the meanings of life. Please don't skip to the end of the book next time.

Greatest thanks to Usman, for being my number one fan. For patiently reading drafts, doing character voices, and listening to me agonise over details. For being there. Thank you for the Paris wanderings, and for never doubting me even when I doubt myself.

To dear Dr Umar Faruq Abd-Allah for showing me the value and necessity of stories, and for your guidance and light.

To the Grand Paris Mosque and all who sail in it. To every soul who chooses courage and truth in the face of oppression and brutality.

And thanks, to *you*. The reader, who ultimately this is all for.

Glossary

Masha'Allah – God has willed it

Insha'Allah – if God wills

Assalamu alaikum – peace be upon you

Fajr – one of the five daily prayers for Muslims, read before dawn breaks.

Madrasah – Islamic school

Quran – Islamic holy book

Adhan – call to prayer

Eid – Islamic holy festival, celebrated twice a year

Muezzin – the person who calls to prayer

Munshid – someone who sings or recites poetry

Seder – Jewish ritual dinner to mark the celebration of Passover